Fowl Play

An Accidental Farmer Mystery

Amy Gregg

Fowl Play

An Accidental Farmer Mystery

Amy Gregg

FOX POINTE PUBLISHING

https://www.foxpointepublishing.com/author-amy-gregg-1

Library of Congress Cataloging-in-Publication Data
Gregg, Amy, author.
Hall, Kiersten, editor.
Town, Scotty, designer.
Johnsen, Krista, cover artist.
Fowl Play / Amy Gregg.
A city socialite turned small-town entrepreneur continues to uncover mysteries, including solving local murders.
ISBN 978-1-955743-79-2 (hardcover) / 978-1-955743-82-2 (softcover)
[1. Cozy Mystery – Fiction. 2. Small Town & Rural – Fiction.
3. Farming – Fiction. 4. Amateur Sleuth – Fiction.]
Library of Congress Control Number: 2 0 2 5 9 4 1 2 7 1

Dedication

For

Tim

We miss you

Love you

Bye click

Chapter One

Lilly decided long ago that preparing for battle was more of a game of wits than brute strength. She stood on the back porch, the morning light barely lifted from the horizon, and donned her armor. The rooster crowed across the farmyard, signaling the arrival of her foe.

She struggled to pull the hockey pads over her legs and cursed her thick shins. Next, she straightened the shoulder guards, yet again, as those tended to slip off to one side. After dashing into the kitchen mudroom for a wardrobe change, Lilly emerged once more, this time wearing a heavy Carhartt hooded sweatshirt under the shoulder guard. The unwieldy apparatus now stayed in place. Finally, she pulled on heavy welder's gloves and flipped the visor down on the matching welder's helmet, obscuring not only her face from view but also her view of much else.

As the rooster crowed again, Lilly tied a deep-pocketed apron around her waist and picked up a battered metal bucket. The chunky fingers of the welder's gloves, a slim wire handle, and a dense payload made for less-than-ideal management of the bucket.

"I'm coming for you, Colonel," she muttered beneath the metal mask as she descended the porch steps.

Lilly clumped and thumped her way across the yard, rubber boots catching on the uneven ground and tufts of grass. The narrow view through the visor also hindered her progress. More than once, she had to reassess her course and adjust direction.

I should have put the visor down when I got closer, Lilly thought as she huffed along, the mask suddenly stifling in the early morning cool. Although I now look like Darth Vader, that will scare him.

Already sweating under her mask and battle garb, Lilly refused to take any piece off. It was the principle of the matter. If she removed it now, she'd lose the battle—and ultimately the war—before it began.

She stood in front of the chain-link fence and its clapboard structure. All was quiet now, the calm before the storm.

Steadying herself with a deep breath, Lilly flipped the metal latch and walked into the enclosure, bucket held firmly at her side. If she lost control of the bucket, all would be for naught. She quickly slammed the door behind her. The chain link rattled, vibrating like a twisted dinner bell.

No turning back now.

A flutter of activity sounded from within the dark structure. Shadows played with Lilly's restricted vision as the sun crept higher in the sky. A tiny, tufted head slipped from the dark, one beady black eye darting aimlessly until locking onto Lilly. The hen unruffled her feathers in a sleepy daze as she ambled down the gangplank.

"Really, Colonel? Sending Marta out first?" Lilly scoffed. "That's low even for you."

After Marta came a flurry of feathers and clucks; the small flock of Sussex hens was always the first to go to breakfast. Two of the hens, each a lovely mottled brown speckle, Suzy and Mrs. Patmore, shoved their way past Marta, the smallest of all the chickens. Her feathers were crisp white with a cloak of gray along her head and at the tip of her tail.

Following the Sussex hens came the two Booted Bantam hens. Whenever she saw the Bantams, she couldn't help but think of over-toasted marshmallows that had sprouted legs. Their tawny brown feathers bore black burnt tips, suggesting scuttling s'mores. Their clawed feet were hidden by dainty tufts of feathers, lending the "booted" to their breed's name. Francesca and Fancy Pants hurried after their lighter flock mates and began pecking at the ground, even if Lilly had yet to scatter the seed.

"C'mon, Satan's feather duster, show yourself," Lilly steeled herself, preparing for the final member of her little flock. She threw seeds from the bucket halfheartedly. Her hens clucked merrily to themselves as they attacked the ground, unaware of the coming battle.

The rooster crowed his battle cry, a strange reverberating sound coming from the bowels of the chicken coop.

He emerged as an iridescent blue-black shadow, with highlights of purple. The Colonel stood at the top of the gang plank and extended his wings, puffing up his impressive plumage to nearly double his size. Silky russet feathers cascaded down from his towering blood red comb. His majestic, jeweled leg feathers concealed razor-sharp talons under midnight booted tufts. The Bantam rooster strutted down the plank and scanned the small fenced-in yard.

His eyes then locked onto Lilly. She adjusted her grip on the feed bucket and met his gaze. "Let's dance, Colonel."

The jeweled rooster flew at her with surprising speed. Lilly continued to toss seed down to the hens, her eyes locked on the Colonel. She swung the bucket in a wide arch before her, seed spilling out with each turn. The hens scattered and erupted into a discordant cacophony of clucks and cackles as the food showered down.

The Colonel, undeterred by the distraction of flying food and feathers, kept his course locked onto Lilly. His hidden talons sank into the hockey pads. When he didn't find his desired target, the rooster dug in deeper and began climbing up Lilly's leg guards until he gained purchase on the long arm of the welding glove.

Lilly tossed the near-empty feed bucket toward the farthest corner of the enclosure. The hens followed, predictably, with wild abandon. The Colonel didn't fall for it. He knew all of Lilly's moves.

The rooster's claws gripped the welding glove tightly, tugging Lilly's arm along with his motion and substantial weight. He succeeded in throwing her off balance. He landed gracefully on the ground, ignoring the plentiful seeds under his feet as she struggled to regain her footing in the oversized boots. Lilly abandoned trying to distract with food and made her way toward the coop. In her haste, she accidentally booted poor Marta as she passed.

"Sorry, Marta!" She scrambled toward the back of the coop shed, hoping to get inside before the Colonel rallied for another attack.

He watched her as she moved, teasing her with his calm demeanor.

She didn't have to wait long for the rooster to make his next move. The rooster crowed and flew into action as she got within three feet of the door. He launched himself at her back, his claws finding a sweet spot just under her shoulder guards. Lilly's pained cry failed to escape the confines of the welder's mask. She felt the sharp points graze her skin even through the thick Carhartt hoodie. Her gloved hand fumbled with the door as she fought off the deranged poultry with the other. Her sight, already altered by the visor, became further skewed through a barrage of wings hitting her head.

The Colonel released his grip on her back and flapped around to her front, intent on going for her face and neck. These areas have historically been prime targets for attack. Now he found an unexpected fortress in the welder's mask. His claws briefly raked the visor before pushing off to redirect his attack.

Lilly saw this small opening and seized it. Her gloved fist shot out and closed around the rooster's feet. He clucked angrily at her, though she heard what she'd classify as Godzilla screams through the welder's helmet. The frenzied flapping of wings blocked her vision and threatened to throw her to the ground once more.

She had caught the winged devil. *Now what?*

Lilly opened the coop with her free hand and backed inside, keeping the enraged rooster at arm's length. She had to time her exit strategy perfectly, lest she end up dealing with a doubly mad rooster in a small space. She ducked further into the coop and closed the door until her hand and the rooster hung outside. Lilly counted to ten, then released the Colonel, slamming the door as soon as her fingers cleared the frame.

Only after the door latched did she raise the visor on her helmet. She blinked in the dim light of the coop. The Colonel's frenzied clucking and scratching were muffled by the door that bore his displeasure from many mornings past. She wiped at her sweaty brow with her glove, smearing dust and feathers across her face. She didn't care. She had made it into the coop.

Soon, the devil rooster will wear himself out, finally eat his breakfast, and reconnoiter with his harem of feathered ladies. Lilly turned to the rows of roosts behind her, housed in a bank of reclaimed doorless lockers her grandmother had taken off the local high school's hands when they remodeled thirty years ago. The straw and feathered nests sat eerily still in the dust-heavy air.

Lilly regarded the empty shelves, worried that none of the hens remained on her roost. It was rare for the hens to leave their roost after laying eggs, although breakfast was a tempting diversion from incubating. She slipped off a glove and moved toward the first nest. "You ladies better have come through this morning," Lilly warned as she plunged her hand under the straw and feathers. "Otherwise, we're having some Kentucky Fried goodness tonight."

Lilly kicked her boots off while still on the porch, grimacing at the feathers sticking to suspicious white smears, and began to tear off her battle armor. Hockey pads and shoulder guards clattered onto the whitewashed wood with a few choice words sprinkled in. She tumbled through the back kitchen door, tangled in the arms of the hoodie, and banged around the cabinets until she came to a stop at the middle island. Even with growing frustration over the early hour, the difficulty of getting her chicken coop clothes off, and knowing that the Colonel merely existed, Lilly still managed to gently put her apron on the island, a scowl on her face.

Only four eggs that morning. Either she needed to figure out how to get her hens to lay more, or get more hens to lay. Could she afford to get more hens? Would the coop and her sanity be able to handle a larger flock?

"That… was impressive."

Lilly rolled her eyes and dropped her shoulders. Given the early hour and the battle she had just endured, one would expect her to be more alarmed by a second voice in her kitchen. Over the last six months, Lilly had become, begrudgingly, accustomed to her hired hand coming and going as he pleased.

"Not now," she growled, side-stepping him.

Ryan had appeared behind her. He chuckled as he leaned on the island. He glanced down at the apron and poked one of the oblong bumps. "Wanna make me an omelet? I like lots of peppers."

"What are you doing here?" She rubbed the bridge of her nose, frowning when she drew her hand back and saw feathers. "Isn't it a little early for you to be an annoyance?"

"I had to see that for myself," he grinned, gesturing toward the back door. "When Faith told me you borrowed her kid's hockey pads, I didn't believe it when she told me why."

Faith Fischer was the owner and proprietor of Grandma's Attic and one of Lilly's closest friends after she returned to Lone Tree and her grandparents' farm all those months ago. Thankfully, Faith welcomed the prodigal daughter back to Lone Tree without so much as a sideways glance, unlike most of the town. She also happened to be her hired hand's older sister, which led to some interesting deviations of conversation.

"I'm surprised you willingly got up this early," Lilly moved toward the coffee pot, thanking herself for prepping it to brew as she was out collecting eggs. The small panel on the machine read six-thirty. Ryan usually arrived at the farm after seven to start his cow chores in the barn.

Once upon a time, she had made it a goal in her life only to see one 'six-thirty' in the day. And that was typically accompanied by TV dinners and *Wheel of Fortune*, or, as she got older, a cocktail and salmon dinner. Over the last few months, Lilly surprised everyone, including herself, by regularly seeing both sixes on the same day. She poured herself a mug of coffee and, after a few moments' thought, poured one for Ryan as well.

"Totally worth it," Ryan dug through the apron and pulled out the eggs.

"Hey, leave those alone," Lilly slapped his knuckles. She slid the second mug of coffee across the island, just out of reach from where he stood. "Those are for the market."

"Four eggs?" Ryan lowered his eyes at her as he stretched over the countertop for his coffee. "You can't even do a half dozen sale."

"The Davenports' are bringing their eggs today, we'll have enough. And I still have some eggs from yesterday." Lilly sat heavily on a stool and drank from her mug. The black happy-go-go-juice seared her throat, and she sighed. "Don't worry about it."

Ryan shook his head and backed away from the eggs. "Who said I was worried?"

Lilly smiled over the rim of her mug. "You wouldn't have commented if you weren't worried about the number of eggs."

He pushed away from the island and took his mug. "Whatever, I gotta start chores."

"She's going to be mad you're waking her up so early," Lilly warned, watching as he moved around her scattered articles of makeshift armor on the kitchen floor.

"No, she's not." He tripped over the shoulder pads and slammed a shoulder into the back door. Ryan swore under his breath. "She loves me."

"Uh-huh."

With a slam of the screen door, the kitchen fell silent. Lilly let out a tired breath and drank more coffee. Her eyes drifted down to the meager offering from the chickens, and she frowned despite her confident words to Ryan moments before. Lilly didn't know if her grand experiment could last much longer.

In the six months since she arrived back in Lone Tree, Lilly pulled off a truly miraculous transformation. Legions of contractors and masons came in steady waves to the farmstead to bring her grandparents' farm back from the brink. Years of wear and tear from weather, use, and age were stripped away. The broken and missing shingles on the farmhouse were replaced, along with some spots on the barn and machine shed. The chicken coop, the long building meant to house her murderous flock, received new windows and a fresh coat of white paint. Within the next week, Lilly planned on moving the fowl back into their proper home from the little shed they lived in now.

The farm from her memories was reborn with a few notable improvements.

The upper level of the barn that once housed the hayloft, and an assortment of dangerous scythes and knives, now held her classroom space. After all the unpleasantness of last April, Lilly decided to jump in with both feet with her "agri-tourism" idea. Her farm officially became 'The Accidental Farmer Experience', a retreat for anyone who wanted to try their hand at farming, whether that involved milking cows, gathering eggs, tending chickens, working in the fields, or even making artisan crafts and foods from scratch. Families, singles, or groups could rent the farm for a week at a time and take over the everyday chores, with herself and Ryan available as mentors and security in case of complications.

As spring steadily turned to summer, only a few brave souls dared to sign up for her classes. But Lilly still held out hope.

Alongside the agri-tourism, Lilly opened Bev's Farmers' Market 2.0, and the residents of Lone Tree responded better than she had hoped. At first, the participants filled the farmyard with booths and tables three days a week, luring locals and travelers alike just off the beaten path to one of the largest farmers' markets in the area. Bev's Market also had a cross-over effect on Lilly's experiment, as shoppers picked out zucchinis and heirloom tomatoes, they also booked their Accidental Farmer experiences.

Soon, much to Lilly's surprise and Ryan's vexation, the farmyard grew crowded with vendor tents and customer cars. To the point that Ryan had demanded the market be shut down or relocated, the extra cars and people on the farm made it difficult for him to complete his regular chores.

And the cars were chewing up the grass.

She rolled her eyes at the memory of Ryan's grumbling over cars parking too close to the barn and pasture, how he nearly got kicked by Peony while he was hanging the milker on her. How many times had he reminded her that if she wanted milk for her soaps and other hipster trinkets, the yard had better be kept in pristine condition, so keep the cars away from the barn. Fortunately, Lilly's friend and Ryan's older sister, Faith, found a vacant lot in Lone Tree that was large enough to accommodate the farmers' market. The location change proved a success with easier access for vendors and customers, and ample parking along the city streets.

Now, as September crept onto the calendar and the weather started to cool, families settled into their post-summer vacation schedules of school and work, and fewer booths were set up on market days. Lilly didn't want to admit that her inaugural summer success was swiftly coming to an end. She wasn't sure how she'd be able to keep the income coming in once the leaves and snow started to fly. The comfortable nest egg her grandparents had left for her had been steadily depleted over the last few months due to all the renovations.

She may have gone a little overboard on some design elements...

Lilly shook the depressing money concerns from her head and took a cleansing drag of coffee. She replaced cash flow woes with images of Ryan trying to handle Dandelion at such an early hour. The temperamental matriarch of the small Holstein herd stuck to a strict schedule, and hell hath no fury like that cow awakened too soon. Lilly smiled a bit sadistically as she ran through the various scenarios of how Dandelion would let Ryan know that this early wakeup call would not be suffered lightly.

Lilly wondered if the bovine read her mind when a muffled, yet angry, bellow drifted across the farmyard and into the kitchen.

As much as she would have liked to witness the aftermath of Ryan's poor choices, Lilly knew she had to get moving. It was market day, and she needed to start setting up. Parking signs and booth identifiers needed to be placed around the town lot. By now, the regular vendors were familiar with their pre-assigned booth locations. However, as fewer vendors started to show up, the layout continued to be condensed and shuffled.

And she had to hurry into town to put up her booth.

She was very proud of her little stand, which sold eggs and homemade merchandise from her animals, as well as a selection of artisan crafts offered as part of the Accidental Farmer Experience. Candles, milk soaps and lotions, regular paraffin soaps, and homemade bread spoke of the wholesome fun to be had with the purchase of a group package. Fun for the whole family or a Girls' Weekend!

It was close to seven-thirty when she emerged from the farmhouse, freshly showered and ready to tackle the day in what she deemed perfect country "every day" clothes. Dark wash True Religion jeans with strategic, intentional tears at the knees, along with a favorite Ralph Lauren plaid shirt in pink and blue pastels that Ryan insisted looked like an Easter egg dye kit exploded over it. And every time she wore this pair of jeans, he never missed a chance to remind her that the only way jeans should get tears is from earning them the hard way.

Just because she lived on a farm in rural Minnesota didn't mean she had to give up her sense of style.

At times, Lilly couldn't believe it had already been six months since her move to Lone Tree, Minnesota, after inheriting the family farm from her deceased grandparents. The former country girl turned Minneapolis socialite, who reluctantly returned home and became a country girl once more—the true makings of a Hallmark Channel Christmas movie.

Perhaps she was only trying to hide from the aftermath of her failed marriage; her ex-husband and his mistress ended up with everything once the divorce was final. True, Lilly had given in to all their demands just to expedite the process. Any extra time spent with those two was the straw to her already defeated back. Given the hell she had gone through discovering her husband had been cheating on her and then served her papers in less than a month, her escaping to the familial homestead for a few months wasn't entirely irrational, was it?

She often thought that her desire to run the farm and her plans to turn it into a thriving cottage industry would fade as the weather got warm. Between near-daily harassment from a farmer demanding his dues, her grandparents' hired hand winding up being her old high school boyfriend who she unceremoniously ghosted when her family bailed for the Twin Cities, and a murder mystery that eventually led to Lilly fighting for her own life against someone she thought was a friend, Lilly honestly wondered how she hadn't run screaming for the relative safety of Uptown Minneapolis.

Spring matured into summer, and now summer was giving way to autumn, and Lilly was no closer to leaving behind her family farm. She smiled to herself as she rearranged the cardboard boxes of merchandise for the farmers' market to ensure that the glass bottles of lotion didn't topple over. The last thing she needed was to lose any of her stock. The one thing that stuck with her the most in her quest to become a maven of the farm-to-table industry was that it took way too much time to make that little product.

Lilly finally settled into the driver's seat of her loaded-up Kia and headed toward town. The market lot sat on the eastern side of Lone Tree along the main road through town, County Road 45/Main Street. It was no more than a weedy gravel parking lot of a long-shuttered feed supply business, yet it served its new purpose superbly. The new location caught citizens heading to and from work, tourists from nearby Fort Ridgely State Park, and those traveling through the area in search of historical and cultural markers. She pulled into the lot and, after maneuvering around the other early bird vendors already setting up, she parked close to the back of the old feed store.

Once she had removed boxes of new stock, Lilly lifted the heavy sandwich board out of her car and dragged it to where the entrance of the parking lot met the county road, ensuring the arrow pointed to the preferred spot for vendors. The ideal place for guest parking was along the county road or in neighboring parking lots, which offered prime spots for vendor tents and parking near their spaces.

With the market sign in place, she walked back to the front of her tent and started setting up. The first vendors of the morning were nearly complete with their staging. The once-bustling lot, crammed with over a dozen booths, now boasted a meager six, including Lilly's. During the last couple of weekends of September, Lilly knew that number would dwindle again. She made a mental note to ask the other vendors if the first weekend of October should be the last of the season.

A wetter-than-normal summer had left the gravel parking lot riddled with pock marks and washboard ridges from tire treads and tent poles. Lilly added calling the excavating service in Sleepy Eye to grade the lot to some resemblance of 'smooth' before winter came, and again in the spring with the thaw. If gravel parking lots were anything like the country dirt roads, the frozen ruts and frost heaves would do a number on any car that traversed them. Her own little Kia nearly rattled itself to pieces over the summer while traveling some less-maintained roads in the area.

The day's farmers' market started without a hitch. Lilly was pleased at the level of traffic that stopped by to snatch some of the season's last vegetables and fruits. Mid-September signaled the subtle end of the growing season and the shift into autumn. And autumn meant more canning and preparations for the upcoming colder season. Lilly remembered her grandmother spending most of September and October canning goods for the winter. If she waited too long, the produce would start to spoil before she could can it, thus rendering the crop useless.

Lilly wondered if she should add a canning course to her offerings for the Accidental Farmer Experience. How many people her age knew how to can, either missing out due to personal choice or not having the opportunity to learn? She flipped to the back of her always-on-standby notebook and scribbled a note to investigate canning DIY videos later that night.

DIY canning could prove more fruitful than DIY soap. Lilly didn't believe her kitchen island would ever recover from all the botched batches of soap she attempted. Pinterest and TikTok made it look so simple. And Ryan still hadn't forgiven her for clogging the mud room sink with a half-melted soap base.

And Ryan still hadn't forgiven her for clogging the mud room sink with a half-melted soap base, although hearing the colorful language Ryan used.

Again, the farm's looming money troubles crept into her mind. Lilly lowered her gaze from the other market vendors lest they see her darkening mood. The other booths were swarmed with customers. The sight of money exchanging hands soured Lilly's mood even more. Interest in the Accidental Farmer Experience was not as piqued as Lilly hoped. She understood that any new business didn't break even in the first year. Or even the second. It took time for word of mouth and marketing to take effect. Marketing online and in newspapers was an area in which she excelled. She posted flyers in the library and even visited the Chamber of Commerce to request publicity in their programs and on posters for the upcoming town festival, Apple Dapple Days.

It was the word-of-mouth and personal testimonies portion that Lilly struggled to master. One needed customers to use their services before they could tell their friends to join in the festivities.

She smiled as a trio of women walked past her booth. Their arms were laden with hand-spun wool from Elvira Johnson's stall. One of the women, the self-appointed Alpha of the group, was telling her companions about the new knitting project she had explicitly selected for the just-purchased skeins of yarn.

"Would you ladies be interested in learning how to spin your own yarn?" Lilly broke into their conversation before she realized she was speaking. "Or perhaps bake artisan breads?"

The trio stopped mid-stride and mid-sentence and turned toward Lilly as one.

"We're offering a special discount on classes as a new attendee," Lilly continued, encouraged by the fact that the women hadn't walked away when she spoke. She had precious seconds to get to the heart of this pitch before their attention waned. "At the Accidental Farmer Experience, there are many fall and winter workshops planned, including yarn work with a spinner's wheel. I think that might be coming up in the first week or so of October."

The Alpha scanned the pamphlets and samples of products and wares Lilly had carefully arranged on her table. Lilly put on her perfected fundraising plasticine smile. If it worked on separating Minneapolis' elite with five to six-figure checks, it surely can work on these women to sign up for a three-hour workshop or two. Maybe even a Girls' Weekend.

"Spin our own wool?" Alpha echoed. Her tone of feigned interest just barely covered the annoyance on her face.

"Susan, that sounds fun!" One of her friends piped up. She tucked an unruly strand of brown hair behind her ear as she reached around the Alpha now known as Susan and took a pamphlet off the table. "Oh! Candle making!"

"Hmm." Susan's response was less than dignified or promising for a sale. "Why would we come out here to do that?"

Before Lilly could reply, the third woman, wearing obscenely large-lensed sunglasses, elbowed Susan gently. "We trekked out to Harmony for your Amish quilts. And we went all the way to New Ulm for the Glockenspiel—"

"And you're welcome," the brunette woman cut in.

"—So why can't we come down here for candle and yarn making?"

"And soaps," Lilly added, hoping to lighten the thinly veiled challenge to Alpha Susan.

"Oh, yeah! I saw a video online about soap making," the Glockenspiel-loving brunette's face lit up like a kid at Christmas. She turned abruptly to Lilly. "Do you think we could make mermaid soap? It's blue and pink and aqua with little starfish pieces and—"

"Enough with the mermaid soap!" Sunglasses groaned.

"I'm certain I can come up with an easy version of mermaid soap," Lilly gave her best smile, already mentally adding another Google search to her To-Do List.

"Maybe next time," Alpha Susan said, taking the pamphlet from Brunette's hands and placing it back on the table. "We need to get going. It's a long drive to the Cities."

With an unspoken command, the trio turned and left, Brunette and Sunglasses following Alpha Susan, looking somewhat deflated. Lilly watched the women head toward a sleek silver SUV and felt an eerie sense of déjà vu wash over her. She remembered those types of friend groups from her time in Minneapolis' higher society. Her ex-husband, Alec, came from old money, and as his then-wife, she had been expected to move within the same circles as well. How many times had she kowtowed behind a similar alpha like Susan, all to jostle for a better social standing and better table assignment at the season's gala or fundraiser?

Lilly shuddered at the influx of memories. It had been a mere eight months since Alec presented her with not only divorce papers but also the reason behind them—Olivia. The woman he'd been cheating with behind her back for who knew how long. Lilly declined to ask for that detail. Then weeks later came news of her grandparents' deaths, along with a hefty inheritance—the family farm in rural Brown County—two hours and a million light years away from her former upper echelon life.

Two short months after receiving those two bombs, Lilly moved back to the farm with hopes of somehow piecing her life back together. Since that fateful April day, she had set her heart on reclaiming her lost youth once spent on the farm, but Lilly still wasn't too sure of her master plan.

As Alpha Susan and her band climbed into the SUV and rolled out of the farmers' market, Lilly felt another piece of her resolve slip away.

What was she doing wrong?

"Can you please get out of my way?"

Lilly's attention snapped back to the farmers' market and the gravel lot around her. After a quick scan of the lot, Lilly found the source of the shrill outburst.

Cecilia Baxter.

Oh crap, now what? Lilly groaned inwardly as she took a tentative step out from under her canopy.

Cecilia Baxter would have been more at home in the upper rungs of the New York social scene than in the rural hamlet of Lone Tree. At least, she tried to convey that aesthetic and lifestyle. Cecilia sold fresh vegetables and herbs at her booth, touting her produce as non-GMO and 100% organic. Complete with informational sheets praising the non-GMO/organic diet while revealing the "truths" of any other product that wasn't hers.

Lilly knew Cecilia meant well, trying to help others live a clean and healthier lifestyle, even if she went about it in all the wrong ways.

"I'm sorry, Cecilia, but you walked into me." A second, equally familiar voice retorted to Cecilia's brash demand.

Angela Stilner, according to Cecilia, is a proud seller of non-organic, possibly genetically modified (GMO) produce, both canned and fresh, as well as eggs from 'caged' chickens. Since the beginning of the market, the two women had been after each other and their offered merchandise. Though Lilly felt Cecilia instigated more than not.

Within a few strides, Lilly stood before the two women. Cecilia had platinum blond hair twisted into a perfect updo to match her 'farmer chic' outfit. Lilly recognized the J. Crew buffalo skirt and black turtleneck over black tights from last winter's line. Impractical high-heeled boots complete the look. She suppressed a smirk, remembering when she still attempted to wear designer clothes around the farm.

Once her dry-cleaning bill started to match the cows' feed bill, Lilly put a stop to that right quick.

Angela stood before Cecilia as her opposite in every way. Dark hair in a messy braid, paired with stained and well-worn jeans and an Allis-Chalmers sweatshirt, allowed her to blend in with the other Lone Tree locals more easily.

"Excuse me?" Cecilia snapped.

"You heard me," Angela shifted the mason jars in her arms.

"Ladies, ladies, please," Lilly slowly positioned herself between the two, arms outstretched. "What seems to be the problem?"

"Wide load here knocked into my cart and one of my jars fell," Cecilia motioned to her bright blue canvas and metal wagon, strikingly similar to the type parents use to schlep their kids around at fairgrounds instead of strollers. A shattered mason jar of preserved tomatoes threatened to be crushed under the metal wheels as they rolled over the gravel.

"Wide load?" Angela's cheeks burned, her whole body bristling from the insult.

Lilly bit her lip, brain churning to stay ahead of the quarreling women. Angela wasn't a large woman by any means, but she was curvy with a solid build, thanks to years of working on her farm. Most people grew a bit stockier as their time doing chores and manual labor increased. Lilly had noticed her clothes fitting differently after only six months of working in the barn and her garden.

"I'm certain it was an accident, Cecilia," Lilly flashed each woman her best measured, retail smile. "Even if it wasn't," she added quickly, as Cecilia opened her mouth, "now is not the time or place for such a scene. We still have customers in the market."

Both women flicked their gazes across the lot, taking inventory of how many pairs of eyes and ears had slowly shifted attention to them. In the case of Elvira Johnson, who was less than ten feet away, the elder woman looked ready to grab a tub of popcorn and settle in for a long cat fight.

Cecilia took a sharp breath through her nose. She leveled her gaze at Lilly. "You're right, Lillian. I do expect to be compensated for my lost product."

"Now wait one minute—" Angela pointed a finger in protest.

"Of course," Lilly cut in, placing herself directly in front of Angela.

"I must get back to my booth," Cecilia bent daintily to retrieve the fallen handle of her wagon. "I would sincerely reconsider having this home-wrecker/pariah/blight as a vendor next season, Lillian. We don't need her kind sullying our good town's image."

With her last verbal barb, she stomped off to her booth, wagon, and mason jars rattling dangerously behind her. Cecilia's exit wasn't as dynamic as she'd hoped, Lilly suspected, as her high-heeled boots caught on the uneven ground and larger rocks, causing her ankles to twist and bend with each sashaying stomp. The woman looked more like a newborn calf attempting to walk minutes after birth than the self-righteous champion of the farmers' market.

"You're not taking her side, are you?" Angela's voice brought Lilly back from her wandering thoughts. "And you can't make me pay for her fermented store-bought tomatoes!"

"No, I'm not. I just don't need another scene between you two," Lilly sighed. Flashbacks of the screaming match from two weeks ago made her stomach sour.

Betrayal flashed across Angela's face as her eyes widened. "You are taking her side. If you think I'm going to give her any money—"

"Angela, no!" Lilly rested a hand on Angela's arm, fearing she'd forgotten about her armload of jars. "I'll pay for it. I won't make you pay for her ego."

Angela took a measured breath and glanced down at her feet. "Are you going to ban me from selling next year?"

"Ban you? No," Lilly shook her head. "I don't know what history you and Cecilia have, but I haven't seen anything that would keep you from being a vendor next year. Though if these outbursts between you two continue, I may have to rethink both of you."

"I knew it," Angela muttered.

Lilly held her gaze. "You both have started some scenes this summer, it's not just you or her. If you two can't play nicely together, then I'm not going to punish the other sellers by having your antics ruin their sales."

Angela let out a heavy sigh. "I guess so."

"That being said, I'm not going to ban you outright just because Cecilia said I should. You both need to prove to me that you're able to act like adults," Lilly tried to give her best reassuring smile. She never realized running a farmers' market involved reminding grown adults how to act.

"Thanks, Lilly," Angela gave a small smile of her own. Lilly could sense the woman's feeling of dread rolling off in waves. "But sooner or later, everyone hears about me and shuns me, deciding the best way to deal with me is to make things so hard that I just give up and get out of the way. It has been nice being a part of this market for as long as I have."

"Angela, what are you—"

The woman turned and went back to her booth without another word. Lilly stared after her, suddenly aware of how exposed she was in the middle of the lot, outside the protective confines of her pop-up canopy. Eyes still lingered on her as she made her way awkwardly back to her booth.

Angela's words haunted Lilly as she settled in behind her table. What did she mean by once people hear things about her? Lilly hadn't heard Angela's name pop up in any of the rumor mills over the last few months. And considering how fast news traveled around a small town like Lone Tree, she had no idea what she was talking about.

But if there was anyone in town to get a skinny on old news, that person could be found at Grandma's Attic Café.

As Lilly pondered the meaning behind Angela's words, a rogue gust of wind surged from behind her. The weatherman had predicted stronger-than-normal wind gusts later that day, though closer to early evening, not before noon.

The gust caught her booth's canopy and lifted it. Her red canopy rose from the ground by a foot, escaping the suddenly inept pole weights, then dropped to its side with a clatter and spray of gravel. Her display table was the next to follow. The tablecloth and pamphlets sailed through the air and littered the parking lot and the adjacent street.

She gaped at the freak act of destruction, too stunned to leap into action. Off to her right came a sharp bark of laughter. Slowly, Lilly turned and saw Elvira Johnson sitting in her camp chair and popping sunflower seeds into her mouth. She held a wicked grin while chewing the seeds, then spat out a clump of black hulls before continuing her harsh laugh.

"I told ya' earlier, ya' needed more weight on those things, didn't I?" Elvira cackled.

Lilly hung her head.

Why me? Why must everything I try turn into an utter disaster?

Chapter Three

Lilly left the broken-down tent, folded table, and boxes of market merchandise in the back of her Kia, unwilling to drag the items across the farmyard and up the porch steps. The farmers' market took more out of her than expected, especially with chasing her booth contents all over the gravel lot, down the street, and across a neighboring field. Even with assistance from Elvira, she was unable to save all her fliers or soaps. And the emotional toll of playing referee between Angela and Cecilia was the final straw.

Today was a definite loss in the business ledger.

She told herself she'd unpack later. It was almost one o'clock, and her stomach constantly reminded her of a lunch missed. And she needed a shower after working up a sweat chasing paper in chaotic winds, which had also kicked up enough dust and grit to negate any earlier grooming.

Lilly slammed the car door as she glanced around the farmyard and stared for a moment when her eyes reached the front of the barn. There was one more truck than usual in the yard. Ryan's half-rust, half-green behemoth sat in its usual spot at the rise in the yard before sloping down to the lower entry and pasture. Next to it sat a newer extended-cab truck with painfully rust-free white panels. Along the driver's side was the detailed announcement that the truck was part of the Wilhelm Veterinary Clinic fleet of vehicles.

She forgot Nathan Wilhelm, head large animal vet, was scheduled for a herd check that day. Ryan mentioned it to her once three weeks ago, blatantly ignoring her requests to write it on the main farm calendar hanging in the kitchen. Seeing the vet's truck jarred that memory loose. Lilly made her way down to the barn, hoping to catch Nathan to discuss herd health matters. Hopefully he wouldn't be elbow-deep in a cow's butt when she found him.

Along with money concerns, the farm now faced health scares within the herd. With autumn just around the corner, Ryan and Lilly worked to prepare the cows for winter, as the colder weather also brought along illnesses. The cows had escaped most herd-wide diseases until two weeks prior, when a batch of recent calves showed signs of lethargy, difficulty breathing, and fever. Lilly wished she had been introduced to the vet under different circumstances than battling month-old calves into standing still to check their temperature. Lone Tree's newest eligible bachelor made learning about bovine respiratory syncytial viruses and "pasture pneumonias" far more interesting.

Lilly slipped through the barn doors into the lower level where the cows were kept. She noticed that the distinct aroma palette of the animals didn't cause such an olfactory affront as it had in recent months. Lilly inherited the family farm and all that came with it. On more than one occasion, she was close to losing her lunch while spending time in the barn. The mixture of dirt, straw, and hay, along with copious amounts of animal waste, blended into a uniquely pungent smell. Being away from the family farm for fifteen years, Lilly's tolerance for those once commonplace smells had waned.

Slowly but surely, she was getting it back.

However, the more graphic aspects of bovine anatomy and husband-ry, Lilly knew she'd never be able to stomach.

Ryan's distinct, monosyllabic responses and grunts came from fur-ther in the barn, close to the maternity pens. Nathan's smooth baritone, using a more structured version of communication, spurred Lilly's feet faster through the straw. As she passed behind a row of tethered cows, Dandelion swung her head back and bellowed at her. The self-appointed matriarch of the herd needed to voice some slight to Lilly, in hopes that she would rectify the situation.

"Put your concern in the complaint box, Dandelion," Lilly patted the large bovine on the rump as she passed. "I have matters to discuss with Ryan and the vet."

The cow let out another long bellow to Lilly's back as she continued to the maternity pen.

She stood at the heavy metal fencing that made the pen and watched as Ryan and Nathan tended to a small heifer. Lilly studied the animal and tried to figure out which cow was in the pen. She knew that Peony's and Rose's due dates were fast approaching. Peony was older, around three to four years, and certainly wasn't this small. This soon-to-be-mom had to be Rose with her first calf.

Ryan and Nathan strolled around the cow. Ryan stayed up by Rose's head, maintaining a hold on her halter to keep the cow from swinging her head back toward the vet. Nathan leaned against Rose's rotund side, moving a stethoscope along her black and white hide.

Nathan Wilhelm, the youngest of the Wilhelms to join the family busi-ness, began working at the local veterinary clinic in mid-summer as the newest large-animal veterinarian. Tall, lean, with the tell-tale Wilhelm blond hair, Lilly firmly believed he was also the most handsome of the clan as well.

The fact that Nathan's elder siblings were at least five years older than he, married, and with a brood of children each hadn't factored into Lilly's assessment, whatsoever.

The dating pool in small towns was notoriously limited. Even more so since Officer Joshua Heimdall left town in early June. Lilly thought there had been the beginning of a connection between the two, though it wasn't enough for him to turn down a promotion to the Mankato Police Department. And perhaps being her ex-boyfriend's cousin might have helped chase him away.

Lilly focused on Ryan Swenson, hired help, and aforementioned ex-boyfriend. She had unknowingly 'inherited' him as the farm hand when she took over the family farm after her grandparents' death. His reception of her had been downright arctic thanks to the grudge he held from high school. She and Ryan had dated for a year in high school before family drama between her father and grandfather caused her family to leave town quickly. Ryan had been sore over their unexpected and one-sided breakup.

Now, fifteen years and six months later, the arctic void between them was beginning to thaw.

"What are you staring at?" Ryan's hard gaze and voice jolted Lilly back to the barn and maternity pen.

"Your fat face," Lilly shot back. It was a slow thaw.

Nathan choked back a laugh.

"How's Rose doing, Nathan?" Lilly asked, turning away from Ryan as he began to open his mouth in response.

Nathan looped his stethoscope around his neck and rolled his shoulders. "She's stable, lungs sound clear, and her appetite is improving. Baby is doing all right, as far as I can tell."

"Thank you for coming out to look at our herd," Lilly gave the vet a pleased smile. She caught Ryan rolling his eyes in her periphery, and she amped up the smile.

"That's my job," Nathan shrugged as he stepped away from Rose. "Ryan also said your milk production is down as well. Have you had the nutritionist out to check your feed, or should I check the rest of the herd?"

"Mark, the feed man, has been out—" Lilly began.

"Many times," Ryan interjected.

"And he says that the wet summer hasn't been the greatest for the cows. The feed is adequate, though last year's dry conditions also hurt this year's dry feed." Lilly fought back her prideful grin at Ryan's face. Pure shock, mixed with a hint of amazement, was visible on his face. "What?" she snapped, "I pay attention."

Starting in July, the small herd of twelve milking cows and six calves had been struck by pneumonia after a prolonged stretch of midsummer rains. Even though she had Ryan clear out the calf hutches of the soaked straw and bedding, the calves still caught the virus, and it was passed to the rest of the herd. Milk production dropped almost in half as the sickness spread through the barn. Most of the older cows bounced back once the weather cleared up, which should have led to an increase in milk as the days and weeks passed. The rally, after being given a clean bill of health, had yet to occur. Two of the pregnant cows, Peony and Rose, have been slower in kicking the nasty bug.

The vet nodded, considering what Lilly had said. "I'll give you a few more doses of Draxxin for Rose and Peony, just to be on the safe side," Nathan said, turning and making his way out of the maternity pen. "I could also offer some supplements for the herd's feed if you're interested."

"Mark said that, too," Ryan countered. "We don't have the assets to be adding anything to the feed rotation."

"Not even for the pregnant cows?" Lilly asked. She felt the heat rise in her cheeks at Ryan's comment. The money problems stemmed from her overspending on the farmstead renovations and the lack of income from her grand business plans.

Had she inadvertently doomed the cows?

"I think your herd will be fine, with time," Nathan offered, as if he read her mind. "We'll focus on the sick cows, give them the Draxxin, and keep them isolated from the rest as much as possible. From what I've seen today, these two are on the mend finally."

"I hope you're right," Lilly bit her thumbnail.

"You need me for anything else, Nathan? I have to get going on the calf chores." Ryan closed the heavy metal gate to the pen.

"I think I'm through here," the vet waved Ryan off. "I have to get over to the Haugens' and check on their new foal. Sounds like what spread through your herd is making its rounds."

Ryan gave the vet a short nod, then left the barn. Lilly noticed how he hadn't offered any parting gesture to her. Though if he had, she'd probably faint away from the sheer shock.

"How much do I owe you for today?" Lilly asked Nathan.

"Don't worry about the bill now," he waved her question off. "You've got other things to worry about."

Lilly gave a tight smile. "We are going to pay our bill, Nathan. I don't want the clinic to think we're trying to short you..."

"We don't," he flashed her a gentle smile.

They walked out of the barn and toward his truck in silence. Lilly's brain spun with numbers and bills, as well as personal and business fires that needed to be extinguished. Between the struggle to launch the Accidental Farmer Experience, finalizing farm repairs, and her sick herd, Lilly wasn't sure if she'd survive the year.

"Earth to Lilly."

She felt a hand on her arm that stopped her mid-stride. Lilly blinked and found herself face-to-face with the metal side of Nathan's vet box at the back of his truck. Her bewildered expression stared back at her from the beveled chrome.

"Oh," was all she could say.

"Didn't want you breaking your nose on my truck," Nathan grinned. "I know how to set a broken cow or horse femur. I'm lousy at human nasal breaks."

"Thanks," Lilly's cheeks flushed. "We will pay our vet bill."

He shook his head, as if to dismiss her last statement. He opened a panel in the metal truck bed topper and began replacing the items he used for the herd check. "Are you doing anything with your farmer accident thing at Apple Dapple Days this weekend?"

She laughed despite herself. "Accidental Farmer Experience," Lilly corrected. "And yes, I will have a booth set up in the vendor fair section of the street. Maybe I'll get some more out-of-town interest."

"Good," he nodded. He opened another side panel and brought out a small glass vial. "Here's more Draxxin for Rose and Peony—same dosing as before. Ryan should still have those instructions. Just follow that until this round is done, and that should be that."

Lilly took the medicine and turned over the bottle in her hand. Somehow, she couldn't help but feel the fate of the farm rested in the liquid within. "I'll make sure Ryan gets this."

"Say, when is the vendor fair done?"

Lilly paused as she went over the Apple Dapple Days schedule in her mind. She had it almost committed to memory, barring any last-minute changes. "It goes from ten a.m. to four p.m. on Saturday."

"My cousin's in a band that's playing in the beer tent on Saturday night, maybe we could go check them out?"

"I didn't know your cousin was in a band." Lilly didn't know much about any extended family members of the Wilhelms'; if she had to be brutally honest, she didn't have a clue about most of the families in Lone Tree. The town's population had undergone significant changes over the past fifteen years.

"Yeah, kid thinks he's going to be the next Slash or Eddie Van Halen. The band does mostly eighties and nineties covers," Nathan explained as he put his medical equipment back in their proper compartments. "Though I think they're experimenting with more rockabilly now. I can never keep up with that kid."

"That sounds more up my alley," Lilly said. She followed him the few steps he took around the rear of the truck.

"Great," Nathan grinned. "Then it's a date." He punctuated his declaration by slamming shut the tailgate.

"Date–?" Lilly stammered as she dumbly followed him to the cab of his truck and watched him climb inside. "Are you sure—"

The truck roared to life, drowning out the rest of her protests.

"Catch you later, Lills," Nathan called to her over the growl of his diesel engine. He winked at her before driving out of the farmyard.

From beyond the house, the Colonel's screeching crow echoed across the empty yard.

"Who asked you?" Lilly shouted.

Chapter Four

"You have a date for Apple Dapple Days?" Faith's incredulous tone was punctuated by the clatter of tableware onto chipped Formica.

Lilly looked up from the disheveled burger and fries barely hanging on to the plate Faith had so ungracefully dropped at her booth. It certainly wasn't how she had figured her lunch would start. "Um, hi, Faith," Lilly straightened out the fries that threatened to fall off the plate. "How are the kids?"

"Don't give me that folksy, down home small talk crap!' Faith hissed as she sank into the booth seat across from Lilly. "Savannah told me that Dr. Nate asked you to the dance Saturday night!"

Lilly's brows drew together as she took a bite of the burger. Melty cheese and savory bacon filled her senses, momentarily distracting her from the poised question. "How does your youngest daughter know about that?"

"She overheard Ryan muttering about it last night when he was over for dinner."

"You mean supper," Lilly corrected.

"No, dinner. The meal that typically comes after lunch." Faith shook her head.

"So, supper," Lilly grinned.

"No. Dinner. As in breakfast, lunch, and dinner." Faith's finger stabbed the tabletop with each word to stress her point. "And don't change the subject. Dr. Nate asked you to the dance?"

"Yes, Nathan did ask me to the dance," Lilly confessed. "I don't see why that warrants this big of a deal to be made."

She caught Faith staring at her for a long moment. Lilly swallowed her food, fearing she had done something wrong. She wondered if this was the 'mom look' her kids always spoke about in reverent whispers. "What?" Lilly asked quietly.

"What about Ryan?" Faith demanded.

"What? Did he want to ask Nathan to the dance?" Lilly took a long draw on her iced tea. Even if it was mid-September and the weather dictated that one's choice of drinks should start with the warm variety, namely all things pumpkin, Lilly couldn't quite let go of her iced beverages yet.

"*Klugscheißer*," Faith narrowed her eyes. "Oh, I dunno, maybe that he's still in love with you?"

A few of the customers in the café swiveled their heads as discreetly as they could, which wasn't at all. Lilly felt her cheeks burn.

Since moving back to Lone Tree, Lilly found herself to be the unofficial "new thing" in town, the default fodder for the town's gossips. Everything she did turned into fair game for the rumor mill. And Faith inadvertently gave them another morsel to devour, and a rather large one at that.

"Faith, shhh!" Lilly leaned close to her friend. Who also happened to be Ryan's older sister. "He is not still in love with me."

"Yes, he is."

"He certainly has a stellar way of showing it," Lilly grumbled as she scratched at the back of her neck. "And how can he be stuck on me after all these years?"

After I broke his heart at fifteen by skipping town suddenly with my parents? Lilly shook her head as she replayed bits and pieces of that day over in her mind. Yeah, that's something that'll keep a heart yearning for all these years.

"The heart wants what the heart wants," Faith shrugged.

"And, if I'm not mistaken, didn't you try to set me up with your policeman cousin right when I came back to town?" Lilly poked a fry at Faith's head.

"Just trying to keep your options open and inspire Ryan to get his butt in gear." Faith snatched the fry from Lilly's fingers and popped it into her mouth.

"Right," Lilly rolled her eyes. "Well, he hasn't gotten his butt out of park for the last five months, so I think you're a little off on this."

"Whatever," Faith fluttered her fingers in a dismissive wave.

"And I thought you'd be happy for me to get out there, to get back into the dating scene," Lilly pushed. "I certainly can do a lot worse in this town than Dr. Nathan Wilhelm, large animal veterinarian."

Faith smiled broadly. "That's certainly true. Maybe this will finally get Ryan off his butt to profess his love for you."

"Ha!" Lilly barked out a harsh laugh that caused heads to swivel once more. "The only professing he does is to tell me how much I mess things up at the farm."

Faith's voice softened. "You're still learning, and the agri-tourism business is still getting its legs under it."

"I hope so," Lilly groaned and bit into her burger once more.

"You need any help setting up your booth tomorrow afternoon? I heard about what happened yesterday at the farmers' market."

Lilly slumped in her booth. She was swiftly turning into Lone Tree's one-woman show. "Who told you about that? Savannah or maybe it was Thomas?" Faith's kids seemed to be everywhere in town and knew the juiciest gossip before it even left the rumor mill.

"Elvira stopped by real quick after the market, last night, before going home. Gave me the whole play-by-play," Faith grinned.

"Don't you have customers to help?" Lilly muttered.

"Oy!" Faith shouted out into the dining area. "Any of you need help?"

A muttered chorus of "no" echoed back. Even Chris, the front-line cook, stuck a thumbs up out the food window behind the counter.

Lilly narrowed her eyes at Faith's beaming grin, "I hate you some days."

"I know," Faith laughed, stealing another fry.

"I think I'll be okay. I'm bringing some cinder blocks from the barn for the canopy. No more surprise, rogue winds will take me down."

"Good."

"Hey, did Elvira also tell you about the little spat between Angela and Cecilia?"

Faith snatched the pickle spear from Lilly's plate. "Did one of them finally throw a punch? Please tell me Angela punched Cecilia in her spring-break-nose-job."

"No one punched her... What?"

"Every spring break, Cecilia and her brood go down to Mexico so she can get discounted plastic surgery."

Lilly's mouth fell open. "No way."

"Oh, yeah. She tells everyone they're going to Cabo San Lucas, but they're going to Mexico City for two weeks. Then the whole family comes back, and mommy has a new nose, lips, cheeks, butt, you name it."

Lilly sputtered a laugh around her French fry. "Wow. I wonder if all those fillers and implants are non-GMO?"

"Hey, Faith! I need your help with the order real quick," line cook Chris shouted through the order window.

"Well, gotta go be boss lady," Faith scooted out of the booth. "I'll be back in a second."

Lilly waved her off and watched as the owner of Grandma's Attic went and performed her job. She wondered, with all the conversations the two had had over the last few months, if Faith talked to all her customers that way, how does she get any work done at all?

Enough for the Attic to become one of the few staples in Lone Tree. Lilly pushed her nearly finished lunch away and brought out a notebook from her bag. Her last-minute To-Do List for Apple Dapple Days. She opened her list and frowned. She'd hoped to be able to establish a new economic staple with the Accidental Farmer Experience. The handful of bookings she'd had over the summer were barely enough to bring the farm into the black. All the renovations to the outbuildings and the rising veterinary costs were threatening the farm's viability.

Lilly shook her head to clear her mind of those looming threats and try to focus on the weekend. One thing at a time. She had cinder blocks, signup sheets, informational pamphlets, and promo stickers. Sample soaps, lotions, candles... she marked the candles with a pen as possible freebies. Hopefully, with the influx of out-of-towners for Apple Dapple Days, interest in her fledgling business will pick up.

She started scribbling down ideas for hashtags to use on her social media posts over the weekend. Apple Dapple Days already had their online tags, and each Instagram or TikTok post made by the festival's marketing committee garnered quite a few likes and views, considering this was a small-town event. Though, as Lilly thought it over, there wasn't much to compete with out in rural farm country, unlike with the various festivals and weekly neighborhood events that took place at any given moment in the Twin Cities. In her old Loring Park neighborhood, there seemed to be a new block party or business soft opening every other week.

The café's entrance bells chimed and broke Lilly out of her thoughts. She glanced up from her notes to see Lisa Hayes enter the Attic. The head of the Lone Tree Chamber of Commerce looked a little worse for wear, with platinum blond hair pulled into a messy ponytail, a long-sleeved shirt, and a puffy vest dusted with dirt and grime. Her usually professional, if not stoic, face looked absolutely drained.

"Hi, Lisa," Lilly gave a little wave. "Missed you at the market yesterday."

Lisa's eyes locked onto her as she made her way through the emptying tables over to Lilly's booth. She gave Lilly a quick once-over. "Yes, well, I've been busy making sure that Apple Dapple Days runs smoothly."

"I can only imagine how busy you must be," Lilly nodded. "Thank you for letting me have a booth in the commerce area for the Accidental Farmer Experience."

"Yes, yes," Lisa looked down at her smartphone as it chirped.

"I think next week might be our last market for the year," Lilly ventured, watching as the Chamber head clicked and swiped away on her phone. "A lot of vendors told me yesterday at tear down that schedules were starting to get busy with home and school activities."

Lisa's eyes darted up from her phone's screen, and she smiled. Lilly knew that smile, and a chill went down her spine. How many times has she seen that smile from her ex-husband's patronizing mother?

"Oh, those are the reasons they're giving you?" Lisa asked. "Hmmm."

"What do you mean by that?" Lilly sat up straighter in the booth.

Lisa leveled her gaze and gave a soft, yet sharp laugh. "Oh, Lilly," she sighed, "You saw firsthand that little fiasco Cecilia had to suffer through."

Of course, she would be besties with Cecilia Baxter.

"No one wants to be around that Stilner woman. How many incidents will the good folk of our town have to suffer through before you see that she needs to go?" Lisa asked.

"Now, you know as well as I that these incidents aren't just Angela's fault," Lilly countered.

"Hmm. Cecilia wouldn't need to debase herself so needlessly if you'd just get rid of Angela," Lisa lowered her eyes and tapped on her phone with her thumbs. "She is just responding to the situation the best a woman like Angela can understand."

Lilly fumed. "What's that supposed to mean?"

"Civil and rational words don't work with a woman of Angela's... background."

"Background? What are you—"

"Just don't let her be a vendor next year, and I'm sure that all of the current vendors, and even more, will be back for next summer's market." Lisa's voice dripped with thinly veiled threats wrapped in plasticine positivity.

"But I don't—"

"Online order for Lisa!" line cook Chris barked from the kitchen window.

Lisa turned to the counter and raised her hand. "Just a moment, dear!"

"Lisa, there has to be some way—"

"I must grab my order and get back to the office." Lisa tapped her phone a few more times before she dropped it into her purse. "Please, Lilly. I don't want to see Bev and Harold's granddaughter drag their

name, and our town, through the mud while trying to help the less for-
tunate," she smiled grimly while flashing air quotes with her fingers.
"You're already on thin ice with the farm and this agri-tourism thing, I'd
hate for that woman to bring you any farther down."

Lilly watched in stunned, yet fuming, silence as Lisa Hayes walked up
to the counter and grabbed a to-go box from Faith. The Chamber head
gave a short wave of her fingers and left the café. The bells announcing
her departure grated against Lilly's ears.

Chapter Five

The incident with Lisa left a sour feeling in Lilly's stomach. And left her more than a little rattled. What did Angela Stilner do that warranted such hatred from Lisa Hayes and Cecilia Baxter?

After her disrupted lunch, Lilly decided she needed a walk to clear her head. A mental palate cleanser before she went back to the farm and met with whatever Ryan's mood du jour was that afternoon. She had other things to worry about than her temperamental hired hand, such as whether or not she should risk keeping Angela at the farmers' market. Would it be worth making one woman mad at her versus bringing down the wrath of two of the most powerful women in town?

Lilly turned down Main Street, away from the Attic and the Apple Dapple Days festival grounds. Flatbeds and city trucks were already lined up on the main thoroughfare through town, preparing to close it down that night so vendors and other festival personnel could start setting up Friday morning. The last thing she needed was another reminder of Lisa Hayes at that moment.

Although now she headed toward the end of town, where the farmers' market was held. Lilly groaned, realizing she was stuck between her very own rock and a hard place. Be mindful of Lisa Hayes' warning or Cecilia Baxter's threats?

Lilly paused at one of the stoplights in town, waiting for the cross-walk signal to indicate when it was safe to cross. Next to the crosswalk button was a green and brown bench, one of the many around town that had been donated by some long-gone citizen's family or by a business. Sitting on the bench was a man Lilly couldn't place. Between becoming almost a regular at the Attic, she figured she'd seen most of the citizens of Lone Tree by now. Perhaps she had missed one. This gentleman preferred to get his food elsewhere than the Attic; maybe the dive bar on the other end of town.

He sat on the bench, head tilted down, as if he were reading or sleeping. Lilly spotted no book in his hands, so she figured he was resting on a slightly balmy September afternoon. He wore the standard clothes of a Lone Tree native, worn jeans and a John Deere shirt. A mix-and-match International Harvester hat sat upon his greasy-looking black hair. The light turned in their favor, signaling for all pedestrians to cross at that moment.

"Sir, the light changed," Lilly called out. "Were you waiting for the light?"

The man did not move. Perhaps he truly was asleep. The crosswalk timer slowly counted down the seconds before it was too late to cross. "Sir, the crosswalk..." Lilly reached out tentatively and touched his shoulder. She hoped to rouse him quickly. After that, she was going on her way. Who was she to interrupt his nap?

"Sir?"

As her hand touched his shoulder, he slumped to the side. And continued to slump until his temple connected with the bench seat. The man's hat fell from his head, revealing two glossy eyes and a dull expression.

Lilly gasped as she scrambled away from the man and the bench. Her mind went blank momentarily as she stared at the man's motionless body on the bench. Slowly, her senses came back to her, and Lilly fumbled with her purse until she produced her cell phone.

"Hello, 911?" Lilly stammered into the phone. "There's a dead body at the corner of Main and Elm…"

"ID found on his person said Owen Perkins," Sheriff Branford flipped through his notes. Tall with dark features and a face she rarely saw crack with any emotion, let alone a smile, Sheriff Michael Branford made for an imposing figure. He was dressed in his uniform, consisting of crisp, dark brown pants and a khaki-colored shirt, which stood in stark contrast to the holster around his waist and the gleaming badge on his chest. "Though we'll run fingerprints and ask around to make sure that's who he really is."

"Any idea how he died?" Lilly swallowed hard.

"Not until we do tox screens and an autopsy." He flipped his notebook shut. "Well, I think I have everything I need from you. Don't leave town."

Lilly laughed awkwardly. "You're… you're kidding, right?" Silence greeted her. "Right?"

"Sir," a police officer walked up to the pair, an evidence bag the size of an envelope in his hands. "We found something under the bench."

"Let's see," the sheriff said, taking the bag from the officer and holding it up. He turned the bagged item over a few times, taking in all the angles.

From what Lilly could see, it looked like a clear syringe. A long, thin metal needle stuck out menacingly from one end. She couldn't help herself and found she leaned in closer to the sheriff to get a better look.

"Ahem," Sheriff Branford's brow arched as he held the bag out of her line of sight.

"Sorry," she whispered.

"Make sure the lab goes over this, see what was in it," the sheriff said, handing the bag back to the officer. The other man walked briskly to a waiting patrol car.

"Did he die from an overdose?" Lilly asked. "Were there drugs in that syringe?"

The sheriff let out a long sigh and looked at her. "Too early to tell."

"Was he a drug dealer?"

"No way to tell that at this time."

"Are there any drug lords in Lone Tree?"

"Lilly, stop!" The sharp tone of the sheriff stalled any other questions on her lips. "Go home."

"But–"

"Do you have a badge?"

A slight pout creased her lips. "No."

"Then go home."

Lilly frowned as she walked back to the Attic and her parked Kia.

Who was Owen Perkins? Was he a resident of Lone Tree? How did he end up on the bench at that corner? And did the substance in that syringe kill him? Was it self-inflicted, or did someone help him off this mortal coil?

Her brain buzzed with questions and possible answers as she drove back to the farm. She was so lost in her world of potential scenarios that she parked and exited her car in a daze. Lilly dropped her purse on the kitchen island and sat on a stool, barely registering that she had done those acts.

Perhaps the shock of seeing–and touching–a dead body finally set in for her. She barely acknowledged Ryan sitting across from her at the island, eating a bowl of mac and cheese.

"Hey, Lilly, you okay?" Ryan asked. "You look a little rough."

Lilly blinked and focused her eyes on him. She opened her mouth to answer, but snapped it shut quickly, a frown furrowing her face. "Is that my extra cheesy mac and cheese?" She blurted out. Ryan grinned and took another bite. "I was saving that."

"I'll buy you some more mac," Ryan swallowed. "What happened to you? See a ghost?"

The tears began to flow as soon as the word left his mouth. He sat in stunned silence as she cried. "Sorry," Lilly sniffed and wiped her hand over her cheeks. "I saw a dead guy on the street."

"Um," Ryan lowered his fork back to the bowl. "Like someone dressed as a zombie?"

"No, a real dead guy," she snapped, still wiping roughly at her cheeks. She filled him in in great detail about finding the now deceased Owen Perkins on the bench.

"Man, you're two for two for finding dead bodies this year," Ryan's mouth turned up in a slight smirk.

"This isn't funny, Ryan," Lilly groaned. "There's a murderer out there!"

"Owen Perkins, right?" Ryan asked, and Lilly nodded. "If it was the Owen Perkins I knew from high school, then he probably did it to himself."

"How could you say that?" she asked, aghast.

"Because Owen ran with the druggies in high school," he shrugged. "I, well, I also got some off-label meds from him after my little accident."

Ten years ago, Ryan had been helping another farmer move bulls and cattle. Being young and thinking himself invincible, Ryan lost track of the farm's most dangerous bull and took a horn to his left thigh. After years of surgeries, therapies, and pain medication, he still walked with a pronounced limp and had chronic pain issues because of it.

"I didn't realize..." Lilly looked down at the island counter.

"It's better now," Ryan shrugged again. "I haven't been a patron of Owen or Henry for a while."

"That's good to hear–" Lilly froze and locked eyes with Ryan. "Owen and Henry?"

"Yeah, they were inseparable in high school."

"Henry... Stilner?"

"Yeah, that Henry."

Lilly grew quiet as more questions fired off in her mind. Perhaps that was the condemned behavior that Lisa and Cecilia hinted at? Angela was married to a former, or not so former, drug user and supplier. That was the unfavorable influence they didn't want associated with the farmers' market.

"Does Henry still supply?" Lilly asked.

Ryan shrugged his shoulders. "Not sure. I haven't talked to either of them in years."

"Good," Lilly said emphatically. Ryan's eyes widened under his always-present John Deere cap. "I mean, I'm glad you're not... that things are better." She let her voice fade into the silence of the kitchen before she said something foolish.

"May I ask why Henry Stilner caught your attention?" Ryan asked after a moment of studying her.

Lilly sighed and relayed the whole messy business of Angela, Cecilia, and Lisa, especially the pointed conversation at the Attic before she discovered Owen's body.

"So you think this has something to do with that whole mess?" he asked. "Henry and Owen were nothing but two bit druggies who thought themselves the next Breaking Bad. And that's a reason to shun Angela?"

"It's my only working theory at the moment," Lilly said. "Unless..."

"Oh, I hate that tone." Ryan lowered his head and took another bite of mac and cheese. "What now, Nancy Drew?"

"What if it was Henry?"

"Henry did what?"

"Kill Owen to get him out of the way," Lilly suggested. "He wanted all the drug business for himself."

"Henry's only doing pot nowadays, at the county fairgrounds and his farm." Ryan continued. "He'd only do enough to get a bad case of the munchies. Same with Owen."

"I thought you didn't know what they were up to now?" Lilly asked, her eyes narrowed at him.

He matched her expression. "My sister's not the only one who hears rumors and things about town."

"Mm-hmm," Lilly pursed her lips together tightly.

Ryan shook his head and focused once more on the bowl of mac and cheese. "Whatever."

"Whatever, my butt!" Lilly took the fork from his hand and shoved the cheesy noodles into her mouth. He stared at her with an expression Lilly hadn't seen on him before. It was hard to place. It made her insides rumble. And she didn't like that one bit.

Maybe she had fifteen years ago in high school.

She swallowed hard and returned the fork to Ryan's still out-stretched hand.

"There's something to Owen's death," Lilly finally spoke, each word precise. "There's more to this than what we're seeing, I know it."

Chapter Six

"Coming through! Move it or lose it!" Faith's booming voice echoed down the Main Street corridor. Festival vendors and volunteers alike parted before the pair in a comically Biblical fashion.

"Faith, we're not winning a prize for who can set up first," Lilly called after her friend. "Slow down!" The collapsible wagon Faith lent her snagged a wheel in a pothole in the asphalt. Jars and lotions and boxes of candles jostled ominously at the sudden stop. "The Friday vendor event doesn't even start until four o'clock, we have enough time!"

"Well, we certainly won't with that attitude!" Faith called over her shoulder, pausing just long enough to adjust the cardboard box of promotional pamphlets she was carrying.

Lilly sighed as she struggled to get her wagon moving once more. Slowly, the path Faith's outburst had opened closed in around her. Pop-up canopies and booths had sprung up along either side of Main Street since eight o'clock that morning, each showcasing the various services and businesses of Lone Tree and the surrounding areas. The displays even spilled from the sidewalk and into the street, trying to make use of whatever space the vendor could eek out without getting cited by the festival officials. Activity bustled all around in a steady stream of bodies and merchandise.

Thankfully, the vendor spots were assigned and not on a first-come, first-served basis. If that had been the case, Lilly's late start that morning would have spelled certain doom for her booth. She'd be pushed to the outskirts of the vendor area, muscled out of the prime customer traffic by all the early birds and diehard sellers. She finally tugged her errant wagon wheel free and cursed the blasted rooster's existence.

If the Colonel could have been a normal rooster and not a territorial psychopath, Lilly could get her chores completed at a normal time. Instead, she has to go through numerous extra steps just to protect herself from the insane fowl. And the fact that she discovered another dead body the day before. That would put a wrench in anyone's plans to get a head start on the day. Thankfully, Faith hadn't mentioned the latest town crisis. Lilly began to wonder if she was just a magnet for bad luck.

Lilly pulled the wagon up to her pop-up canopy and tables. She had gotten them set up by herself before running into Faith. Being a set-up crew of one at the time, Lilly trudged the canopy and each table three blocks from where she parked her Kia. Main Street had been blocked off with orange and white construction barricades in preparation for the festival, so motorized traffic—even for vendors—was prohibited. Faith had been chatting with a neighboring booth's proprietor when she spotted Lilly struggling with her last table. Though it was September in Minnesota, summer's heat was holding on for a few more days. Sweating through her clothes and feeling like the drowned rat she knew she resembled, Lilly finally accepted Faith's offer of help.

Faith had her box unpacked and organized on the table by the time Lilly arrived with the errant wagon. Her heart sank at the sight. Not that Faith did anything wrong. Seeing the booth set up and almost festi-val-ready in such a short time made Lilly's doubts from the last few days rear their ugly heads once more.

Perhaps she was out of her league with the Accidental Farmer Experience? Everything around her suddenly felt suffocating and tumbling down on her head.

"Why the sour face?" Faith asked as she rearranged the pamphlets to make space for the newly arrived lotion and candles. "Is it the whole finding another dead body thing?"

"Wondered how long you'd last before you brought that up," Lilly muttered, smiling despite herself. "I'm proud you lasted this long."

"I am anything if not a pillar of self-restraint," Faith declared.

The wagon handle fell from Lilly's limp hand. "Am I kidding myself here?" She blurted out.

Faith regarded her for a long moment. "No."

"That's it? Just 'no'?" Lilly handed over candles from the wagon. As far as she could tell, none were damaged on their shaky ride from the car.

"I said what I said," Faith replied.

"It's been five months and I've sunk so much money into this stupid idea with nothing to show for it." Lilly lamented. "Nothing but a handful of bookings and rising debt."

"You had those bookings – that's nothing to sneeze at," Faith flashed her a grin. "Welcome to running your own business."

"Oh, right. Have you ever gone through anything like this? The Attic is packed almost every day of the year with people."

"Not in the beginning," Faith countered. "After I bought the place and word got around that the Attic was under new management, the regulars stopped coming for almost a year. It was rough going for a long time."

"Really?"

"The people of the town, even though they knew me, weren't the most trusting people. They had to see how things would pan out after I bought the Attic." Faith arranged the candles into a quaint pyramid. "They wanted to wait and see what I'd do with the place, if I were going to keep it status quo or turn it into a kale karaoke bar or some stupid thing."

Lilly laughed. "If you were in downtown Minneapolis, a kale karaoke bar would have a decent go."

"I'm not in Minneapolis, thank God," Faith breathed. She caught herself and gave Lilly an apologetic look. "No offense..."

"None taken," Lilly smiled.

"What I mean is that you're not in Minneapolis. Things in Lone Tree move at a completely different pace and run by their own rules. Even if those rules make no sense." Faith continued. "You just have to give things time to settle. You're still new here."

"But I'm not new. I was born here," Lilly stressed.

"You were gone long enough for people to see you as a stranger." Faith arched a brow, "And before you go into that whole family drama rehash, I know it wasn't your fault you left. You were a teen, and you had to go where your parents were, blah blah blah. That minor detail doesn't mean a lick around here."

Lilly frowned and let what Faith said sink in. It was true that there was nothing a rural community loved more than juicy drama, and to remind those involved in it of their new outsider status at any given moment. The sooner any drama was resolved, the quicker boredom settled in among the populace. Some didn't care who was hurt to keep the drama alive, as long as the town had their real-life soap opera to keep them entertained.

"Good afternoon, Sheriff Branford!" Faith suddenly called out, waving.

Lilly turned and watched as Lone Tree's sheriff, and her mother's cousin, walked through the crowd toward her booth. "Hey, cousin Michael," Lilly gave a small wave.

He stood beside Lilly and surveyed the booth before he spoke. "You decided to take a stab at Apple Dapple Days?"

Lilly bristled at what her fragile self-esteem took as a slight. Since coming back to Lone Tree, Lilly hadn't found reconnecting with the estranged family on her mother's side easy. She constantly wondered if they were complicit in the talk around town about her parents' sudden departure from Lone Tree all those years ago, and the reasoning behind the rift between her parents and grandparents. And then, when factoring in the messy business of her finding a dead body last April on her farm, it was hard to break through and make new friends.

"Yes, I'm taking a stab at it," Lilly replied, forcing her best smile. "What brings you out here during setup? Are you window shopping for Katie?"

Sheriff Branford shook his head. "No, Katie didn't send me down to look for her. She's on the planning committee and knows what's all here."

Lilly's smile faltered. Of course, the sheriff's wife would be on the Apple Dapple Days planning committee.

"I'm looking for Lisa Hayes," the sheriff continued. "I have to finalize security for this weekend with her."

"Does a small-town festival like this really need security?" Lilly looked around the street. "What could possibly happen at Apple Dapple Days?"

Both the sheriff and Faith leveled telling gazes at Lilly. She glanced at each in turn before the blush crept up her neck. "Oh, yeah. Owen Perkins yesterday... Sorry."

The sheriff cleared his throat and tilted his head toward her. "We'll have an influx of out-of-town folks as well as citizens of Lone Tree. And the committee went ahead with the beer tent, despite my petition not to have it. All those elements together mean the heightened risk of incidents."

"You did not petition for the removal of the beer tent!" Faith howled with feigned distress.

"I invite you both to help out in the dunk tank tonight and Saturday night," Sheriff Branford offered. Lilly almost swore one corner of his mouth twitched up in a slight resemblance of a smile.

"No, thank you," Faith said, holding up her hands and going back to organizing the merchandise. "And you have another murder to solve!" Faith continued with a smile. "Better than worrying about the silly beer tent."

Sheriff Branford eyed her. "Yes."

"Any new leads on Owen?" Lilly asked.

"None yet," the sheriff said. He then shook his head, as if catching himself. "And certainly none I can share with you."

Faith shot Lilly a telling glance.

The sheriff glanced down at his wristwatch and shook his head. "I should get going, I have to find Lisa before she gets caught in something I can't pull her away from."

With a sharp nod, Sheriff Branford left the two alone in Lilly's booth. She watched him disappear into the frenzy of festival preparations, not envying him for needing to speak with Lisa Hayes. Lilly remembered the icy conversation she had yesterday at Grandma's Attic and could only imagine how frayed the woman's patience would be today.

"Hey, Faith, what do you know about Angela Stilner?" Lilly asked abruptly.

Faith froze mid-organization. "Wait. You don't know?"

"Know what?"

"You've only hung out with the woman all summer at the farmers' market! How can you not know?" her friend demanded.

"I don't know, Faith, maybe I'll have to ask her next time I see her why she didn't reveal to me why the whole town seems to hate her?"

Faith's cheeks flushed for a moment. "She was Lone Tree's scandal *du jour* after your family left."

Lilly stood silently, arms crossed over her stomach, and waited for Faith to continue.

"Do you remember Henry Stilner? He was a year ahead of you and Ryan in high school." When Lilly finally nodded her positive memory, Faith resumed, "Angela didn't go to Lone Tree High; she is originally from Sleepy Eye. During their senior year, Henry and Angela started dating casually, but after graduation, they became serious quickly. Within the year, they moved in together, and by three years, they were married."

"That doesn't seem too bad," Lilly shrugged. "A lot of people marry quickly after high school."

"It gets worse," Faith warned. "So by this time, Henry and Angela are living at the old Stilner farm, just south of town. Henry's parents had given up farming, sold the crop land, and moved to New Ulm. Henry took over the building site."

"Still not seeing the issue," Lilly urged.

"Even though they don't have crop land, the building site is big enough for small livestock, sheep, goats, pigs, the like. So Henry and Angela keep a small flock of sheep on the farm that she uses for yarn and wool to sell, and eventually the sheep get processed for meat and other such things."

Lilly pondered this information momentarily. Angela always brought vegetables and eggs to her farmers' market booth, and sometimes yarn or wool.

"So Angela and Henry hired a guy to help with the sheep, and also with Henry's tractor repair business, which he started up in the large machine shed on the property." Faith continued with her tale. "This was ten years ago, the first of many hired men to cycle through the Stilner farm. There's an old mobile home on the property that Old Man Stilner used for their previous hired hands when they had crop land. Although soon it's not just sheep and tractors these hired men are helping with."

Faith paused, shooting Lilly a dramatic look.

"You mean... Angela..."

"Is getting more than just her livestock needs met."

"Faith!" Lilly gasped.

"The rotating roster of hired men finally stops five years ago when the most recent help is brought on. Not only is he practicing more than animal husbandry, but Henry has been kicked out of his family's farmhouse and is now living in the hired help's trailer. New Mr. Side Piece is shacking up with Angela in the main house."

"What!?" Lilly's mouth hung open despite herself.

"Angela and this new man have been living in the main house as an item for the last five years." Faith lowered her tone as she cast glances around them, as if now she was worried about eavesdroppers, "In her husband's family's house."

Lilly gaped at Faith in disbelief. "Angela has been cheating on her husband?"

"Pretty much since the 'I Do's,'" Faith nodded solemnly. "If not longer."

"I had no idea..." Lilly's brows furrowed. "And everyone knows about this?"

"Both Henry and Angela act like this is some sort of state secret, but we all know. Worse kept secret in Lone Tree."

"They just go on with life as if nothing is wrong?" Lilly couldn't help but gape. Her mind was spinning from this new revelation.

"Most people tend to act like they don't know, to help Henry and the Stilner relations save face. He's a son of Lone Tree, you know."

Lilly's frown returned. "But Angela doesn't get that courtesy? Because she's not from here?"

Faith shook her head.

Lilly continued, "Do I know this hired man slash homewrecker?"

"I think his name is Jacob?" Faith ventured. "He doesn't come into town much. I think he fears the lynch mob that would form if he did."

Lilly chewed her bottom lip as she processed what Faith said. For being such a soap opera-worthy story, she wondered why no one else in town offered to enlighten her about the Stilner cheating scandal. People seemed so set on telling her to stay away from Angela, but never gave their two cents as to why.

Probably because she was still part of that gossip network, whether she wanted to be or not; being newly on the Lone Tree rumor circuit kept her from knowing about the other juicy tidbits floating around town. Thankfully, Lilly didn't think her situation was quite on par with Angela Stilner. However, it was never enjoyable to be talked about behind one's back. And now Angela was somehow attached to Owen's death, at least peripherally at the moment. Her husband was friends with the victim. Could there have been bad blood between the two drug pushers? Could there be more going on with the drug-addled past of Henry?

Lilly took a slow breath. "Do you think I should ban Angela from the farmers' market?" Each word was carefully measured. *Focus on the now. Not on a crime that may or may not have happened.*

Faith paused for a moment, settling her hands firmly on her hips. "Cecilia and Lisa putting pressure on you to kick her out?" Lilly only nodded. Faith stared off into the distance, eyes not focusing on the festival around them. Lilly almost swore she could hear the gears churn away in Faith's mind. It was unusual for Faith not to have an immediate reply.

"What do you think?"

"Hey, I asked you first," Lilly pouted.

"So, take out the salacious personal life, what does that leave us with?"

"Angela is just trying to make a living at the farmers' market, just like everyone else," Lilly replied.

"Exactly. Strictly business," Faith nodded.

"If we're going to demonize Angela... then we should also look at Henry," Lilly offered. Faith's brows shot up. "Think about it. He's also part of this weird love triangle. He's been living with it for over a decade. If he wanted to change his situation, why not divorce Angela?"

"Fair question," Faith nodded. She opened a lotion sample bottle and sniffed the contents. "Ooh, sandalwood. I love this!"

"Back to my dilemma, please," Lilly plucked the lotion from Faith's hands. "So, Angela is cheating on her husband, who seems to be okay with their unorthodox arrangement. Why are we vilifying Angela and not Henry? Seems like they're both guilty in this whole absurd ordeal."

"Say it louder for those in the back, sister!"

"What's good for the goose is good for the gander."

"I think you might need to swap that, the gander for the goose... or the goose for the gander... what's good for Angela is good for Henry?" Faith snatched the lotion back. "Are you saying Henry needs to have an affair?"

"No, no, no. That if we're going to point fingers at Angela, then Henry needs some pointed at him as well."

"So, did I answer your question?" Faith asked as she tossed the empty cardboard box over the table.

Lilly caught the box and shook her head. "No. You didn't. I did." She put the box in the wagon. "Angela stays if she wants."

"Good," Faith grinned. "You have other things to worry about now than the busybodies of Lone Tree anyway."

"Like what?"

"Like what you're going to wear to the dance tomorrow night to knock Dr. Nate off his feet?"

Chapter Seven

Lilly arrived on the farm well after lunch. Her stomach rumbled as she pulled her car to a stop in front of the farmhouse. On top of running behind with her morning chores and setting up her festival booth, Faith insisted on grilling her about what outfit she planned to wear to the dance the following night. Lilly's sudden date with the eligible and hunky veterinarian was, regretfully, the last thing on her mind at the moment.

Unexpected commotion in the yard distracted her from seeking out immediate sustenance.

Lilly climbed from her car and started toward the barn. Ryan's rusted and green truck was parked in its usual spot. Now it had company. Two trucks, each with a two-wheeled trailer hitched to the back bumper, had backed down to the lower barn door. Her hunger was momentarily forgotten as she walked to the barn. Male voices she didn't recognize came in as shouted echoes from the depths beyond the white doors.

She walked between the trucks and trailers and made her way into the barn. Dandelion was the first to acknowledge her. The large cow voiced her displeasure with a long, mournful lowing.

"What's all this, girl?" Lilly stood next to Dandelion and scratched her forehead. That seemed to calm the cow's nerves somewhat. "Who are all these strangers in your barn, huh?"

Two men Lilly hadn't seen before moved around in the back of the barn, where the younger cows of the herd were hooked up. New to the barn, these few cows were new mothers getting milked for the first time. Being in the barn, rather than the relative peace of the pasture, often caused considerable stress to the one- and two-year-olds. Keeping the more experienced cows closer to the higher-traffic areas by the doors helped maintain the herd's sanity.

"There you are!" Ryan's voice reached her before she saw her hired hand. He followed behind the pair of men as they walked a reluctant heifer down the main walk behind the other tied-up animals. Lilly watched the animal as it struggled against the halter around its muzzle.

"What's going on?" Lilly asked, ignoring Ryan's outburst.

"Where have you been?" Ryan stopped behind Dandelion and rested a forearm on the cow's substantial rump. "I needed you here to help with this move."

"Move?" Her eyes narrowed. "Where is Sapphire going?"

"Her new home," he pulled his trademark John Deere cap from his head and rubbed a hand over his sweaty hair. The filtered light through the open barn doors caught his features, causing his skin to glisten. Which in turn did things to Lilly's insides.

She cleared her throat and lowered her gaze. "Sorry. I got delayed setting up the booth at Apple Dapple Days."

"I needed you here," Ryan grumbled as he jammed his hat back in place. He jerked his chin to the two men at the back of the trailer. "Thankfully, James brought his own help."

Lilly turned her head and caught the last of Sapphire as she was loaded into one of the waiting trailers. Sapphire was a one-year-old heifer, prime for breeding and milk production, given her deep pedigree. One of the few things that Ryan instructed her on over the summer was milking breed pedigrees and optimum breeding for maximum herd health. As this heifer left to improve another herd, a new cow would be bought or born into their barn to do the same for their herd.

It still hurt to see one of the animals leave, though.

"Looks like you have everything under control," Lilly said. The trailer gate slammed shut, and she flinched. Sapphire gave out a confused *mrroooowww* as the truck doors closed shortly after. She never liked seeing the cows leave the barn, even if it was a good move for both parties involved. "I would have only gotten in the way, like always."

Ryan snorted, "You're getting better."

Lilly turned on him, brows sharply arched. "Why, Ryan Swenson, was that a compliment?"

He grunted and lowered the brim of his cap lower on his head, casting his stubbled face into further shadow. "C'mon, we have to go help Jefferies with the chickens."

"But what about the other trailer?" Lilly glanced around the barn. She couldn't see another cow being moved from her stall. "Did they move the other cow already?"

"The trailer's not for a cow…" Ryan sighed.

He pushed off from Dandelion and walked briskly out of the barn. She followed him out into the yard, after a quick goodbye scratch for Dandelion, and hustled to catch up with Ryan. He was halfway to the chicken coop by the time she exited the white trimmed doorway.

For a man with a severe limp, Ryan moved surprisingly fast when he wanted to.

"If the trailer isn't for a cow, then what is it…" Lilly pressed her lips into a tight line to fight back her grin. "It's for the chickens?"

"Damn yuppie 4-H parents," Ryan muttered under his breath.

"He seriously brought a cattle trailer to pick up chickens?" Lilly's laugh couldn't be contained anymore.

Ryan's mouth pulled into a deeper frown. "Didn't want to ruin the upholstery in the extended cab."

As the two approached the chicken coop, Lilly's amused smirk turned into a grimace. The man Ryan had identified as Jefferies stood within the fenced-off chicken yard, surrounded by a flurry of feathers and shrieking poultry. She took in the scene before her, the four hens scurrying around in a frenzy and the Colonel strutting in front of the middle-aged man, challenging him to make the first move.

"I think I'm going to go grab lunch…" Lilly took a step back.

Ryan grabbed her wrist and pulled her closer to the coop, closer to him. "Not a chance." He turned to her with a devious smile. "You're bait."

"Bait?" Lilly shouted.

"Stupid Jefferies went in there without me, and the Colonel got to him, as you can see," Ryan needlessly explained. He tugged her over in the direction of the door. "I need to get that blasted rooster distracted so I can help Jefferies gather the hens."

Lilly glared at Ryan as he slowly lifted the latch to the chain link door. The four hens continued to cluck wildly as their wings churned the air in a panic. The Colonel kept Jefferies pinned in a corner against the coop. His puffy L.L. Bean vest was pocked with claw marks, fluffy cotton batting mingling with detached feathers.

"Swenson!" Jefferies shouted. "Get this blasted rooster away from me!"

"I told you to wait," Ryan shot back. "Serves you right."

"Why is he getting hens anyway?" Lilly asked as she took her position behind Ryan. This would be her first time going into the pen without her egg gathering gear. She wondered if Jefferies would mind waiting as she went to the house and suited up. The mere thought of facing the Colonel in plain clothes left her mouth dry and made her feel positively exposed.

"Jefferies' girls are showing two hens at Apple Dapple Days for the 4-H poultry contest tomorrow," Ryan said over his shoulder.

"And they are not going to be anywhere near show-ready after all this!" Jefferies barked.

"I told you to wait!" Ryan shouted back.

Jefferies shrank against the coop.

Ryan turned to Lilly. "You ready?"

"No!" She spat.

"Good."

Ryan kicked open the door and pulled her into the coop behind him in one fluid motion. With his firm grip still on her wrist, he yanked her around him and pushed her toward the rooster. Sensing new victims behind him, the wild-eyed rooster spun around with wings spread wide. As Ryan broke for the hens and Jefferies, Lilly stumbled right into the Colonel's path. She swore under her breath as the diminutive terror ran toward her with a shrill screech. She cursed Ryan's name as she ran away from Ryan and Jefferies, hoping to give them a reprieve from the rooster.

"Go get the chickens!' Lilly screamed at the man in his silly torn vest as she sped past him. After a moment, the man hurried over to the other side of the fenced yard with Ryan.

Lilly knew the only safe place for the rooster was back in the chicken coop. She ran to the door as the Colonel took to the air and landed on her back. Talons dug through her shirt as she fumbled with the door latch. Finally, the door opened, and she tumbled inside, with the rooster firmly settled on her back.

In a fit of exasperated rage, Lilly kicked a foot behind her to slam the door shut. She reached over her head and took hold of the rooster's flailing wings and pulled up.

The momentarily stunned fowl seemed to lock eyes with her as she hurled him over her head and across the coop. The rooster landed in a jumble of wings and feathers. As the Colonel scrambled to his feet, Lilly reached over and hit the lever that lowered the fox-proof inner door for the chicken ramp. The door slid down the wall only to jam before it cleared the top of the frame. She hissed out a curse and risked a glance at the rooster. He apparently had the same idea, to leave the coop via the outside ramp. The two raced toward the last exit, and the bird would have made it out into the yard if Lilly hadn't kicked sawdust and straw bedding at the Colonel.

Panicked by the sudden projectiles in his face, the Colonel floundered in his escape. Lilly heard the chain link door clang shut, signaling that Ryan and Jefferies had made it out of the fence. She spun on her heels and made a less-than-graceful exit from the coop shed. The crash sent her back into the door as it thundered shut, muffling the rooster's protests and scratching claws. In the bird's blind hatred of her, he forgot that the door to the ramp was still open to him. Lilly used that one-tracked distraction to her advantage and slinked away from the coop and out of the fence door.

By the time the rooster screamed down the ramp, she latched the door behind her.

Jefferies and Ryan stood just outside the fence, each holding a hen, mouths slack and eyes wide. She stood before them, covered in dust and feathers, clothes ripped, and skin scratched.

"Damn, girl!" Ryan breathed.

Jefferies took a step forward, pulling at his ruined vest. "Look at this mess! And the chickens—"

"You." Lilly twisted toward him and leveled a finger at his face. The man took a step back and clutched the hen, Fancy Pants, tighter. "Not a *word* from you."

"Lilly, uh, you're bleeding," Ryan began softly, but swallowed the rest of his words when she turned her wild gaze on him. He adjusted his hold on little Marta and lowered his eyes.

"Don't anyone talk to me until I've showered and have eaten," Lilly ordered. She darted a hard look at Jefferies. "And you and your chickens need to be off my property by the time I reach the back porch."

Lilly stomped away from the two men, not waiting for an answer. With each step, the adrenaline from facing the Colonel in bare combat swiftly dissipated, leaving her more than just a little woozy. The pain from the fresh claw marks on her upper back and shoulders roared to the center of attention. She hoped they looked better than how they felt.

As her shoes touched the back porch steps, Lilly barely registered the rumble of diesel and spray of gravel as truck and trailer jostled off the yard and down the driveway.

Chapter Eight

The quiet of the farmhouse was a welcome respite between the recent poultry chaos and the chaos of the Apple Dapple festival to come. Lilly sat at the island counter in the kitchen and stared at the half-eaten peanut butter and jelly sandwich in front of her. During her shower, her appetite finally returned, pushing aside the sting of the Colonel's claw marks on her back. From what she saw in the bathroom mirror, the souvenirs from the rooster looked worse than how they felt. She wouldn't suffer any permanent damage, she hoped, from the temperamental rooster.

His date with the fry pan had been postponed. For now.

Lilly leaned back on the stool and absently braided her damp auburn hair. Keeping her hands busy helped her mind focus, and with all the jumbled thoughts bouncing around from the last few days, she needed all the help she could get.

In less than two hours, Lilly needed to report back to the Apple Dapple Days festival for the vendor fair. She'd be stuck in town for the rest of the day and well into the evening, only to repeat it all over again for Saturday. Meaning she had almost two whole days of forced proximity with the people of Lone Tree, who, no doubt, had heard from Jefferies all about the chicken fiasco and her less-than-neighborly outburst. If she knew his type, he'd have told anyone who would listen all about his harrowing trip out to the Schmidt farm, the devil rooster, and the equally hellish owner.

"Never mind that it was *his* fault," Lilly grumbled. She tied off her braid and picked at her sandwich.

So much for the fresh restart she hoped for.

After the mess she found herself in the previous spring with death threats, land disputes, and a murder plot, Lilly believed that that was all behind her. Months had passed, the rumor mill slowed down, and she felt the community at last started to warm up to her. Then that damned rooster dared to exist.

"Maybe we'll be having some fried chicken soon," Lilly glared out the kitchen windows in the general direction of the coop.

"Fried chicken does sound good," Ryan entered abruptly through the back door. "I, a hundred percent, endorse that idea."

"I hate that damn rooster," Lilly groaned.

Ryan straddled the stool across the island from her. "Just have to wait until the end of fall. Then that 4-H kid will come collect him and he'll no longer be our problem."

She rubbed her hands over her face. "Why did I agree to house 4-H projects again?"

"Because you're a people pleaser and don't know how to say 'No'," Ryan picked up the untouched half of her peanut butter sandwich and took a bite.

Lilly gaped at him. "What is it with you and your sister constantly stealing my food?"

"We had a large family," he shrugged. "If you didn't grab what you could fast enough, you didn't eat."

She shook her head. "What am I going to do? Am I screwed?"

"How so?"

"With Jefferies and the rooster attacking him," she prompted.

Ryan took another bite. "No worries. He knows the dangers of farms. And everyone he's told already knows he's an idiot, so they know it's all his fault no matter what he says."

"Really?" Lilly allowed herself a faint smile. "Are you sure that's what they'll think? I'm not exactly the town darling as of late."

Ryan said nothing, only cramming the rest of the sandwich into his mouth.

"I'm already doing business with Angela Stilner, so why not add assault with poultry to the reasons why I'm the town pariah?" She hung her head.

"Why do you care about what other people think now?" Ryan asked. "Never stopped you before."

She leveled a hard stare at him.

"It's true," he continued, "you decided you were going to run this farm and start your agri-tourism business without checking with anyone first." He flashed her a wide grin. "Especially me, your hired hand."

Lilly made a face.

"You know, small towns like Lone Tree love their gossip. Half of it isn't even true, and everyone gets their britches in a bunch over nothing." He licked the peanut butter from his finger.

"That's easy for you to say," Lilly frowned. "You closed yourself off to any human emotion or connection years ago. You're more cow than human."

His dark eyes narrowed under the brim of his John Deere cap.

Lilly cleared her throat. "Uh, sorry..."

Ryan glanced down at his watch, sighing. However, Lilly wasn't sure if that move was an attempt to hide a smirk. "Don't you have somewhere to be soon?"

Lilly tapped her phone screen to life and noted the time with a muttered curse. "Crap," she breathed. "I'm going to be late!" She scrambled to collect her phone and purse from around the kitchen, then froze to look at him. "Do you need any help here before I go? I've been so focused on the market and festival that I haven't been around for you, er, the farm."

"I'll be fine," Ryan waved her concerns off. "I have some 4-H kids coming by to help with the calf chores and second feedings before the last milking of the day."

Lilly hesitated, rocking side to side on the balls of her feet. "Are you sure?"

"The farm will survive without you," Ryan stood from the island stool. Without another word, he disappeared out the back porch door.

Lilly hurried out the front door and to her car. As she maneuvered her little car down the gravel driveway, Ryan's last words echoed ominously in her head.

The farm will survive without you.

She knew what he meant. The farm and he would be fine without her for the afternoon. Indeed, that was the message to help ease her mind about rushing off to town.

Right?

Even if her booth wasn't the most popular of the Apple Dapple Days vendor market, that Friday afternoon wasn't a complete bust. She consoled herself by looking at the bright side of a slow stall: people watching. She had fifteen years of town gossip, family dynamics, friend group drama, and overall tantalizing chatter with which to familiarize herself. And what better way to get a crash course than a small-town festival?

Thankfully, her return to town and the subsequent legal and criminal drama from six months ago had died down enough for Lilly to feel she was no longer the main topic of the rumor mill. However, that meant someone else was being set up to take the top spot as she sat there, enjoying the late summer sun. Right now, it was Owen Perkins' death. Tomorrow, who knows?

A never-ending cycle.

Lilly mulled over her recent conversations with Lisa and Faith. It seemed the town's go-to backup topic of the day was Angela Stilner and the current state of her marriage. Over the summer of working with Angela at the farmers' market, Lilly wasn't able to get to know the Stilners well enough to form much of an opinion, so rumors she had heard were nothing more than that—nasty rumors.

Lilly shuddered in the shade of her pop-up canopy, despite the mild September heat. To have the whole town know—or think it knew—all the dirty laundry of your marriage, and then have it thrown back into your face while you just try to make a living. She hadn't heard any whispers or rumors about her ex-husband's affair. She had been delightfully clueless until the day Alec shoved divorce papers in her face with his mistress hanging off his Armani-clad arm. If there had been any whispers circulating in their social circles, again, she was unaware.

But then, who of her so-called friend group had known of the elephant in the room, and remained silent? How little did her friends regard her that they kept her husband's known cheating from her?

Neither option of being the town's public scandal or an oblivious secret sounded like the lesser of the two evils. Lilly shook her shoulders to break free from the unwanted memories and ruminations. It was all in the past now. No good will come from dwelling on Alec and his side piece, Olivia.

Further distraction came in the form of visitors to her booth: a pleasant-looking woman and her detached teen daughter. Lilly reigned in her excitement, feigning professional detachment as she answered the pair's questions. The inquiries came more from the mother than the daughter; Lilly wondered if the girl would look up from her phone's screen during the whole interaction. She learned the pair was in town from Mankato, visiting a set of grandparents who resided in the senior living center in nearby Sleepy Eye. The mother reminisced about her summers in Lone Tree and the previous incarnations of Apple Dapple Day.

Over the years, the late summer town festival had gone through some reinvention from its initial celebration as the Harvest Moon Festival, and even before that, as Town Founder Thaddeus J. Longford Days. As society and sensibilities progressed, the idea of having a festival honoring a genocidal and racist town founder was less than ideal. Now, the town of Lone Tree celebrates local producers, farmers, artisans, businesses, and, of course, the apple orchards on the north side of Lake Lone Tree and the nearby river valley.

Lilly listened intently and nodded when appropriate as the mother continued to lament that her daughter had not experienced the old festivals and her grandparents' farm in its prime. The woman's parents had sold the farmland and moved into town years before their granddaughter was born. Lilly risked a glance over at the teen girl, wondering how she was handling being the center of the conversation. Again, the girl's eyes were locked onto the phone screen, fingers and thumbs tapping away at unseen buttons. Lilly smiled as she handed the mother registration forms.

That gesture finally tore the girl's attention from the screen, eyes widening with prerequisite teen angst as her mother signed the whole family up for a half-day Accidental Farmer Experience later in October during a long school break.

The mother paid the registration fee and whisked her horrified daughter away to a nearby booth. Lilly waited until they were far enough away before she grinned in triumph. Another customer signed up. She glanced down at the list of registered patrons, and her grin waned at the handful of names on the sheet. It wasn't as many as she hoped for, certainly not enough to help get the farm out of its money problems.

But it was a start.

Her smile faltered as her eyes fell on an approaching figure. Cecilia Baxter's polished figure cut a swath through the festival crowd. Her impractical heels strode purposefully down the street, seemingly right to her booth. Lilly steeled herself for another impassioned rant about Angela Stilner's participation in the farmers' market next season. The closer Cecilia came, the tighter the knot in Lilly's stomach grew. The woman looked out of place at the small town festival. Lilly remembered when she first came to Lone Tree, dressed in designer outfits that would equal the food budget of one Lone Tree household. Second-hand embarrassment washed over her as she watched Cecilia walk by, looking more at home in New York or L.A.

Had Lilly looked just as ridiculous and pretentious?

The woman's fierce eyes were narrowed, laser-focused on something beyond Lilly's booth. As subtly as possible, Lilly followed Cecilia's path, determined to see whomever the unlucky soul was at the end of that icy stare. She shifted her stance, pretending to scan the vendor traffic, though really, she was keeping the Cecilia drama in view.

"Oh, lord," Lilly groaned as she discovered the unwilling target of Cecilia's ire.

Angela Stilner stood a few yards down the way, casually surveying the wares of another booth. Next to her was a man Lilly had never seen before. Was this man Angela's husband? Or alleged lover? He was a tall, thin man, drowning in oversized denim overalls with a tattered and stained tank underneath, an International Harvester hat perched high over a pinched face. Lilly fought the visceral instinct to grimace, remembering the same type of hat that had slid off Owen's face. This man was not what one would consider classically handsome enough to be a leading man.

Eh, to each their own, Lilly conceded.

"You have some nerve!" Cecilia called out as she neared Angela. Lilly started at the booming voice from the usually proper woman.

"Cecilia?" Angela stammered as Cecilia's hand lashed out and clamped vise-like fingers around her arm. "Ow! You're hurting—"

"That's rich, coming from you two," Cecilia spat.

By this time, most of the shoppers along the vendor booths turned to stare openly at the three. Whispers already started behind raised hands and shoulders.

"Cecilia, please," the man's eyes searched the crowd quickly. Lilly had a hard time hearing him, whether it was due to the distance or his soft voice, she wasn't sure.

"Don't talk to me," Cecilia turned sharply and focused on the man.

"Let's go, uh, somewhere..." he began, eyes still scanning.

It appeared as if Cecilia had suddenly awoke from a deep sleep. Her eyes darted around the gaping faces, and her cheeks flushed deep crimson as she remembered where and who she was. With her attention split, Angela pulled her arm from Cecilia's grip.

"Yes, let's go," Cecilia murmured.

The trio left as one, continuing their conversation in hushed tones. Lilly's mouth slackened as she watched them go, annoyed that she couldn't follow. What was *that* about?

Slowly, the crowd returned to a semblance of normal. Lilly watched in awe as they went about their business again as if nothing had just gone down right in front of the whole town. Or perhaps scenes like what just unfolded were more common in this town than what she'd been led to believe.

"Hey, you look like you've just seen a ghost."

Lilly jumped as the voice broke through her thoughts. She turned and saw Nathan Wilhelm perched in front of her booth. The initial shock wore off quickly as he broke out into an easy smile. Lilly felt her cheeks warm as she caught her eyes scanning the impressive veterinarian in stained jeans and a faded gray Wilhelm Veterinarian Clinic polo. She had a strong idea what those stains were on his jeans, and even though she'd normally balk at their origins, seeing him with proof of his profession made him appear even more rugged.

But Ryan has gunk like that all over his clothes. Why doesn't that make your stomach flip?

Lilly cleared her throat loudly, afraid that thought was less internal than she hoped. "Nathan, hi! I didn't, uh—"

"Catching the latest episode of *Real Housewives of Lone Tree?*" He picked up a milk lotion sample jar and took a drawn-out sniff. "Hmm. Lotion from milk. The wonders never cease."

"So, uh, what's up with those three anyway?" Lilly fought the urge to play with her hair as he perused the booth table, inspecting her samples and wares for sale. It wasn't as if no one had stopped by her booth all day and appreciated her work. Her stomach continued to flip giddily at each approving noise the gorgeous vet uttered.

"These are great, Lilly," Nathan shot her a glance as he put a sandalwood and rose milk candle back on the table. "I'll have to tell my sisters about your place. They've been looking for a new thing to do on their yearly Girls' Weekends."

Lilly shook the puppy love look out of her eyes. "Oh, that'd be great, Nathan, thank you." She winced at how overly eager her voice made her sound.

"As for the Stilners and Cecilia, they have a long and vibrant history. One never knows if what they're fighting about is something new or old history rehash."

"Stilner..." Lilly frowned. "That was her husband...?"

Nathan laughed, and her stomach tumbled once more. "Don't look so surprised, Ms. Schmidt."

"But I thought... the affair?" She willed the ground to swallow her up so she'd stop stammering like an idiot.

Nathan's laugh died away, and a muscle twitched along his jaw. "Oh, no, no. That's good old Henry Stilner himself. The one and only."

"I guess that makes sense why she'd find someone else..." Lilly muttered. Nathan leveled his gaze at her. "Oh! God, that was horrible! I mean, I... well..."

Nathan's gaze darkened as he palmed another candle, reading the label absently.

Lilly could not believe what she had just said. Henry was nothing compared to the hunky vet before her, but that didn't mean his looks alone dictated his marriageability. Long-hidden memories and thoughts from her divorce spread out from the back of her mind. Visions of her ex-husband's new love interest, Olivia, danced through her head, and nausea washed over her. Alec's new woman was 'model attractive', with flawless skin, shimmering black hair, and a body that men and women envied. Was she Alec's 'Henry'? He traded her in for the shiny new model, just as she assumed Angela was doing.

"When should I pick you up tomorrow?"

Lilly blinked and saw Nathan's disarming smile once more. "What?" She blurted out.

He took a step sideways to stand directly in front of her. "You didn't forget our date, now did you?"

Lilly swallowed hard at his intense gaze. "No, I didn't." Again, her skin flushed from her neck on up. She started talking nervously, her hands fidgeting. "I just... well, don't be too disappointed, okay? I haven't gone on a date since my husband, my ex-husband—"

Nathan snatched one of her flailing hands and held it with both of his. Two strong, warm, yet work-worn hands wrapped her tightly, protectively. At the touch, Lilly's stomach and her mind went dangerously still.

"Don't worry about that, Lilly." his voice was low and steady. "We're just two single adults going out for a night of dancing, drinks, and fun. Nothing more. Nothing less. Right?"

"Right." The word escaped her lips without her permission.

"Then I'll pick you up at seven on the nose," Nathan's eyes danced with his smile. He gave her hand one last squeeze. "Now, I must leave you. I have some new foals to vaccinate and a steer to deworm before I see you again."

He was off before she fully acknowledged his departure. Lilly was too emotionally jumbled and flustered to register what he had said fully, though she did not envy his To-Do List one little bit.

Chapter Nine

Lilly stared at the stranger, in the mirror before her. The features and clothes were familiar, yet she knew not from whence this woman had emerged. Although much to her concern, the mirror did not and could not lie.

She fretted all afternoon about what to wear for the Apple Dapple Dance. A department store's worth of clothes exploded from her closet and now decorated the floor and bed in haphazard piles. Lilly finally settled on a sundress. Though now that she stared at the image reflected, her confidence in her choice wavered.

Her long auburn hair, freshly washed and secured in a messy braid, looked extra coppery thanks to the olive-green tones of the sun dress. In what she learned was the latest in cottage core style, the shin-length garment boasted an embroidered hemline, off-the-shoulder sleeves, and a cinched waist that showed off all the right curves... maybe too many of the right curves. Between the revealing waist and sleeves, Lilly wasn't sure what look she was going for. The sweet farmer's daughter next door or sultry divorcée?

At least it had pockets.

Lilly glanced over to the country chic clock on the bedroom wall—the bedroom that had once belonged to her grandparents, where they had spent over fifty years together. That thought weighed even heavier on Lilly's mind as she quickly gathered last-minute accessories for her outfit before rushing downstairs.

It was almost seven. Nathan would be outside at any moment. Lilly bit her lower lip and willed the butterflies to settle in her stomach. It'd be better if she waited for Nathan on the front porch. She reached for the front door and reflected on the last time her nerves were this frantic before a date. Lilly hadn't felt this since—

"Ryan!" Lilly nearly collided with him as she hurried out the door.

"Hey—"

"What are you doing here?" Lilly asked as she stumbled back a few paces. He was dressed in his usual jeans and tattered T-shirt, all stained from questionable human and bovine sources. She glanced down at the front of her dress, hoping none had transferred to her outfit. "I thought evening chores were done?"

"They are." Ryan's curt response was nothing new.

However, his gaze lingered on her for far longer than she deemed necessary. Lilly raised her hands and pulled her purse up to her neckline, hoping to hide the rising heat there. "Then what are you doing here and not in your truck on the way home?"

Ryan blinked, his gaze once more meeting hers. "I was coming inside to get ready for tonight."

"Tonight?" Lilly heard tires grind up the gravel drive, followed by the increasing growl of a powerful diesel engine. "What's going on tonight?"

"The dance," Ryan pushed past her and into the main hallway. "I thought you'd know that, since you got all *hussied* up for it."

Lilly's jaw dropped. She turned and stomped after him. "Excuse me!"

"Something wrong, Lilly?" Nathan's voice came from the doorway.

She turned mid-stride and walked back to the door. He stood framed in the entry, wearing blue jeans and a dark olive-colored button-down shirt, which did nothing to calm her butterflies. "No, no, nothing wrong, Nathan." Although she caught Nathan's eyes focusing beyond her in the hall. "Ryan was just leaving..."

"Swenson." Nathan's voice came out unusually flat.

Ryan returned the sentiment. "Wilhelm."

Lilly cleared her throat and stood close to Nathan. She put a hand on his chest and applied the faintest of pressure to his sternum. She glanced back at Ryan and saw the shadow pass over his face under that John Deere cap.

Her hired hand quickly turned and walked toward the kitchen. "Have a good night, you two," Ryan called over his shoulder as the kitchen door closed behind him.

Nathan looked down at Lilly, his brows raised as his arm slid protectively around her shoulders. He guided her out to the porch and shut the door behind her. "Wow, he's a great conversationalist, huh?"

"Yeah... well..."

He led her to his large vet truck, parked at the top of the horseshoe driveway in front of the main farmhouse. It sat idling, the growling engine echoing throughout the whole yard. She heard a couple of the cows *mmrrrrrooowwwww* in response.

"Is it true you used to date him?" Nathan asked as he held the passenger door open for her. "Seems like you dodged a bullet with that one."

She absently took his offered hand and allowed him to help her up into the tall vehicle. What was it with guys and insanely tall trucks? Nathan hurried to the driver's door and hopped inside with ease. They were halfway down the driveway before Lilly finally answered.

"Yeah... dodged a bullet."

The Beer Tent had been transformed into a farmer's dance hall paradise. The tent itself took up most of the intersection of Main Street and Fifth Street West. All roads leading into downtown Lone Tree were blocked off for the Apple Dapple Days festival. Between the vendor fair taking up Main Street from Fourth Street West to First Street North, the limited selection of carnival rides on Oak Street one block over, and the giant half-block-long Beer Tent, all crucial access points to Lone Tree were disabled for three whole days.

The Apple Dapple Dance was more of an outdoor bar patio with temporary walls than a dance. Wooden picnic tables from the adjacent park, along with the long white tables from Our Lady's Grace church basement, filled the center of the tent. Along the walls, sporadic straw bales offered more places to sit. At one end of the tent, closest to the designated entrance, sat a long wooden bar. It boasted all the liquid refreshments of Axes 'n Ales Bar & Grille, the newest bar to open out on the edge of town. Neon signs hung from sagging tent supports, highlighting the shelves heavy with multi-colored bottles of spirits.

Lilly and Nathan settled on a picnic table closest to the far end of the tent. Here, wooden pallets had been reassembled into a makeshift dance floor, where few patrons partook of the music. On the risers that Lilly feared would not last the whole dance, the live band played. Nathan's younger cousin stood at the very edge of the platform, strumming his guitar with singular determination, for his entire music career rested on this one performance.

The fast-paced rockabilly tempo was just too much to warrant actual dancing. The few brave souls to grace the dance floor bopped and swayed to the upbeat tune, more staggering than dancing. It was half past seven, and Lilly had a strong feeling that most of the people in the Beer Tent had partaken of the potent libations too liberally and were in no shape to dance to the quick beat properly.

"You're quiet," Nathan leaned over suddenly, his mouth right next to her ear.

Even with his mouth that close, Lilly barely made out his words. "It is a little loud in here," she responded.

"What?"

"It's a little loud in—" she started, only to realize the song had ended during her shouted reply, causing her voice to carry over the whole tent.

Please have the ground just swallow me whole, now... Lilly begged silently as dozens of eyes focused on her.

Nathan chuckled. "Sorry. The only open tables were these closest to the stage, and the band's surprisingly loud speakers."

"Like good Lutherans, no one sits in the front rows," Lilly grinned.

The band's lead singer mumbled directly into the microphone, reminding Lilly of Charlie Brown's teacher, accompanied by shrill feedback, a garbled announcement of a quick break for the band. At least that was her guess as the four-member band all shuffled off the risers and congregated in the closest tent corner.

"Your cousin's band isn't too bad," Lilly turned to Nathan, swallowing her following words as she realized his face was still dangerously close to hers. "S-save the questionable stage presence."

Nathan smiled. "They're good kids and take it pretty seriously," he said as he shifted in his seat, pressing his side into hers. "Though I do think we should take advantage of the next slow song."

So far, she enjoyed Nathan's company, and the conversation was adequate, given they hadn't had many discussions outside the health of her dairy herd. For the first post-divorce date, it was a most pleasant experience. Her stomach still flipped at the idea of their eventual slow dance. She hadn't been that close to a man who wasn't her husband in ages.

"Oh, of course," Lilly stammered.

"You're cute when you blush."

Her grin deepened along with the color in her cheeks.

"Kevin, we're switching seats. *Now!*" Cecilia Baxter's sudden outburst shattered the intimate moment, her grating voice carrying over the din of the crowd.

"Now what?" Lilly joined the rest of the townsfolk in the tent, witnessing Cecilia boldly remove her husband from his seat and shove him toward another table with open seats. Steadily, the crowd turned back to their affairs as Angela and Henry Stilner took possession of the newly vacated seats.

"Well, tonight's going to be interesting," Lilly said, taking another sip of her drink. She kept a stealthy watch on the Stilners in her periphery.

Between the two, Angela was the spouse who was aware that something had happened upon their arrival. She hugged her purse closer to her side and lifted a gauzy scarf over her head, as if she were a movie star trying to hide from the paparazzi. Lilly found herself admiring the bright design of the scarf, with its tropical flowers and leaves, which balanced out the dominating blaze of yellow from the pineapples. Henry, now dressed in cleaner and less tattered overalls and a T-shirt, seemed to be dressed up for the occasion. Once seated, Henry chatted with their new tablemates in a nonchalant ease that Lilly found herself jealous of.

"Who is Henry Stilner?" Lilly asked Nathan. "How did he get Angela to marry him? To me, she settled."

Nathan lifted his long neck beer and took a drag. "You mean someone of Henry's less than stellar looks can't land someone like Angela? Way to adhere to toxic beauty standards, Lilly."

Lilly elbowed him in the ribs. "You know what I mean."

"I know, just busting your chops a bit," Nathan smiled. "She is out of his league, I'll admit that."

"Then what's his deal? Is he super rich? Arranged marriage? He's got a huge..." Nathan's brow arched, "... plot of farmland?"

Nathan replied with a snort. "He's rich. The Stilners are old money in Lone Tree." Another long drag from his beer, then he put the empty bottle on the table. "The Stilners have been a fixture here in Lone Tree for generations, some even claim that the family was here back during the founding of the town and the Indian Uprising. Henry has earned the reputation of being the town's favored child because of who his daddy and granddad are, people kiss the family's ass to curry favor with the eldest patriarchs."

How did Daddy Stilner feel about his boy associating with drug dealers?

"Lovely," Lilly grimaced. She didn't remember the Stilners from her time growing up in Lone Tree over fifteen years ago. However, she was familiar with the idea of old money. When she married her then-husband over seven years ago, she was introduced to one of Minneapolis's premier families, similar to the Pillsburys and Washburns. She could easily see the appeal of aligning oneself with one of the town's founding families. Perhaps Henry did charm Angela, and their marriage was solid, built on mutual love and respect. Their union could also be only as profound as Henry's bank account.

Which would certainly be fertile ground for an unhappy wife to seek affection elsewhere.

Maybe that's what happened to Alec and me, his glint and glamour wore off, and he decided to move on before I realized it.... Lilly slammed the remainder of her lager in one swallow.

"Whoa, whoa, slow down," Nathan chuckled, taking the bottle out of her hand. "I want to slow dance with you, not drag your passed-out dead weight around the dance floor."

Lilly's cheeks burned fiercely. The alcohol soured in her stomach at the talk of dead weight. Owen Perkins' lifeless form flashed in the front of her mind again. Did Nathan not know about Owen's death? Or that she was the one to find him? Maybe he was blissfully unaware of the latest town drama. "Sorry... I was just... lost in thought."

His eyes narrowed. "Must've been some thought." He gestured toward the stage. The ramshackle band hopped back onto the stage, with gangly teen limbs, to continue their set.

The lead singer mumbled something directly into the microphone again, causing yet another squeal of feedback throughout the tent. Lilly figured the singer felt more comfortable singing than speaking into the mic. Thankfully, his singing voice was far less headache-inducing. The band started their next song; after a few chords, Lilly recognized it as *"Can't Help Falling in Love"* by Elvis Presley.

Nathan nudged her with an elbow as he rose to his feet. "Lilly, may I have this dance?"

How could she turn down such a request?

He offered her a hand, and she accepted. Quickly, he maneuvered her to the dance floor, a hand at the small of her back and the other hand clasped firmly around hers. Other couples joined in for the dance as well, which helped to ease Lilly's nervousness.

Lilly braced herself for a fumbled first dance with Nathan. Her nerves threatened to derail any communication she attempted with her limbs. However, much to her surprise, their dance was uneventful at first. Pleasant, if Lilly even dared to allow herself to go that far. The sheer presence of Nathan soon swept away her anxieties. His hands held her close as he led them around the dance floor. His scent of sun-warmed leather and straw filled her head more than the lager.

She allowed herself a moment to admit that she missed being that close to a man.

Their dance was lovely, though short-lived, as a manicured hand reached out through the crowd and tapped Nathan on the shoulder. It was Cecilia Baxter. Lilly stared daggers at the woman as she and Nathan stopped dancing.

"Nathan, darling, I hate to interrupt you during your uh—" she cast a withering glance at Lilly "—your time, but I just have to ask a huge favor of you."

"What?"

Lilly wasn't sure if Nathan's response was an honest inquest into what Cecilia's favor was, or one of incredulous disbelief over what was happening.

"Isabelle's prize-winning rooster has fallen ill. There is something amiss with him," Cecilia said.

"Well, I..."

"Please, Nathan," Cecilia pleaded, her hand wrapping around Nathan's bicep. "I'd hate for something to happen to the rooster before tomorrow's competition."

"Just go," Lilly gently pushed a hand on his chest. "Hurry back."

"Oh, thank you, Nathan!" Cecilia squealed as she pulled him off the dance floor. The vet shot Lilly an apologetic smile as he followed Cecilia through the crowd.

Lilly shuffled off the dance floor, slowly making her way back to the table. Being a single dancer amongst the other couples was beginning to draw looks. Or that was from the crowd watching Cecilia essentially rooster-block her with an actual rooster. Either was not a pleasant prospect. Lilly scanned the crowd, looking for a friendly face to sneak a seat next to. She caught Angela's stern gaze. Mrs. Stilner still sat next to her husband, who looked like he had partaken of the libations too much that evening. Lilly figured Angela's odd expression was from embarrassment over her husband's public drunkenness. Lilly started to walk toward Angela when the other woman averted her gaze sharply, almost holding up a hand to block the side of her face. Henry got up on unsteady legs and made his way to the exit of the dance tent. His wife slowly made her way to follow him.

Feeling her cheeks burn, Lilly turned abruptly to head back to the table she and Nathan had commandeered. She almost made it out of the throng of dancers before a strong hand grabbed hers and pulled her back onto the dance floor. She yelped before she recognized the man who roughly pulled her close.

"Ryan—what are you—"

"About time that other guy left," Ryan graced her with a brief flash of a grin.

He held her close, closer than Nathan danced with her. His hands placed her hands on his shoulders before resting firmly on her hips. She glared at him, finally taking in the sight of her hired hand—and one-time high school boyfriend.

Dark blue jeans and a clean button-down shirt replaced his usual stained and tattered farm clothes. And for the first time in what she believed to be years, Ryan was without his signature John Deere hat. She started at the sight of his dark hair, looking sinfully rakish in the dim lights of the beer tent. Lilly blinked as she took in this upgraded version of Ryan.

"What?" he asked as he glanced around. "Is Nathan coming back?"

"No," Lilly shook her head. She found herself unable to form proper sentences. "You're just... well..."

Memories of high school and their one official dance came flooding back without warning. Their freshman homecoming dance, fifteen years ago, made their relationship official, as they declared their boy-and-girlfriend status at the homecoming football game earlier that night. They danced as if they were the only couple in the school's gym, all the lights, fog machines, and streamers just for them.

Six short months later, her parents would leave Lone Tree suddenly after the discovery of a family scandal. Lilly and Ryan's romance was short-lived and soon forgotten over the years, until her sudden return six months ago.

"I told you I clean up good when I want to," Ryan smiled.

Lilly's stomach flipped. Hard.

"Did you get Cecilia to come over here to get Nathan away from me so you could cut in?" she asked.

"No, I wish," Ryan snorted. "That was just pure luck. I certainly won't interrupt a couple's dance, but I'm gentleman enough to see the dance all the way through."

"Oh," Lilly bit her lip. Why was it so hard to talk to Ryan?

The Elvis song came to an end, only to be replaced by another slow dance. Couples either left, stayed, or moved onto the dance floor. Ryan and Lilly stood in the same spot, arms and hands still in the same positions as during the dance. Ryan tentatively started swaying and couldn't hide his smile when Lilly followed suit.

"So, um, Lilly," Ryan cleared his throat.

The noise broke whatever spell had come over Lilly. She glanced around the dance floor and the tables beyond. People were talking, whispering, and pointing. Were they talking about her and Nathan and how she was now dancing with Ryan? A few pairs of eyes looked in her direction. Oh, they were talking, talking about them.

"Lilly, I wanted to uh, well, I was..." Ryan's voice ebbed around the sound of the music and the murmur of the crowd. She saw his lips moving but didn't understand what he was saying.

Ryan paused and stopped dancing. His dark eyes pierced into hers. "Lilly, are you okay? Do you need to sit?"

No, I'm not okay. I came to a dance with one man, and now I'm dancing with another, who just happens to be my employee and my old high school boyfriend, no less. I'm going to be the town's next Angela Stilner for sure!

Lilly's thoughts raced faster than she could process them. For some reason, at the thought of Angela, Lilly sought her out in the crowd. She wasn't sitting at their table. Nor was Henry in sight. Where did he go? There she was, along the far wall. Angela hurried toward the entrance of the tent, quickly picking her way along the straw bales and among other Lone Tree citizens.

Where was Henry? Lilly glanced around the crowd. Perhaps Angela was slipping out of the dance to go meet up with her other beau?

Heat rose up Lilly's neck, and her stomach sank. "I have to leave," she blurted out. She pulled away from Ryan.

"Hey, Lilly, wait—" he reached out for her hand.

"No!" Lilly shouted.

The tent went motionless. Even the band stood silent.

"Oh, Lord..." she breathed.

"Shh!" Ryan hissed, gripping her hand tighter. "Someone just screamed."

Another scream broke through the tent walls. Lilly hadn't heard the first scream, for her shout came at the same time.

"Help!" The woman who belonged to the mysterious voice entered the tent, face frantic and pale. "Help! He's dead! Henry Stilner's dead!"

Chapter Ten

"Henry Stilner's dead?"

The question had been repeated in some form or another in the hour after the deceased had been found. The festivities of the Apple Dapple Dance had come to an abrupt halt, and a whirl of colored emergency lights, blockades, and police tape appeared within minutes after the 911 call was made. The festival grounds were now a designated crime scene and covered in emergency vehicles and police personnel. The sheriff's patrol car rode over grass, around vendor booths, and blockades with a singular purpose to reach the poultry tent.

While Friday night's main event was the dance, Saturday's affair was the much-applauded Apple Dapple Day Poultry Show. This show allowed children enrolled in 4-H, Future Farmers of America, and other similar clubs to showcase their prized hens and roosters. The entrants spent months raising and working with their chosen fowl to bring out the highlights of their breed's qualities. Two of the hens in Lilly's little flock back home, Marta and Fancy Pants, were set to take part in this year's competition.

As well as the Colonel, if they could ever tame that flame-broiled, hot-headed rooster.

Although now, as she joined the crowd of festival goers pressing against the yellow police tape fluttering around the tent, Lilly doubted the poultry show would go on as planned the following day and surrounded by the blue, white, and red colored lights of the ambulance and police cars, which clashed with the darkness of the evening. Dim conversations ebbed and flowed among the crowd, punctuated by occasional calls from police or crime scene technicians. Lilly barely registered Ryan's hand wrapped around hers loosely. Murmurs flowed through the tightening crowd around them, everyone eager to catch a glimpse of the stretcher with Henry Stilner's body as it was loaded into the back of the coroner's van.

Morbid lookie-loos.

"Do we have any idea how it happened?" Lilly asked quietly.

"I don't know," Ryan gave her hand a quick squeeze.

A woman standing in front of the pair turned around, "I heard he was strangled." Lilly had seen her around town over the last couple of months, though her name escaped her now.

"Shirley Larsen, how do you know that?" Ryan pressed.

Shirley didn't balk at Ryan's stern voice; instead appeared pleased with having juicy news to share. "Luann Murphy. She found him in the poultry barn."

Lilly blanched, remembering her own experience with discovering a dead body. Lone Tree, being a small Midwest town in the middle of Minnesota farming country, wasn't used to having the discovery of dead bodies be a regular occurrence. However, as of that minute, Lone Tree could now count three murders in six months. Not a very good ratio for the police department to see increasing.

"What was Luann doing in the poultry barn?" Ryan's brow creased. "She doesn't have any kids in 4-H or FFA anymore. She shouldn't have been in the tent looking around the chickens."

Shirley Larsen's proud expression faltered. "I don't know why she was there," she harrumphed.

"Luann was the one screaming before," Lilly said absently.

"I heard she found him sitting in a rooster row, right in front of the metal crates. Poor birds were trying to peck at him." Shirley continued to relay the salacious information. "And there was a scarf around his neck, strangled him. It had tropical fruit on it. Pineapples, maybe."

"Shirley, jeez, c'mon," Ryan's eyes narrowed at the woman as Lilly squeezed his hand.

"Pineapples?" Lilly's attention snapped to Shirley. "Are you certain it was pineapples?" The longer she held the woman's gaze, the more she came to recognize the rumor monger. Shirley was part of the library's weekly senior card game group, the group that somehow seemed to spread the most gossip around town.

Shirley was startled at Lilly's intense gaze. "Y-yes. Well... It was what Eddie had heard from the sheriff himself."

"The sheriff?" Ryan scoffed. "He told Eddie important information about a possible murder case?"

"That's what Eddie said!" Shirley doubled down with a frown. "He was in the crowd outside the poultry tent when the police were loading up the body."

"Eddie," Ryan shook his head. "Like he'd know what a pineapple was."

"Eddie didn't see the scarf," Shirley snapped. "He heard the police talk about the pineapples." With that last statement, she huffed off into the crowd.

"Why are you so interested in the pineapples?" Ryan turned to Lilly. "You almost bit Shirley's head off when she mentioned them."

"Angela was wearing a scarf tonight. It had big yellow pineapples on it." Lilly replied quietly.

"Oh."

A stillness fell upon the two. The crowd around them began to thin as the emergency vehicles started to leave. Lilly noticed several Lone Tree police officers make their way through the crowd, ordering people to disperse. The evening's festivities were now officially over.

"So, where's Nathan?" Ryan broke the silence.

"I... I don't know," Lilly glanced around the remaining faces and empty festival grounds nearest to them.

"He just left you?"

Lilly flinched at the accusing tone in his voice. "Well, no. I don't think he just left. He was called to examine Cecilia Baxter's children's rooster. He went to the poultry tent right before..." Lilly's mind worked hard to put the pieces together of the night's events.

"He left your dance to go look at a rooster?" Ryan's brow arched. "He was in the poultry tent before Henry was found?"

"He's the town vet," Lilly replied through a frown. "It was an emergency, according to Cecilia."

"A bad hair day is an emergency for Cecilia Baxter," Ryan muttered.

"Maybe he saw something," Lilly returned. "He's off talking to the police. If he were in the tent so close to the murder, they might be questioning him."

"To see if he did it?"

Lilly elbowed his side. "To see if he saw someone going in or out of the tent before Henry was found."

Perhaps Nathan had seen something and was speaking with the police and the sheriff. Maybe he was checking on the rest of the poultry in the tent now that their restful night was disturbed by a murder and crime scene technicians stomping through the tent. But how long did it take to talk to the police? How much of the crime had he seen before Luann came in? Where was Cecilia in all this? Had he gone off with Cecilia elsewhere besides the poultry tent?

Lilly shook her head, mind racing and throbbing with the beginning of a possible alcohol-induced headache. She had always been a lightweight when it came to alcohol. Her socialite friends back in Minneapolis always made fun of how few drinks it took for her to call it a night. Slamming her lager before her dances and now a possible murder didn't allow for thinking too clearly.

"I don't know why he's not back," Lilly said softly. "Maybe I should go look for him..."

"No, you stay here." Ryan gripped her hand tightly. "Maybe he is being questioned. He didn't have a pineapple pattern on his stupid shirt, did he?"

She recognized his jealous tone. "Nathan is wearing the same thing you are wearing, jeans and a shirt. What's so horrible about his choice in color?"

Ryan cast her a side-eye glance. "It was awfully green. And he's tall. Eddie could have mistaken him for a big unripe pineapple."

"Shut up, Ryan," Lilly re-introduced her elbow to his side, forcefully this time, while gripping his hand like a vise.

"Ow!" He hissed. He hugged his side and pulled his hand free from her grip. "Just saying. He doesn't pull off green well. Not like you."

Another, more poignant silence fell over the pair. One that stretched out to the point of being painfully awkward. Lilly took a sideways step to put some more space between her and Ryan.

"Are you sure Angela was wearing a scarf with pineapples on it?" Ryan broke the silence again.

"I'm pretty sure," Lilly's head still swam from the night's events. And the still-too-close closeness of Ryan.

"Well, there's a lot of room between 'pretty sure' and 'really sure,'" Ryan shrugged. "Again, who knows what Eddie supposedly saw or heard from the police?"

"Could... Angela have?" Lilly couldn't find the strength to finish her thought. She didn't know Angela very well, though the few interactions the two had shared while working at the farmers' market were pleasant enough. Angela certainly didn't scream "murderess" when one looked at her initially.

Was Angela Stilner capable of murder?

"You think Angela did this?" Ryan asked.

"Her marriage to Henry wasn't the best, was it? That's the latest rumor going around town, right?" Lilly asked, swallowing. "A woman in a bad relationship is capable of almost anything."

"Would you have killed your ex?"

Lilly pursed her lips.

"You think Angela did it?" Shirley Larsen's shrill voice surprised both as the woman suddenly appeared out of the darkening festival grounds. She had apparently completed her tour of the remaining pockets of morose spectators.

"What? I—"

"Angela Stilner killed Henry!" Shirley's voice reached new octaves as it rang out over the street. Heads turned swiftly in their direction; some townsfolk even began to move closer to the trio.

"We don't know that for sure!" Lilly started.

"You said it! You said she killed her husband!" Shirley pressed harder.

"No! I didn't say that!"

"Angela Stilner killed Henry!" Shirley turned quickly and hurried off to the approaching group of festival stragglers.

"Oh no..." Lilly closed her eyes and hugged her arms to her stomach. "This is so bad. So very bad."

"Nah, what makes you think that?" Ryan asked. Lilly shot him a withering glare that chased the grin off his face. "It's not as bad as you think, Lilly."

"Lillian!" The sheriff's booming voice echoed off the vendor and exhibitor tents. Lilly froze as she saw Sheriff Mike Branford's tall frame cross the police tape and stomp towards them. His dark eyes pierced hers in the night.

"Or... it could be that bad," Ryan gave her shoulder a quick squeeze. "Sorry."

"I'd like to talk to you, Lillian." The sheriff pointed a pen at her, then at Ryan. "You, too, Mr. Swenson."

"Great," Ryan hissed, dropping his chin to his chest.

Lilly sighed and looked up at the star-filled sky. "This is not how I wanted my date to end tonight."

Ryan dropped her off at the farm after the unofficial and unfortunate end of the Apple Dapple Dance. Sheriff Branford was less than pleased to see her at the perimeter of a new crime scene. Considering she had discovered Lone Tree's other two deaths, her presence at this latest one didn't bode well.

"I don't have to remind you about snooping around my investigation, do I?" The sheriff had asked after he took both Ryan and Lilly's statements of what they saw transpire that evening.

Word of her amateur sleuthing got around quickly, much to her law enforcement relative's annoyance.

"No, you don't," she had replied, fidgeting with the edge of the yellow police tape, to which Ryan choked back a laugh. She kicked him in the left shin.

Nathan Wilhelm had been a no-show since the discovery of Henry Stilner's body in the poultry tent. Tired and emotionally drained, Lilly hadn't put too much emotional effort in to asking the retreating crowd of morbid spectators if anyone had seen the hunky vet or even Mrs. Cecilia Baxter, the last person she saw him with. After the coroner's van left the scene, taking Henry's body away, she decided to call it a night. She would call Nathan in the morning to check in on him.

Which led to Ryan taking her home.

Again, not the way she'd envisioned this date ending.

Ryan pulled his old Chevy truck up to the front of the farmhouse and threw it into Park. Lilly knew it was time to get out of the truck cab. But something kept her in the idling vehicle.

"That was kind of like old times," Ryan said with a sideways smirk.

Lilly gaped. "Old times?"

"Didn't a few of our dates end with one of us chatting with the police?" His dark eyes glinted in the dim light of the truck.

"Oh, yeah..." Lilly stammered. "But this... is... it wasn't a date."

"Right, right," Ryan's face sobered as he nodded. "But where was your date tonight?"

"I—" Lilly bit her lower lip to force herself to pause. "He was called away for animal health matters. And then probably got caught up in the crowd after Henry was... was found."

"Mmm-hmm," Ryan scoffed. "Right."

Silence fell between the two, fueled by the annoyed growl of the truck's diesel engine and the strange electric energy emitted from each of them.

"Well, I have to get up early for chores," Ryan announced suddenly, as he put the truck into Drive.

Lilly gaped at him for a moment, then quickly unbuckled her belt. "Thank you for the ride home," she said softly.

"Yeah," Ryan replied.

Lilly climbed out of the truck and closed the door swiftly. Once the door latched, Ryan pulled away from the farmhouse and roared down the driveway. She sighed and trudged up the front porch steps.

Just when she thought the relationship between her and Ryan had started to smooth out since her return to Lone Tree, hiccups and road-blocks always seemed to pop up at the worst possible times. They had been working better together the last month, the stand-offish, awkward truce beginning to melt. It wasn't easy for either of them to work so closely together after fifteen years apart. Former friends and one-time couple, their thick-as-thieves friendship had been shattered all those years ago.

And for every step forward in getting to a more civil relationship, be-yond just farmer and hired hand, there were times like tonight that set them back two steps.

Was Ryan actually jealous of Nathan? That she went to the festival with the vet and not him? Well, the vet asked, he didn't. Was Faith right in that Ryan still had feelings for her? She thumped up the stairs to her room and forced all the thoughts of any relationships—former, new, or dysfunctional — out of her mind for the black voice of sleep.

The previous night's events seemed a distant, foggy memory as Lilly went through the morning's chores on autopilot. The animals must have sensed a change in her as the chores were completed with few interruptions and in record time. An odd, uneasy feeling settled over the farm-yard that morning. The cows were abnormally quiet as Ryan parked his truck by the barn and then began his milking chores. Even the Colonel behaved as much as he could. He only pecked relentlessly at her boots and leg guards, instead of a full-body assault.

Lilly sat in the kitchen, putting the day's eggs away in cartons, listening to the Apple Dapple Days Vendor Group Chat blow up on her phone. The thin black box pinged with each new message. Lilly had stopped looking at each notification and latest addition to the chat a few minutes ago, tired of the endless stream of non-information and rehashed questions that would never be answered. The vendors and organizers were all frantically seeking an answer to the same question: Was the Vendor Fair still on for this morning?

Other Apple Dapple Day questions, about the festival as a whole or at least the poultry barn, were scattered in as well by the festival organizers. People were even wondering where Lisa Hayes was, as she had stopped responding to texts and inquiries at seven o'clock that morning.

Lilly could only imagine the chaos the Apple Dapple Days committee was going through that morning. Who knew if the police would release the poultry tent for the festival and any planned events for the rest of the weekend? Would just the tent be shut down, or would the entire spot where poor Henry was found be shut down? Or would the whole weekend be canceled?

Too many questions for one person to handle that early in the day. And Lisa Hayes was not the right person to be asking in the first place. The police and crime scene technicians were the only people in town who knew the answers to the questions plaguing Lilly's phone. Lilly did not envy Lisa Hayes' job that day. The Chamber of Commerce head had put so much effort into the Apple Dapple Days festival, only to see it ruined by the strangling of Henry Stilner.

Lilly frowned as her thoughts strayed to Henry and Angela. Strangled by a scarf with pineapples on it. At least that was the preliminary gossip being spread by the gossip mongers the night before, no thanks to her.

Angela had a pineapple scarf before she and Henry left the dancing tent. Then the scarf was missing when Lilly caught sight of her later—a pretty straightforward conclusion to have been made by the townsfolk. How many episodes of *Dateline* had she watched that pegged the spouse as the number one suspect in the other's murder? Over two thousand and seven hundred episodes of Keith Morrison couldn't be wrong.

Lilly grabbed her phone and opened the group chat, if only to clear away the mounting number of text notifications. She scrolled through the chat randomly, but didn't see any new information about the festival's status. She figured she would continue with her day as if the regularly scheduled events were still going forward.

As she began to put her phone down, another ping alerted her to a new message. The chat had been blissfully quiet for a few minutes. Maybe Lisa finally rejoined the chat after her hours-long hiatus. Lilly opened the chat to see what the newest, repeated question would be.

> **5075551234**
>
> Where is Lisa? Should we talk to the police station about whether the festival is going on?

> **5075555678**
> She's dealing with enough this morning; give her a break.

Lilly Schmidt
I'm planning as if the festival is still going on until I'm told otherwise.

> **5075559101**
> You're related to the sheriff, Lilly. What do you know about the festival? You heard something?

Lilly Schmidt
No, I haven't heard anything. I don't know any more than you guys do.

> **5075555678**
> You knew about the pineapple scarf! You know more than you let on.

5075559101
What scarf?

> **5075555678**
> The one Angela used to kill Henry!

Lilly Schmidt
Hey, guys, we don't know that for sure. I only heard about the scarf from Shirley cuz she was Saying she heard it from Eddie.

> **Cecilia Baxter**
> Don't believe a word she says, ladies. Lilly is linked with Angela Stilner. She probably is helping to cover things up for her friend.

Lilly put her phone down and closed her eyes. She let her head fall forward so her chin hit her chest. Of course, Cecilia was part of this chat. So many of the other participants that Lilly didn't have in her phone were just nameless numbers. Her phone must have pulled Cecilia's information from the Farmers' Market contact list.

> **5075559101**
> OMG Lilly helped Angela cover it up??

> **5075551234**
> OMG LILLY???

> **5075558910**
> who's lilly?

"Oh my God..." Lilly muttered. She hit her forehead with her phone. "Cecilia... what the... what are you—" She ended her thought with a loud, disgruntled scream.

> **Lilly Schmidt**
> I did NOT help anyone do anything. I know as much about this as you guys. Don't listen to Cecilia. She doesn't know what she's talking about.

Cecilia Baxter
Are you calling me a liar!?

Lilly Schmidt
Does the last season Prada heel you've been wearing fit?
Then yes.

The chat exploded into a cascade of shocked emoji faces and gifs of people eating popcorn.

Lilly turned the phone to silent and put the screen down on the island counter, her face froze in a pale expression of disbelief. She may have bitten off more than she could swallow with that last response. As much as she was shocked that she sent that text, she was proud of herself. For too long, Cecilia and her holier-than-thou attitude had been terrorizing her all summer. And she doubted she wasn't the only one who had been victimized by Cecilia's gigantic high school diva ego. And now claiming that she was somehow involved with Henry's murder? Lilly couldn't let that stand without some sort of retaliation.

Suddenly, her phone started to vibrate. Someone was calling. Lilly's stomach dropped to her feet as she watched the phone shake. It almost looked like the phone was going to vibrate itself off the island counter. The vibration stopped just as suddenly as it had begun.

Hopefully, whoever called wouldn't leave a message.

Lilly bit her lower lip as the phone began to vibrate again, as another call came in. The phone vibrated and stopped through three more phone calls. Finally, on the fifth call, Lilly swallowed and picked up the phone.

Cousin Mike the Sheriff – CALLING

Along with three logged voicemails from the same number.

She gnawed on her top lip, wondering why the sheriff was calling her. No, scratch that. She knew precisely why her cousin, the sheriff, was calling. Cecilia Baxter. Make one bad joke about a lady's off-season shoes, and she resorts to calling the cops? Lilly shook her head. The woman needs to get a grip.

Reluctantly, Lilly tapped the green answer button before the call went to voicemail. Again. "Hello?"

"Lillian." Michael Branford's voice came across the phone as crisp and serious as if he stood with her in the kitchen.

"Hey, Mike, how's it going?" She hoped her voice sounded nonchalant. Though deep down, she knew it didn't. It was pitchy and strained—a dead giveaway.

"I need you to come down to the station."

"Oh, really? Uh... why?"

"Lillian."

She signed, knowing the charade wasn't working. "What time?"

"Now."

Chapter Eleven

The Lone Tree Police Station was housed in a turn-of-the-century red brick building. Along one prominent corner sat a pale marble cornerstone that marked the start of construction in 1906. In more recent years, a new wing had been added to the building, with its cornerstone indicating that construction had taken place in 1992. In the newer section of the building were the city offices of the mayor, comptroller, city utilities, and the like.

Lilly blanched at the sight of the newer edition, noticing the architect's lack of foresight in trying to match the older building's aesthetic.

She walked up the cracked sidewalk to the large cement stairs that led up half a story to the main floor. She wondered if this would be classified as a "walk-up", like New York's famous brownstones. The lower floor of the 1906 building housed the few jail cells that the small town seldom used. Lilly wasn't looking forward to even setting foot into the police station, let alone even considering the jail cells below.

Ever since the little cat fight on the vendor group chat, her phone had been blowing up with calls and text messages from friends and foes alike. She was sure that Faith would be stalking the town looking for her if she didn't return at least one of her messages. Cecilia's supporters came out in full force to defend their leader. Lilly considered how these people all had her number. They weren't part of the vendor or the farmers' market chats. Cecilia must have given out her number willingly to her posse.

The old wooden door proved heavier than expected, but Lilly pushed her way through the entrance and into the foyer of the police station. She cast a wary look around, trying to catch a glimpse of the sheriff. She wanted to get this over with as soon as possible. Sitting in the waiting room of the police station, it just screamed "Guilty!" to her.

Even though she did nothing wrong.

Right?

You couldn't get arrested for calling a woman's shoes ugly in a group chat... right?

Lilly walked over to what she thought was the reception desk. Beyond the large wooden desk and its matronly occupant were other desks in an open layout. Various police officers, either in uniform or dressy casual street clothes, sat busily typing away. Even further behind the sea of desks were closed-off offices and hallways that led into the deeper bowels of the police station.

Seated at the deception desk was an older woman wearing a Lone Tree Police uniform. Her close-cut curls were a salt-and-pepper tangle upon her head. Lilly wondered if she still went out on patrols or was a permanent fixture behind the desk. The wood and metal name plaque bore the name 'Boyle', as did the badge on her chest.

Lilly took a long stride up to the desk. "Uh, hello, I'm here to see Sher—"

Boyle looked up and leveled dark blue eyes on Lilly. Her eyes almost matched the crisp LTPD uniform; usually, Lilly would have complimented the woman on the color combination, how the uniform brought out the deep blues of both her eyes and the blue-black highlights in her hair. But the fierce gaze dried any words before they reached her tongue.

"He's waiting for you," Boyle's tone was as sharp as her stare.

"Wh-who?" Lilly knew she sounded like an owl. But the woman unnerved her more than anything she could recall in recent memory.

"The sheriff."

"Oh." Lilly swallowed. "Should I wait here—"

"Down the main hall, second door on the left." Boyle lowered her gaze back to her computer monitor.

And as quickly as that, she was dismissed. Lilly made her way swiftly around the large desk and hurried through the maze of short cubicles to the back hallway. She hoped the police present in the station and at their desks were too busy with actual crimes and police work to notice her as she passed through their space. A few less-than-covert glances followed her as she walked by, telling her that word of her visit—and the *reason* behind it—had already spread to the precinct.

So much for fading out as the local gossip talking point; she had just started getting used to fewer and fewer sideways glances as she moved about her business in town. But this morning's snafu in the group chat had changed everything in an instant. Indeed, once she made it to her cousin's office, they'd all start chittering about her like her hens back home.

Lilly found the second door on the left, marked in gold leaf as the 'Office of Sheriff Michael Branford' on marbled glass. She took a deep breath to still her thumping heart and remind herself that she had done nothing wrong. Cecilia's lies or whatever were being spread around town were nothing more than catty women having a little spat.

"I see you in the hallway, Lillian." The sheriff's voice came from the other side of the door.

Just get it over with, she told herself as she turned the knob and entered the office.

The sheriff's office was almost a carbon copy of any office seen in any TV police procedural. Filing cabinets covered one wall, no doubt holding important information on staff and ongoing cases. Taking up almost the whole office was a twin to Boyle's large desk, the top of which was scattered with files and notebooks, numerous pens, and empty disposable coffee cups. A large bulletin board took up the wall behind the sheriff, covered with newspaper clippings from local papers, as well as some from around the state. Headlines proclaimed the heroism of a local cop after he saved a child from near-death or told of strife caused by a criminal who eventually faced justice.

Lillian slowly moved around a threadbare chair in front of her second cousin's desk, noting the concerning number of empty coffee cups around his desk. As she sat, she caught a glimpse of his notepad. Her name, along with Cecilia Baxter's, was listed numerous times and underlined. Some to the point that the pen had ripped through to the sheets underneath.

Oh boy.

Lilly took a deep breath and decided to dive right in. Tell her side of the story before anything else is discussed. "So, what happened this morning—"

"What did you do to tick Cecilia Baxter off now?" He stared at her over the wire rim of reading glasses.

"I didn't do anything—*now?*" Lilly spat.

"Do you realize that I field more complaints about you from that woman than I care to count?" Branford asked. Lilly shook her head. "All because you decided this summer to let a certain someone be part of your farmers' market?"

"I can—"

"So imagine my surprise when half the town is suddenly calling me this morning, telling me that you had something to do with Angela Stilner killing her husband?"

Lilly felt the color drain from her face. "I did no such thing!"

The sheriff stared at her for a long moment. "I know you didn't do anything. I took your statement, along with Ryan Swenson's, last night. And there were plenty of other people at the dance tent who could confirm that you were nowhere near Henry when he died."

"Then... then why am I here?"

The sheriff sighed again, taking off his readers and massaging the bridge of his nose. "Because I need your statement."

"But you said you already have my statement from last night!" She protested.

"I know, I know." Branford put his glasses back on. He flipped through the topmost manila file folder on his desk until he came to a clean sheet of lined notebook paper. "I need you to write your statement, *again*, this time with any of your involvement—or lack thereof—with Henry's death."

Lilly gaped as he handed her the file folder and a pen. She stared at the paper and felt her stomach plunge as her face flushed with heat. "All this because I called her out on her lies?"

"Lillian..."

"The group chat... Cecilia said I was helping to cover up something for Angela. All of this because that woman can't stand Angela..." Lilly's eyes burned as she began writing her latest statement.

This time, she included the group chat, trying to recall what was said and by whom. She wasn't sure if she could pull it up on her phone to write things down verbatim. Cecilia's lies and hatred allowed people to run wild with the idea that she was somehow involved with a murder. Lilly's handwriting was nigh illegible by the time she signed her name at the bottom.

"I can send you screenshots of the chat," Lilly offered, her voice strangely small.

"Please do," Sheriff Branford nodded. "I fear some of the 'evidence' sent to me already has been doctored." He used finger quotes around a particular word.

"Can't I press charges against her for harassment or something?" Lilly shouted, suddenly rising from the chair.

The manila folder in her lap spilled all over the floor. She dropped down to her knees to gather the scattered papers and photos. Lilly realized too late that the folder was the complete investigative folder for Henry's murder. She caught unfortunate glimpses of crime scene photographs before she could force her eyes to look away. There was no denying that glossy photo of gauzy pineapples near the collar of Henry's shirt. She placed the photo on top of her statement and reached for another. This one caught her eye, and she paused. In the straw-covered grass of the poultry tent lay an oddly shaped cylinder with one end capped in orange and the other in blue.

Her cousin cleared his throat sharply, then snatched the haphazard folder from her hands.

"Sorry," she whispered as she sat down again.

"Unfortunately, you can't get Cecilia arrested for this," Branford said. He straightened and reordered the contents of the file folder. "You could go the civil route, sue her for libel, spreading falsehoods about you without evidence, and those falsehoods harm or damage your livelihood."

Lilly fell against the back of the spare chair. "Maybe. That might end up opening up a bigger can of worms with this woman."

"It might."

Silence fell upon the two. Lilly's mind was too busy trying to make sense of the jumble of photos and notes she had seen accidentally, especially if that photo was truly of Angela's scarf from last night. Her cousin cleared his throat sharply. However, another part of her mind was wondering if she was being silenced into leaving.

A passive-aggressive dismissal.

"I guess if there's nothing else… I should get going," Lilly rose from the chair.

"There is one more thing before you go," the sheriff tapped the top of his desk with the closed folder. "No more interfering."

"Hmm?"

"You know what I mean." He leveled a serious stare at her. "I don't want you anywhere near Angela, the chicken tent, any of it."

She blinked her eyes at him.

His sigh was as explosive as his curse. "Dammit, Lillian! You have already been linked to this case by hearsay and a prior relationship with the deceased's spouse. I don't want to hear a *whisper* of you looking into this like you did with the Carpenter matter a few months back."

"And don't even think about looking into Owen's death. I know he and Henry are connected from childhood, and both are dead within twenty-four hours of the other. But you're *not* a cop."

"Yeah, but that guy died on my land. I kinda had to ask around about him…" Lilly knew her defense was flimsy as soon as it left her mouth. "And I found Owen, too…"

Sheriff Branford pointed a finger at her. The way she jumped, it might as well have been the barrel of his service gun. "No. Interfering. Period. Got it?"

"Got it," her voice barely left her throat.

"Now, you're dismissed."

"You're not really going to butt out of this, are you?" Faith demanded.

"Oh, heck no," Lilly shook her head as she took a long drink from her Diet Coke.

Despite being one of the town's latest pariahs, Lilly made her way to Grandma's Attic after her uncomfortable visit with the sheriff. Lone Tree's quintessential small-town café was the place to see and to be seen. It was also the best place to hear the town's gossip and latest news. Naturally, the small eatery was abuzz with talk of Henry Stilner's and Owen Perkins' deaths, and the fate of the Apple Dapple Days festival.

The added ammo of the group chat blunder only made more eyes look at her as she entered the café and found a place to sit at the main counter, near the register. She felt eyes burn into her back as she tried to enjoy her cheeseburger. Lilly could have found a back booth to sit out of most lines of sight, but this way, she could be closest to the best source of town scuttlebutt, Faith Fischer.

"You know the sheriff isn't going to like you poking your nose where it doesn't belong," Faith reminded her as she rang up another customer's bill.

"I know," Lilly shrugged. "But I'm already a part of this whole mess anyway, thanks to Cecilia. Cousin Mike can thank her for further confusing the murder plot I'm supposedly covering up."

Faith rolled her eyes. "You're only involved because Cecilia is bat crap crazy."

"That's what's been bugging me about this whole situation. Why does she hate Angela so much anyway?" Lilly asked. "It can't just be because of the rumors that Angela is cheating on her husband."

The restaurateur shook her head. "I don't know. She's hated Angela and Henry since high school."

"Wait—she hated Henry, too?" Lilly frowned. "But she always directed her ire toward Angela."

"That's because Henry is one of Lone Tree's golden sons," Faith said. "A Founding Father Family and all that patriarchy crap."

"That doesn't explain why, though," Lilly pointed out. "Something must have happened between those three to warrant that level of disdain."

"Which is weird, since Cecilia and Henry used to hang out in high school a lot." Faith shrugged.

"Cecilia used to hang out with Angela?"

"Not Angela. She went to Sleepy Eye High," Faith corrected. "Those two are a year ahead of you and Ryan in school, so you probably didn't remember Cecilia and Henry hanging out. Well, not so much as hung out, but they were seen at the same house parties together."

"And I left after my freshman year, remember?" Lilly took a giant bite of her cheeseburger.

It was common knowledge that Lilly and her parents had abruptly abandoned Lone Tree fifteen years ago, following an unknown falling out with her paternal grandparents. The family has lived in Minneapolis ever since.

"True, there was that, too," Faith grinned in return. "All I remember is that Henry and Cecilia would go to the same parties in high school. I think that's also how he met Angela along the way."

"Something happened between those two, maybe three, in high school." Lilly tapped a French fry against her lips as she pondered the new information. If Henry and Cecilia were at the same parties, it would be safe to assume that Owen was also there. How were those three connected?

"And don't forget the sister's death," an older voice piped in cryptically.

Lilly and Faith turned to the voice, coming from a diminutive woman sitting to Lilly's left. The newcomer wore a bright lavender tracksuit with a brilliantly bejeweled matching flower in her dark black hair. Two eyes, as large as an owl's, stared back from behind thick-lensed glasses.

"Good day, Elvira," Faith set a coffee cup and saucer in front of the woman and poured a fresh cup without being asked.

Lilly smiled at Elvira Johnson, the town's reigning busybody. However, one couldn't always trust half of what she said, as she was known to put her own bias into the latest to come out of the rumor mill.

"What about a sister?" Lilly leaned over toward Elvira, knowing she was about to hear more even without prompting. "Who's sister?"

"That Baxter woman, of course," Elvira answered with a nod of her head. "Although, back then, she was a Schimmel before she married that limp noodle, Kevin Baxter."

Lilly pressed her lips together into a tight line to keep from laughing. From the few times she had interacted with Cecilia's husband, she thought the same thing. He was definitely the *silent* partner in that relationship. "Can you tell me what happened to Cecilia's sister?"

"Of course I can, and I will!" Elvira gave Lilly a conspiratorial wink. "She was the younger of the two. Now, what was her name?"

Lilly shot Faith a discouraged look, silently pleading with her friend to help fill in the blanks. Faith only shrugged as she slipped through the rubber doors that separated the front of the café from the kitchen. Lilly turned back to Elvira. "Well, we can figure out her name later."

"Abigail!" Elvira shouted suddenly. "That's it. Abigail Schimmel. She'd sneak off with her sister to those awful parties to hang out with the bigger kids. Got involved with some not-so-good people. Did all sorts of naughty things."

"Like underage drinking? Drugs?" Lilly offered.

"All of the above and then some," Elvira shook her head. "Those parties caused the sheriff, his name was Rutger back then, oh, it caused Sheriff Rutger all sorts of trouble trying to stay ahead of those parties. Always being held in some abandoned field or vacant storefront."

"What about Abigail? How did she die?" Lilly prompted. Her burger and fries settled roughly in her stomach. She hated how she sounded, too interested in this young woman's death.

Elivra shook her head, her lavender flower glinting in the café's lights. "At one of those parties. She died; I think of an overdose. Drug or alcohol, I can't remember which. Poor thing just wanted to be like all the cool kids, I suppose."

"That's horrible," Lilly said solemnly.

She could only speculate what went through Abigail's mind as she tried to prove she was cool enough to hang with the high school crowd. And all it got her was an early grave. Suddenly, Lilly's frustration with Cecilia shifted to a more saddened understanding. Losing a sibling that young would have been devastating. Lilly was an only child, so she could only imagine what Cecilia went through as a teen. Maybe she rushed too quickly into thinking Cecilia was just a nasty woman for no reason.

"Didn't just affect the Schimmels, either," Elvira took a long drink from the coffee that Faith had set in front of her. "The people who held the house party got caught up in all sorts of hell because of it."

"How so?"

"Their boys were blamed for the death initially, but it was ruled as an accidental death by the medical examiner." Elvira sat back on the stool and scratched her chin in thought. "Though Minne Miller was certain to her dying day that the death wasn't accidental. She, along with many people in town, thought that way. Still do. But Mildred Ashby, she's the medical examiner's ex-wife — they were married back then. So, when Mildred said it was an accident, people believed her 'cause why would her then-husband lie?"

"Who held the house party?" Lilly asked, hoping to keep Elvira on topic. Once she started bringing other busybody ladies' names into the conversation, a tangent was forming quickly.

"Why, it was always those founding fathers' family boys putting on the parties. Stilners' boys were always causing trouble with them. And those too-big-for-their-britches veterinarians outside town, what's their name... the Wilhelm boys... Travis, David, and Nathan."

Chapter Twelve

The group chat started going off again Saturday afternoon after lunch. Thankfully, this time Lilly was not the focus. The Chamber of Commerce and festival officials finally decided on a course of action for the remaining day and planned events for Apple Dapple Days. The vendor and craft fair would go on as planned. The chicken and rooster judging had to be cancelled. The police needed the poultry tent for longer than anticipated.

Lilly sat at her Accidental Farmer Experience booth, leisurely checking the group chat and the numerous missed texts from Faith. She sighed at the news of the cancelled poultry show. That meant that Jefferies would be bringing back little Marta and Francesca in the morning. The police were allowing certain 4-H families into the poultry tent in shifts to minimize traffic congestion near their crime scene. She shot Ryan a quick text to check with Jefferies on when he planned to bring the small Sussex hens back to the farm. Hopefully, this time they can avoid another fowl disaster.

She gazed at the nearly empty street over her neatly arranged table of lotions and soaps, pamphlets, and signup sheets. Barely anyone had come out for the last day of the Apple Dapple Days, even though Saturday traditionally was the busiest of the three days. No one wanted to come out to the vendor fair the day after the murder. And if they did, they only did so to glean the juicy gossip that was surely floating around town.

A whopping two people from out of town stopped by her booth in the handful of hours since she started her shift. The husband-and-wife team was not interested in a weekend getaway for two, packed full of learning how to create artisanal soaps or how to milk a cow by hand. They were only interested in learning if the police knew more about Henry's and Owen's deaths. News had finally traveled beyond Lone Tree's borders and into the surrounding communities.

However, Lilly couldn't blame the town for its obsession with the deaths. A member of one of the town's most prominent families was killed during a town festival. And his long-time friend was found dead the day before. That was a better whodunnit plot than what one could find on television nowadays. She was also spending more time reviewing the tidbits of information she had just learned from Elvira Johnson.

Henry and, presumably, Owen attended the same parties as Cecilia Baxter in high school. One of the said parties was where her little sister overdosed on some illicit substance and died. Henry is allegedly the one who supplied said substance. The hosts of the party where the death happened were the Wilhelm brothers.

One of whom was Nathan, who, along with the still-grieving sister and the other associated party, was all in the poultry tent at some point. Were they in the tent at the same time or in varying combinations of the associated parties? Did Cecilia lure Nathan and Henry out to the tent with the intent of hashing out her decades-old trauma, and something went wrong? How did Owen fit in with these players, as he was found in broad daylight on a city bench?

But where did Angela fit in with her scarf? Somehow, her scarf got around Henry's neck. Right now, that was the figurative smoking gun. Lilly chewed absently on her lower lip as she pondered. And what about the weird orange and blue cylinder in the grass? She couldn't figure out what type of poultry care device the cylinder was designed for. It is too small for a water bottle to hang in a cage and, indeed, not the right shape for a roosting perch.

Lilly mulled over her questions while trying to put the players on a timeline. Owen was alone on a park bench when he died. Or was he meeting someone there, and the meeting went south quickly? How did the syringe play into this, and what was in it? Henry and Angela left the dance tent before Cecilia snared Nathan away. Did she know Henry would end up in the poultry tent? Was Angela with him in the tent? How does Cecilia fit into all of this?

"I'm surprised you're showing your face after this morning."

Speak of the devil.

"Good afternoon, Cecilia," Lilly returned with a strained smile.

"Because of you, I had to go to the police station and give some sort of testimony." Cecilia stood in front of Lilly's booth dressed as if she were going to a red-carpet event, in what Lilly knew were knockoffs of designer leather pants and a leopard print cardigan set. She wondered how much Cecilia had spent to look so obviously out of place. Or maybe that was the plan?

"Well, that's what you get. Teach you not to say someone is linked to a murder when they're not," Lilly grinned. Knowing Cecilia had to sit in the police station, looking like that—being subjected to routine police procedure for taking a statement, paraded through the maze of lookie-loo police officers, made Lilly happier than it probably should have.

Small, blotchy red spots crept up Cecilia's neck and cheeks, doing their best to show through her layers of foundation and contouring. "I'm still not convinced you weren't in league with her."

"Watch what you say, Cecilia, you may get called into the police station again," Lilly shrugged. She didn't have it in her to be fake-kind to the woman anymore that day. Not after the ordeal she had gone through herself with being made out to be Suspect Number Two.

"The truth will come out," the woman warned.

Lilly eyed her for a moment. "Like the truth of what you were doing with Nathan Wilhelm in the poultry tent minutes before Henry was found? Where were you during that time, Cecilia?"

Cecilia's makeup lost its fight with the blotches. "My daughter's chicken needed assistance." The words came out clipped and forced.

"Right."

"I didn't see anything!" She cried. "All I saw was the area my daughter's chicken was in. I went out there after Henry and Angela showed up at the dance tent, needing some space from those people. When I saw my daughter's chicken, it looked unwell, so I figured I'd ask Nathan to take a look at it. He did his little examination or whatever, figured the chicken was just dehydrated, probably from the stress of being in a new place with all sorts of people around. We gave the chicken some water, then we left. I walked past Henry and Angela on the way back to the dance tent. But I didn't see where they went after that."

"Then you'd have known I didn't have anything to do with Angela and Henry. I wasn't with them when you saw them." Lilly pointed out. "But yet, you saw Angela and Henry, not too long before he wound up dead."

Cecilia pressed her lips into a tight line. "What are you getting at?"

Lilly bit the inside of her lip, unsure if she should play her only card. She realized Cecilia was flustered, thrown off her usual game by being summoned to the police station. *Now is a good time to put everything out on that table.*

"Abigail."

Now Cecilia's complexion blanched.

"What do you know about her?" Cecilia's words hissed through clenched teeth.

"Just that Henry and Nathan have links to her death," Lilly replied slowly. "And seeing Henry leave would make a good chance to get the gang back together."

"And supposedly what for?"

"To discuss that night," Lilly ventured. "To finally get some closure after all these years."

Cecilia bristled, rising to her full height in her impractical high heels. "Now, who's accusing someone falsely, Lilly?" She snapped.

"Am I?" Lilly asked. Her stomach flopped as she realized what she had done. She better tread carefully, or she'd have more to contend with than a gossipy group chat. "I'd be wanting to get closure from the man or men responsible for her death."

"Henry killed Abigail. Of that I am certain," Cecilia suddenly said. Her tone was soft, her breath clipped, but there was years' worth of venom in each word. "I can't prove it, and it's been eating me up all these years, that no one has been able to prove it, either. He's been able to live freely, while my sister died too young because of a stupid mistake. No one in attendance at that party gave up the person who supplied the drugs, but everyone knew it was Henry. He knew he would never get in trouble just by the merit of his family."

Lilly swallowed hard, feeling the emotion with each word. "I'm sorry."

"Save your sympathy," Cecilia said.

She suddenly slumped, appearing as if she was deflating. It was one of her heels shifting beneath her weight that caused her ankle to roll. Cecilia's rolling hip bumped into the table. Her purse, once perched precariously on her shoulder, slid down to her elbow and knocked into the table, spilling its contents out onto the surface.

"Oh, let me help you—" Lilly began as both women reached for the items. Cecilia huffed but allowed Lilly to assist. Lilly collected a few tubes of designer lipstick and eyeliner, pens, and a long, thick cylinder from the tabletop. This cylinder was too large to be used as a makeup applicator.

One end was blue and the other orange.

Lilly held the cylinder out to Cecilia, though she was hesitant to let it out of her grasp. "What's this?"

"My son's EpiPen. Blasted thing, always falling out..." Cecilia snatched it quickly from Lilly's hand. Swiftly, it disappeared into the depths of her purse. "He has a severe nut allergy. I need it wherever we go."

"Oh, I had no idea..."

"Are we quite done here, Lilly?" Cecilia shoved the rest of her purse's contents roughly back into their compartments. "Done playing detective?"

"Only if you're done accusing me of being associated with a murder," Lilly countered.

"But you do seem to attract... victims." Cecilia looked her up and down with a scathing glare. Without another word, she turned and walked down the street, hobbling slightly on her rolled ankle. Lilly watched her leave, her stomach finally falling to her feet.

Did she just inadvertently accuse Cecilia of killing Henry? She certainly had the most motive Lilly could determine. Could Cecilia also be responsible for Owen's demise?

And the orange and blue EpiPen more than placed her at one scene.

Lilly returned home after an uneventful remainder of the vendor fair. Many vendors ended up closing and tearing down their booths before the official closing time of four o'clock. Lilly was one of those vendors. After her run-in with Cecilia, she just didn't have the heart to try and convince the few people there to explore agri-tourism when all they wanted to hear were stories of murders in chicken tents and on city benches, or if what Cecilia Baxter recently said in the group chat was true.

The petty side of Lilly wasn't too torn up about their previous conversation, knowing how uncomfortable and on the spot it made Cecilia.

"That's what she gets," Lilly muttered. She hefted a box of farm-fresh lotions out of the back of her Kia. She'd have to go back to town to get her canopy; it didn't fit in her Kia as nicely as it had before when Faith had helped organize the Tetris puzzle in the back of her small car.

"I should get a bigger car," she huffed as she set a lotion box on the front porch.

"Make sure it's a truck," Ryan's voice preceded him through the front door. The screen door slammed behind him as he made his way down the steps.

Lilly noticed he was biting into an almost finished apple. One of the apples she had just bought. Her eyes narrowed. "Don't you normally use the back door?" she asked.

"Afraid I'm going to get barn funk all over your house?" he asked.

"Actually, yes," she replied.

He stood at the bottom step, watching as she continued to unload her car. "Do you need some help?"

Lilly looked at him for a moment. "Don't you have chores to do?"

His eyes narrowed under his John Deere cap. He took one last, large bite out of her apple before he responded, "Cows have been milked, fed, and stalls cleaned. Now they're out in the pasture while the manure cleaner runs. I'm good for a while."

Lilly sighed, amazed that she understood what he said around the masticated apple. She finally nodded toward the car. He moved around her and grabbed two small boxes of milk soap. "Sorry, I haven't been around to help with the barn chores lately," she offered after a few moments of silence.

"You've been busy with the vendor fair and the farmers' market," Ryan said.

"That doesn't mean you have to run everything by yourself," Lilly said as she pulled a box of pamphlets from the back.

"I did fine before you showed back up," Ryan shrugged. "Hey, where's your tent?"

Ryan's first words struck her in the pit of her stomach. She swallowed hard, remembering that Ryan had run the farm by himself when her grandparents had hired him to be their farm hand. After their death, he was the sole caretaker of the grounds and the animals. He had been doing fine without her meddling.

"Oh, the tent is back at the street fair," she replied. "I couldn't get everything to fit in as nicely as your sister." Ryan shot her a look. "What? I couldn't get it to fit!"

"I'll drive you back in the truck." Ryan jerked his chin toward the car. You should have gotten that tent back in there just fine."

"I know..." Lilly sat on the steps amongst the boxed-up reminders of her floundering business. "I think I just needed to get out of there."

"Cecilia giving you problems?"

Lilly looked at him sharply. "How did you know about that?"

"The group chat. Almost everyone in town knows about that by now," Ryan said with a smile. "And Faith has been texting me about it all day."

Lilly shook her head. "No, it's more than that now. She stopped by my booth."

"Is she harassing you?" Ryan asked.

"Not more than normal."

"What did she accuse you of this time?"

Lilly felt her cheeks burn. "Well, it was more of what I accused her of..."

"Lilly..."

"I may have suggested she had reason to kill Henry because of her sister Abigail."

"Lillian!" Ryan cried. He took off his cap and raked his fingers through his hair, all while taking a slow, supposedly calming breath. The two fell into an uneasy silence. Ryan finally broke it by letting out a swift breath and sitting in the empty back area of her car. "I'm impressed you did that."

"Really?" Lilly looked up at him in shock. Usually, he'd be shouting and admonishing her about her impulsivity and how it was going to get, or had already gotten her, into trouble.

"Maybe she'll lay off you now, knowing you're not afraid to talk back."

"You think?"

"Or you just brought down the full wrath of Cecilia Baxter onto you."

"But you see where I got the connection, right?" Lilly asked. "She was in the poultry tent, and somehow Henry was in there, too. Maybe she bumped into him after dealing with the chicken emergency with Nathan."

Ryan humphed. "And I bet you're going to connect her to Owen, too?"

"She has more reason than anyone to kill Henry and Owen, if it's true that either provided the drugs that Abigail OD'd on."

"What about the scarf that's supposedly Angela's?" Ryan pointed out.

Lilly bit her lower lip as she tried to organize her thoughts. "Henry and Angela left together, maybe he got her scarf for some reason."

"That's pretty thin speculation there, Nancy Drew," Ryan smirked.

"Stop calling me that."

"Once you stop playing TV detective," Ryan countered as Lilly stuck out her tongue at him.

"But who else would have a good enough motive to kill Owen or Henry?" Lilly asked.

"The beleaguered wife, perhaps?" Ryan offered.

"Ooh, big word!" Lilly smiled. It was Ryan's turn to stick his tongue out at her, though he also threw in a particular finger gesture along with it. "Just because they have a challenging marriage doesn't mean anything. Is the talk of her cheating true then?"

"As far as I've heard," Ryan shrugged.

"If the cheating and horrible marriage is a motive, then he'd have more reason to kill Angela." Lilly countered. "Jilted husband, knowing his wife is seeing other guys. Knowing the whole town knows about it? I'd put him as a better suspect for trying to off her."

"Maybe he tried to," he suggested. "Got her out in the poultry tent, alone. It's quiet out there 'cause everyone else is either home or at the dance tent. He tries to kill her somehow. But she ends up turning the tables and strangles him with her scarf."

"Then it'd be self-defense, not murder," Lilly tapped her chin with her finger.

"Then why did Angela run?" Ryan asked. "She wasn't anywhere near the poultry tent when Henry was found, nor was she the one who called the cops after. If it were self-defense, she would have stuck around."

"She freaked out?" Lilly said. "I'm not sure I'd think straight after accidentally killing someone, self-defense or not."

"Why did you say 'or not?'" Ryan's brow arched under the brim of his cap.

"I'm... I'm covering all my bases?" Lilly fumbled.

"Is the group chat right?"

"No!" Lilly cried. "I was nowhere near the tent when he died. I was with you."

"Doesn't mean you didn't have some prior knowledge of it."

Ryan's grin poked the stone that formed in her gut. No matter what she did, what she said, she wasn't going to get rid of the lie that Cecilia spread, or the hold it had on people: Blasted Cecilia and her insidious smear campaign.

"Unfortunately for Cecilia, just because I am being a decent person toward Angela doesn't mean I'm suddenly close enough to her to be a trusted confidant for a murder plot."

"That hasn't stopped that woman from making your life hell," Ryan quipped.

"Shut up, Swenson," Lilly grumbled.

Ryan opened his mouth to reply, though he was interrupted by a loud bellowing from the barn. Both sat straighter at the sound, heads turning toward the barn and the pasture. Another bellow followed, sounding more anguished than what Lilly had ever heard a cow utter—even one giving birth.

"Is someone calving?" Lilly asked.

Ryan shook his head. "No one is due for over a month."

He stood up from his seat in her car and slowly made his way to the barn along the gravel driveway. His left leg limped more noticeably after he had sat on the rugged bumper of her vehicle. After another bellow, the farm hand bolted as fast as he could down the lawn, his limp and sore muscles long forgotten. Lilly joined him in his race to the barn, though at a considerable distance behind.

Chapter Thirteen

"A twisted stomach?" Lilly blanched at the diagnosis. "Do I even want to know what that is?"

She, Ryan, and Nathan all stood before cow Number 346, as indicated by the yellow tag pierced through her left ear. Ryan had told her that the cow came from another farm just before her grandparents' death and had not been appropriately named or registered. Unfortunately, Grandma Beverly passed away before she could bestow a name on the new cow family.

Lilly decided, while they waited for Nathan to arrive, that she would name the cow and start a new family name on the farm. Most of the cow families were named after flowers, as seen in herd darlings Dandelion, Peony, and Pansy. The other naming choice, besides flowers, was to name each subsequent generation a name starting with the same letter. Lilly had already started an 'E' family line with a young heifer calf named Envy, born to mama cow Emerald.

What to rename Number 346?

Now Nathan stood next to 346's distended side, stethoscope buds in his ears. He moved the silver disc along the cow's rib cage, pausing to tap in between and along each large rib.

He had arrived almost thirty minutes after Ryan and Lilly found 346 lying on her side in the pasture. Even to Lilly's untrained eyes, she could tell the cow was in distress. It took the pair the full thirty minutes to coax the sluggish cow to her feet and into the barn. The cow moved stiffly on her feet, her eyes sunken and listlessly taking in the action around her. By the time Ryan got 346 tied into her stall, Nathan's large white vet truck pulled up to the barn doors.

Lilly could not get over how distended the cow's flank was; it protruded unnaturally as if the cow were merely pregnant on one side.

"You know cows have a four-chambered stomach, right?" Ryan asked. He leaned back from the cow, resting his hip on the metal stall stanchion.

"Yes," Lilly answered slowly. It had been over a decade since she had been quizzed about the anatomy of cows.

"Well, those suckers like to move around sometimes. Especially if the true stomach gets displaced during pregnancy."

"Pregnancy? 346 just had a calf?"

Ryan nodded. He held up a finger as she opened her mouth. "Yes, you can name mom and baby."

Lilly smiled, then gave Ryan the side eye, unsure if she should believe what he told her. "The true stomach?"

"Where all the main digesting happens," Ryan smirked at her apparent disbelief. "The true stomach part can get displaced by the baby calf. Much like how in human women their organs get all rearranged as the baby grows."

"It basically rolls over on itself," Nathan chimed in as he stepped away from Number 346. Lilly looked at him as if he had suddenly spoken Russian. "How long ago did 346 calve?"

"A month ago," Ryan's tone took on a sharp, defensive edge. "Unfortunately, it's not readily noticed right after birth. The symptoms are similar to those of many other ailments a cow can experience. I've just started noticing 346 has been off her feed for the last two days."

"Hmm." Nathan nodded and said nothing else.

Ryan's eyes narrowed.

"So, how do you fix a twisted stomach?" Lilly asked, hoping to distract the two men from laying blame for the cow's distress. She stared at the protruding flank and grimaced. "Do you just make her burp to get the stomach to go back down or just push on it?"

Ryan coughed to cover his laugh. She eyed him and tried unsuccessfully to kick him from the other side of 346. Nathan smiled, polite enough not to straight up laugh at her lack of knowledge. "If it is caught soon enough"—a meaningful glance to Ryan, who looked away with a scowl—"we have to move the stomach back down to the normal spot surgically. And if needed, I may have to stitch in place. Since it moved once, it'll be more likely to move again."

"Surgically fix it?" Lilly asked. "Do we need to get her to the vet's office?"

"Not at all," Nathan smiled. "We can do it right here."

He turned around to a large tackle box that served as his medical tote, which sat behind him in the main walk of the barn. Nathan started digging through the various compartments until he found two blue-wrapped parcels, a couple of scalpels, and two syringes. He opened one of the blue wrapped packages, producing a large surgical drape. He handed it to Ryan, and without a word, the hired hand started to wrap it around the cow's face, making sure to cover the eyes.

"Don't you have to put her under or something?" Lilly asked, the panic clear in her voice.

Nathan unwrapped the second blue package, revealing a second large surgical drape. He placed it over the cow's back and flanks. He ensured that a premade cut in the drape lay over a predetermined spot that he had quietly selected as the incision point.

"A local nerve block will do fine," Nathan answered. "Ryan, can you go out to my truck and get a bottle of lidocaine and xylazine?"

Ryan left the barn without a word. Lilly's head reeled at the strange medical terms. Apparently, Ryan was familiar with the specific medications that the vet rattled off. Lilly wasn't even sure she could spell them.

"Do you want to watch?" Nathan asked as he pulled out another blue package. He quickly opened it to reveal a large blue smock, and suddenly looked more like a human doctor than a large animal veterinarian. He gave her a reassuring smile as he pulled a long latex glove over one of the sleeves. "I promise, it's a quick procedure but terribly interesting."

"Umm..." Lilly stammered. "I'm not very good with blood." She swallowed hard as her mind raced ahead to what awaited Cow Number 346.

Ryan came back into the barn with the two requested vials of medication. He stood next to Nathan, who took the vials and handed off a set of long latex gloves and a smock to Ryan. The hired hand quickly donned the surgical accessories and looked over at Lilly, one of his usual smirks pulling at the corner of his mouth.

"Is she staying?" Ryan asked, jerking his thumb at Lilly. He snapped the gloves over the sleeves of the smock. The loud sound caused Lilly to jump.

"She says she doesn't do well with blood, which I can respect," Nathan responded. He drew two syringes from his collection of tools and filled each with exact amounts from the vials Ryan had retrieved from the truck. He started administering the shots to the back and flank of Number 346. The cow let loose a startled bellow of annoyance, perhaps even pain, and flinched at the pinch from the needles.

"Given how she gets green when I run the manure collector during barn cleaning? I'm not surprised," Ryan nodded.

Nathan smoothed the surgical drape and positioned his scalpel next to the cow's skin within the drape's opening. "Well, you'd better decide quickly. The procedure is about to start."

Ryan leveled a hard stare at Lilly. "Once we start, we can't stop to tend to you passing out or puking on the barn floor." There was a hint of amusement in his voice.

At that, the blade sank into the cow's flesh, and a thin line of red followed the descent of the scalpel. Lilly suddenly felt her stomach flip. "I-I think I'll go up to the house." She swallowed hard. "Let me know when the surgery is done."

The two men didn't respond as she quickly disappeared out the barn doors.

Lilly chose to distract herself from the surgery happening in her barn by playing around with new scents for her milk lotion line. She had the typical scents of lotions: lavender, sandalwood, vanilla, and eucalyptus. But those came from the limited selection of essential oils she had accumulated over the years from friends who had been drawn into multi-level marketing schemes and the latest fads. She needed to find a scent that was quintessentially *farm*.

She sat in the kitchen, surrounded by tiny vials of essential oils and boxes of shea butter and moisturizing oils. Lilly picked up each little bottle and made a face, not impressed with the choices set before her. How to make a scent that just screamed of life on the farm?

And... what was that scent?

Lilly gazed out the back kitchen window toward the northwest, where the crop land surrounded the farm site. Between the grove trees and the outlying buildings, she spied plumes of dust rising above the earth. This time of year was still a little too early for complete harvesting. However, it was now time to complete the last hay harvest of the year.

As she watched the spirals of dust travel above the tree line, she could just catch a glimpse, or the imagined glimpse, of the scent of fresh cut hay through the back screen door. Instantly, Lilly was transported to her teenage years in suburban Minneapolis. Almost every weekend, the neighborhood was filled with the sound of whirring lawn mowers, spreading the sweet aroma of grass throughout the air. Then she was sent even further back to memories of summer evenings on that very farm when her grandpa cut the grass with his John Deere riding mower. If she were extra good, she'd get to ride along the last few passes as he finished up the lawn.

Such pleasant memories filled her with a sense of peace and calm that she hadn't felt in days. Lilly knew precisely what would become the next featured scent of her lotion line. But she had to figure out how to bottle the smell of fresh-cut grass.

She turned to everyone's favorite answer giver: the internet. Lilly searched for fresh-cut grass and essential oils made from fresh-cut hay, with varying levels of success. As she dug deeper down the rabbit hole, her mind began to wander back to the question of Henry's and Owen's murderer's identity... or identities.

Thankfully—hopefully—she was no longer on the list of suspects. But who was on the police's list of persons of interest? Angela Stilner, obviously. Any faithful follower of true crime would never overlook the possibility that the spouse might be the primary suspect. Cecilia Baxter had a pretty strong case for being suspect number two. She made it painfully clear her dislike of Henry, Angela, and anyone who associated with those two.

Was there anyone else besides those two?

Angela had been in an allegedly awful marriage. Killing Henry meant that she bypassed a possibly nasty divorce. And with the allegations of unfaithfulness on Angela's part, the divorce would not have gone her way at all. Lilly herself had gone through a divorce, though hers was reasonably civil and only took a couple of months to finalize. Alec, her ex, had already moved on with his mistress. They made plans to move into their Minneapolis loft and take most of the marital possessions. Lilly only wanted a handful of items that she had brought into the marriage, and let them have whatever they wanted. Whether that would prove to be the wrong decision as time moved on, she could only guess. Lilly only wanted to get away from her cheating husband and start over quickly.

Murder never crossed her mind. At least not any notions she'd follow through on.

Lilly's online search finally yielded a source of essential oils that would enable her to create fresh-cut-grass-scented items. She also found oils that would prove fruitful for new candles for the winter season. Campfire and cedar smoke definitely sparked her interest, so naturally, they were added to her online cart. As the cart total tallied up, Lilly's hope for the new scents faltered.

The amount of money she was investing in her Accidental Farmer Experience venture was not generating revenue for the business. She reluctantly clicked the Complete Order button and hoped this investment would pay off. Lilly swallowed down the lump in her throat as she closed her laptop and pushed it aside on the kitchen island. At the thought of possibly losing the farm because of her overspending, albeit for much-needed repairs to buildings and the lofty Accidental Farmer Experience upgrades she concocted, her stomach soured. Lilly wasn't sure what she could do to keep the farm running. Would she sell off land? Sell some of the livestock? The idea of losing the farm, just a handful of months after taking it over, made her blood boil.

Lilly's mind turned suddenly to Angela and Henry. Would blood-boiling thoughts lead one to murder?

Perhaps the marriage between Angela and Henry was not as idyllic as the town's golden son wanted everyone to think. On top of the rumors of infidelity, maybe money troubles also festered among the couple. Angela had quite a few side hustles at the farmers' market, where fresh produce, eggs, and sometimes fresh goat cheese and wool were for sale.

What did Henry do for a living, besides riding on the coattails of what his ancestors accomplished centuries ago? How did Owen fit into this? Was he killed for his drug links to the party? Or was someone not happy that Henry and Owen were business partners?

She needed more answers. And who better to get the answers to her questions than from her good friend Faith? The restaurateur overheard bits and pieces of conversations in her café, everything that one could want to know about the latest gossip in the town's rumor mill.

Lilly needed to get back to town anyway and get her pop-up canopy soon. She gathered her phone and purse and glanced at her watch, realizing she needed to get to town sooner rather than later. The vendor fair officially closed in half an hour, at four o'clock. She hadn't realized how much time had been spent dealing with the ailing cow.

She would have to hear from Ryan later about how the surgery went.

She left the kitchen by the back door and stepped out onto the wrap-around porch. This made for an easy escape without having to navigate her way through the main house. Even though she had lived in the house for a while, little had changed since her grandparents had lived in the farmhouse. She was slow to replace decorations and furniture to what suited her style and needs. The memories in each room were still too strong to allow her to make any drastic changes.

Lilly wasn't sure when the farmhouse would finally feel like hers.

The drive to Lone Tree from the farm was quick, though once she got downtown, the traffic on Main Street slowed to a crawl. Large flat-bed trucks lined the streets, ready to take away the tents, tables, barricades, and other festival accessories. Amazingly, Lilly found parking by the Attic, though it would still be a bit of a walk to where she left her canopy.

On her way to her spot, the street was a bustle with vendors who had been there all day. By the tired and downtrodden expressions on their faces, Lilly guessed the choice to stick it out had been a fruitless one. Lilly walked into her spot, the barren asphalt shaded by her canopy, and she began to tear down her tent. She opted to ignore the sideways glances and some outright stares from the other vendors. Lilly knew those women from the vendor group chat and knew they were still upset about what had happened earlier in the day.

Whatever Cecilia Baxter said was gospel to some people.

How long until she shook the association with an alleged murderer? Lilly frowned as she clumsily took down her tent. Just because she knew Angela Stilner and was decent to her didn't mean she was in league with her. Suppose she *did* murder her husband, which was still yet to be determined by the police and a court of law. Perhaps Lilly would file a libel suit against Cecilia. In a matter of minutes, with just a few words, the woman caused almost irreparable damage to her reputation and any credibility her fledgling business hoped to gain.

Lilly stuffed that line of thinking deep down for now, much like how she attempted to stuff her canopy back into its carrying bag. It wasn't pretty, but the bag finally zipped around the tent and was stowed away. Avoiding the constant stream of side-eyes, Lilly pulled her tent back to her car near Grandma's Attic. After a few more clumsy minutes, the tent bag was settled squarely into the back of her Kia.

Now on to her reconnaissance mission in the Attic. Surely Faith would have heard something juicy by now. Hopefully, she'd be able to clear the confusion as to why someone would want both Henry Stilner and Owen Perkins dead.

She slammed her back hatch shut with an unladylike grunt and then turned to the front doors of Grandma's Attic. It was late enough in the day that the café would be empty, allowing Faith time to discuss her current murder theories. And be reasonably free from any unwanted side-eye glares.

Upon entering the café, the aromas of grilled meats and fried foods wafted toward her, also carrying the lingering afternotes of plowed earth and hay. The local farmers like to sneak into the Attic for a quick meal as they drove their tractors to and from the fields, or ran loads of hay and alfalfa to the feed auctions. Surprisingly, the two differing scent palettes blended well, invoking pleasant memories of summer nights spent on her grandparents' farm.

"Hey Lilly, find yourself a seat and I'll be right there," Faith called from behind the counter as Lilly made her way from the front doors.

Lilly found her usual back booth empty and swiftly slid into the long bench seat. Knowing Faith, she'd arrive shortly with either her usual order of a cheeseburger and fries, or just an iced tea. Given she had barely eaten that day, she hoped her friend would bring the former.

Lilly balanced the individual creamer tubs into various pyramid shapes as she waited for Faith to arrive. The aimless activity gave her time to think over her mental murder board. Hopefully, she'd have her theories in order before Faith started picking them apart.

Who were the top suspects in these latest murders? Number one was the unfortunate wife, Angela Stilner. Rumors of an unhappy union and infidelity on the part of Angela seemed to be good fodder for the sudden end to the marriage. But why kill his friend, too?

The second suspect was Cecilia Baxter. The younger sister of Lone Tree's most fearsome busybody allegedly died of an overdose at a party thrown by Henry, Owen, and others, and Cecilia had held onto that grudge for decades. Why wait until now to exact revenge?

"I see that hamster wheel spinning away," Faith grinned as she slid into the opposite bench seat. She placed a large plate of French fries with seasoned dipping sauces between them as she settled into the booth.

"Ha, ha," Lilly stuck her tongue out as she snatched a steaming fry from the heaping plate. "New sauces?"

"Yeah, trying them out for a little bit to see if we should add them to the menu permanently," Faith nodded as she dunked a fry into the sauce. "Toby stopped by a place in Iowa, and they had sauces similar to these, and he couldn't stop raving about them until I came up with my own."

Lilly nodded between bites of fries. The new seasoned dip was mayo-based but tasted more like the robust cousin of ranch. Toby, Faith's husband, was a long-haul truck driver and often brought back new menu ideas for Faith to try from his various trips. "I think Toby was right about this one, Faith. I'd keep it."

"You're not the only one to tell me," the restaurateur nodded. "So, what theories have you come up with so far?"

"Theories?" Lilly pouted. "What theories?"

Faith narrowed her eyes. "You know very well what theories, Lillian Marian Schmidt."

"Ooh, the full name treatment," Lilly chuckled as she bit into another fry. "Careful, Faith, your Mom Mode is showing."

Faith sighed and ran her hand through her dark hair. "Sorry. Toby's been gone for a week, and the kids have been on my last nerve."

Lilly nodded sympathetically and could only imagine the chaos of trying to raise three kids and run a restaurant while being down one parental unit. "You should see if their uncles could use them at the different farms," she suggested.

"The only uncle who hasn't banned them from farm duties is Ryan," Faith leaned back against the booth's cushions.

"Bring them out to the farm this weekend, I bet Ryan would love to have them help out."

Faith eyed her. "Are you sure?"

"I could use Savannah's help with the chickens. Thomas and Morgan could help Ryan in the barn with the cows and calves."

"I'll run it by Ryan first," Faith replied with a noncommittal nod. "So. Murder board theories. Spill them or I'm going back behind the counter."

"Fine, fine," Lilly scrunched her nose in annoyance. "I have two main suspects: Angela, the allegedly unfaithful wife, and Cecilia Baxter, the sister who wants revenge for a wrongful death."

"Seems plausible for both," Faith popped a sauce-drenched fry into her mouth. "But..."

"But what? But why would Angela kill Henry instead of just divorcing him? If she was unhappy in the marriage, why not leave? How does Owen play into this if just her husband had to die?"

"What if he wasn't giving her the divorce?" Faith countered. "He has to sign the papers as well. Divorce goes both ways."

Lilly frowned slightly. Having recently gone through a divorce with her cheating ex, she had fresh experience with needing two signatures on the divorce papers. "So, say Henry was holding out on signing the papers… why? What would he have to gain from staying married?"

Faith sat in silence for a few moments, using her finger to scrape the last of the seasoned mayonnaise sauce out of the little plastic cup. "Or what did he have to lose in getting divorced?"

"Lose?"

"Seriously, Lilly, sometimes I wonder about the state of the hamster running on the wheel in your thoughts," Faith shot back. "You went through a divorce. You had to split assets with Alec."

"I let Alec have pretty much everything," Lilly narrowed her brows.

"Not everyone has such a clear-cut divorce as you did. Some are downright nasty." Faith pointed a fry at her. "Henry's family is loaded, thus he is loaded. Putting aside pre-marital assets, Henry had a mechanic business, which he ran from their farm, that he started after they got married. She would have every right to ask for half of that business. Half of the farm was where they lived. Angela could have cleaned him out, adding insult to the cheating injury."

"Is there even proof of her cheating?" Lilly asked sharply. She pressed her lips into a tight line, confused as to where this sudden need to defend Angela came from. The two women were barely acquaintances, let alone good friends. Yet something about Angela's predicament called to Lilly, who was unable to believe the woman was entirely the unfaithful type.

Even if Lilly personally thought she had settled for Henry and could do a world of better in the husband department.

"Only the town scuttlebutt," Faith shrugged.

"There you go!"

"And the strange men in strange cars seen at the farm," Faith's grin curled snakelike across her face.

"Strange men?" The seasoned fries settled hard in Lilly's stomach. "And who has seen these alleged strange cars with strange men?"

"Lots of Henry's customers," Faith replied. "A few of them have come in here after getting their farm trucks worked on, carrying on about super fancy cars that have no business being out in the country like that."

"Start naming names."

"Are you asking me to give up the names of my sources?" Faith gasped, hand clutching at the base of her neck. "Never."

"Then Angela's dropping to suspect number two on my list. Cecilia has the better motive to kill him than anyone."

Faith harrumphed. "More so than a wife stuck in a horrible marriage with no way out?"

"Give me one name of someone who saw these alleged fancy cars?" Lilly demanded.

"Gregory Fitz," Faith said around a mouthful of fries.

Lilly shot her a look. "Now, see, was that so hard to give up a name?"

"Won't do you any good, though," Faith smirked. "Greg's on the road to Madison right now with a load of cows sold at auction. So if you wanted to ask him about what he saw, you'll have to wait until he gets back tomorrow."

Lilly sighed and watched Faith as she gloated in her apparent triumph. She grabbed the last cup of seasoned sauce from Faith's fingers and started spooning fingerfuls of the tasty dip into her mouth as she mulled over her options. Was she willing to wait a whole day to get the answers that she was looking for? Did she want to waste time by tracking down Gregory Fitz when he returned and ask him what he saw—allegedly?

"Why should I wait for Gregory Fitz to get back?" Lilly asked as she scraped the bottom of the sauce cup with one of the last fries.

"Because you said you wanted proof of strange fancy cars at the Stilners' place?" Faith reminded her.

Lilly slapped Faith's hand as her friend tried to steal the last fry from the plate. "Why should I trust your source when I could just go there?"

"Go where? Madison?" Faith gaped.

"No, not Madison, forget Gregory Fitz." Lilly bit into the last fry. She wasn't sure if her following grin was due to winning the fry or bypassing Faith's supply to the rumor mill. "What's stopping me from going out to Stilners' place and getting answers from the source?"

Chapter Fourteen

Maybe Lilly should have listened to Faith before heading off on her latest adventure.

Her friend's voice kept playing over in her mind as she drove out to the northwest side of town and Lone Tree Lake. As her Kia rattled over the uneven gravel road that led out to the Stilner farm and mechanic shop, Lilly bit her lip and wondered if it was too late to turn back and go home.

"Isn't your cousin the lead investigator on this case?" Faith had asked before she left Grandma's Attic.

"Yes," Lilly had responded sheepishly.

"And after your little stunt with Cecilia Baxter over group chat, I'm betting he told you to stay out of the investigation?"

"How'd you know about the group chat?" was all Lilly could say.

She *had* told her cousin, Sheriff Branford, that she'd stay away from the case. Was it a full, legally binding promise not to ask around? Technically, no. Lilly knew that if Ryan were there, he'd be calling her some TV or book-related detective and giving her a scolding for poking her nose where it didn't belong.

Hadn't she learned from a few months ago to stay out of murder investigations? Her shoulder still hurt from where the assailant's hammer had struck. Was she willing to risk another life-or-death struggle with a murderer to prove... to prove what, exactly? Lilly's mind wandered almost too far with questioning her motive that she nearly missed the driveway for the Stilners' farm.

Only two miles away from the shores of Lone Tree Lake, the farm sat not too far from the main road, meaning the likelihood of a long, unkempt gravel driveway was lessened. Resembling many of the other farms in the area, a large square turn-of-the-century H-frame home sat almost in the middle of the building site, with acres of farmland surrounding the small island of barns and sheds. As Lilly navigated her Kia up to the main house, she noticed a large machine shed that had been converted into a mechanic's shop. The heavy garage doors were open, revealing numerous bays full of trucks and tractors in various states of repair.

Beyond the machine shop was a small red barn, one far too small for housing cows. Lilly remembered that Angela always had a steady supply of eggs and vegetables for her farmers' market stall. However, she couldn't recall at that moment if the Stilners also kept any livestock. Perhaps if she were lucky, she'd have a moment to inspect the barn and the rest of the outbuildings.

Someone had to be on the property, right?

Lilly parked her car in front of the main house and got out of the vehicle. She followed the flagstone walk up to the front porch; it wrapped around the whole house much like her farmhouse. Her kitten heels thunked against the porch boards, strangely the only sound in the farmyard. She swallowed hard and pressed on. She made it this far; now there was no sense in chickening out.

She walked up to the front door and rang the doorbell, straining her ears to determine if the bells chimed on the inside of the house. After a few moments, she rang the doorbell again and knocked on the outer door.

"Angela?" Lilly called out. "Are you home?"

Feeling suddenly exposed, Lilly stepped away from the main door and made her way around the wrap-around porch. Perhaps there was a back door, like the one at her home. Maybe Angela was somewhere in the large house, which made it hard to hear any knocking.

As she made her way around to the back of the house, Lilly's pace slowed until she stopped mid-step. Behind the house was a single-wide trailer, raised on stilts and cinder blocks. White prefabricated picket white fencing was attached to the bottom of the trailer to hide the expanse beneath. A set of haphazardly built stairs led to the front door, framed by sun-faded lawn decorations. The site of the trailer wasn't the most astonishing part of the scene before her. Many farmers had multiple generations living on the same farm site. Lilly heard of some farmers offering on-site residencies for their farmhands.

Lilly shuddered quickly at the idea of Ryan living within a stone's throw of her home.

The sight that made her freeze in her tracks was an expensive black car—a Lexus SUV to be exact—sitting to the side of the trailer on a small patch of gravel. That would certainly constitute a "strange fancy car". Lilly gaped at the luxury car, mind spinning as it tried to formulate reasons why such a car was out in the middle of the country instead of the urban streets of a metropolitan city. Was that Angela's car? Was it Henry's? How could either one afford such a car on a farmer's or mechanic's salary?

But that certainly gave credence to Faith's source's claims of strange cars at the Stilners'. Lilly walked toward the porch railing to get a better look at the vehicle. It had recently been on the gravel roads, the clean lines of the car dirtied by gravel dust, the molten rubber of the tires more tan than black.

"Who do you belong to?" Lilly whispered.

A screen door on the trailer opened and slammed shut behind two people as they left. Lilly's mouth went dry, and her throat seemed to squeeze shut as she saw Angela walking slowly down the trailer's steps.

Followed by a well-dressed and attention-grabbingly handsome man.

Angela's gaze suddenly lifted and locked immediately onto Lilly's. The woman stopped in her tracks, causing her male companion to bump into her from behind. "Lilly!" The color went out of Angela's face. "What are you doing here?"

"I... I..." Lilly stammered. Her mind went blank as to why she had come out to the farm in the first place. "I just wanted to... uh... see how you were doing with... everything."

She wasn't planning on catching Angela in the act!

"You came to check on... me?" Angela's words were flat and measured. She glanced up at the tall man behind her.

Lilly smiled her best smile, hoping to put Angela and her companion at ease. "I know we're not the closest of friends, Angela, but I just wanted to stop by and see how you're doing with everything. I can only imagine how hard this must be for you."

Angela stood silent for a moment, then nodded her head as tears glistened in the corners of her eyes. "I can't believe he's gone," she choked out in a whisper. The man behind her put a hand on her shoulder and gave a squeeze.

Well, that certainly doesn't scream of spousal guilt, Lilly thought. She reached out and placed a gentle hand on Angela's arm. "Is there anything I can do?" She knew the question was useless as soon as it left her mouth, but she couldn't think of anything else to say at the moment. It was the thought that counted, right?

Angela pressed the heels of her hands to her eyes and took a couple of deep breaths. "There's nothing... well, there is one thing..." Angela took a shaky breath. "I know you wanted registrations for next year's farmers" market in a few weeks, but..."

"Oh, no, no!" Lilly shook her head and gripped Angela's arm tightly for a moment before finally letting go. "I'll save you a spot, and you just let me know if you want it when you're ready."

"You'd do that?"

"It pays to know the market organizer," Lilly gave her a little wink and a smile.

"You're not worried about what Cecilia will say about you holding me a spot?" Angela asked.

"No," Lilly hoped she sounded more convincing than she felt. She wasn't sure how many more times she could cross that woman without more dire retributions coming her way.

A long pause fell over the three suddenly, each seemingly wanting the other to continue the conversation. The tall man behind Angela cleared his throat softly.

"Oh, I should, we should..." Angela stammered, glancing from Lilly to the man and back again. "Uh, well, this is..."

Your lover?

The man extended his hand to Lilly. "I'm Jakob," he offered with a smile. "With a 'K.'"

Lilly took this time to get a better look at the man with Angela, trying to place him in the ever-evolving drama that was the Stilner marriage. She scanned him from head to foot. He had thick, brown hair and dark eyes that seemed to take in everything around him constantly. Jakob's lean build was hidden behind tailored clothes, also in black to match his SUV. The crisp line of his black trousers and leather coat stood out not only against the rural scenery but also against the mid-September temperatures.

Lilly guessed he must be sweltering in all that dark clothing. Or under the weight of his ego. *Really? Jakob-with-a-'K'?* She had to fight the smirk that pulled at the corners of her mouth. "Jakob, nice to meet you," Lilly returned the firm handshake. "I'm Lilly Schmidt. I operate the local farmers' market and agri-tourism start-up in town."

A look of confusion mixed with intrigue crossed Jakob-with-a-K's face. "Agri-tourism? I'm not sure I've ever heard of that before."

Angela glanced down at her wristwatch and cleared her throat loudly. "Well, you'll have to pick Lilly's brain about it another time," Angela interjected, tugging on the sleeve of Jakob's coat. "We have to meet the sheriff in town. For our statements. Remember?"

Lilly couldn't place the flash of expression that crossed Jakob's eyes before he nodded with an amiable smile. "Of course. Can't leave the good sheriff waiting."

"Have the police given you any leads as to who..." Lilly found herself unable to say kill or murder in front of Angela. "Who did this to Henry and Owen?"

Angela's skin paled as she took a step down the stairs. "No, they haven't. Now, if you'd excuse us, Lilly, we really must be going."

Lilly took a step back and allowed the two to exit the stairs and make their way to the SUV. "Oh, sure. Yeah..." Lilly swallowed as she saw her window of opportunity with Angela dwindle quickly. "Maybe I can stop by again, Angela. Just give me a call. Anytime."

Jakob slid into the driver's seat as Angela opened the passenger door. She looked back at Lilly, her lips pressed into a tight line. Lilly wasn't sure, but she could have sworn Angela looked almost worried as she glanced between the car's interior and her. Was she scared to be leaving with this Jakob person? Or was she scared to leave Lilly alone on the property?

Lilly gave them a small wave as the SUV finally left the farmyard. As the crunch of tires on the gravel faded, Lilly glanced around as she suddenly found herself with two options. Leave the Stilner farm as any normal, rational person would do after the owners had vacated the property. Or snoop around, knowing that no one else was around, like any self-respecting amateur sleuth.

Unsurprisingly, Lilly went with option number two.

After a quick hop up the trailer steps, Lilly determined that the trailer was indeed locked and then continued to walk around its perimeter. She had hoped that Jakob and Angela were like most residents who lived on the outskirts of Lone Tree and hadn't bothered to lock the door to their abodes. However, this time her luck ran out. Nothing stood out along the outside of the trailer, and there was no other entrance.

Her next option for sleuthing was the outbuildings. Lilly narrowed her scope on the machine shed, knowing that was the center of Henry's home-based mechanic business. Surely, Henry would have kept business papers in the machine shed instead of the house.

As she neared the machine shed, noises came to her from the barn. She slowed her walk and listened, still unsure of what livestock—if any—

the Stilners had on the farm. Her quandary was soon answered when multiple shrill bleats came from within the barn. Goats. Of course, the Stilners kept goats. Lilly suddenly remembered the few times Angela had brought goat cheese to the farmers' market, and how she'd said making cheese was a time-consuming task, so she didn't offer it as often as she'd like.

Lilly kept that mental note for her agri-tourism offerings. Would the risk be worth the benefits of adding such a complicated endeavor? With the money troubles of the farm, perhaps cheese production offered a solution she hadn't considered. She'd have to check with Ryan about the logistics of doing cheese production at the farm. She knew he would denounce her idea before even running the numbers.

Promising herself to catch a quick glimpse of the goats on her way back to her car, Lilly continued to the machine shed. The imposing metal building loomed before her, four garage doors open like gaping mouths of a steel monster. Two of the bays held farm trucks in various states of repair. Hoods stood open, and tool chests sat next to the vehicles, waiting for the mechanic who wouldn't be coming back.

Didn't Faith say that Henry had an associate to help with the repairs, Gregory Fitz? No, he was only a customer of Henry's business who had seen sketchy cars come and go on the Stilner farmyard. And he was out of the state, so he was of no use to her.

Lilly walked into the machine shed and headed toward what she thought was a walled-off office. Thankfully, Henry wasn't as security-minded as his wife. The metal door stood wide open, like the bay doors and toolboxes. If he was lackadaisical about safety measures with the machine shed, what precautions would be in the office for sensitive information, such as customer details or financial ledgers?

Lilly's kitten heels click-clunked dully on the second-hand linoleum flooring within the office. The warped and cracked tiles made walking treacherous, as she had to watch out for any askew tiles or curling corners. A long metal desk sat along the back wall of the hastily constructed office space. She could tell the metal walls were not part of the original building. Open gaps between the office walls and the main building allowed light to enter, highlighting columns of dust. The top of the desk was a disaster zone of paper: piles of manila folders, open checkbooks, outgoing invoices and incoming bills, catalogs of vehicle parts and tools, all stacked into indistinguishable piles to all except for their originator.

And he was no longer capable of helping to decipher the chaotic filing system, if one could call it that.

Lilly stared down at the chaotic piles and frowned. Perhaps she chose wrong when it came to snooping. She would be the first to admit she didn't have a clue what she was supposed to be looking for in the first place. With a long sigh, she rifled through the closest pile of papers that had what appeared to be an invoice scrawled on carbon duplicates. Perhaps she could get an idea of who his clientele was and ask them questions. What type of man was Henry to work with? Did he do quality work? Did he spend most of his time bemoaning the fact that his wife was cheating on him with 'Jakob-with-a-K'?

Lilly's hand paused over a loose piece of lined paper. It looked like a shopping list with the name "OWEN" printed on the top. She picked it up and scanned the list. "Adderall, Klonopin, Ativan, codeine, THC, acetaminophen..." Lilly read off the beginning of the list until her throat went dry.

It was a shopping list for drugs. Owen and Henry were obviously still in their old high school habits.

"And really–how dense was he if he thought he could just leave a list like this out in the open?" Lilly demanded of the dusty office.

The slam of a car door brought Lilly out of her ponderings. She frantically looked around the office for a clock, remembering her cell phone was in her purse on the front seat of her car. Stupid, stupid Lilly, not to bring a safety line with her. Lilly wasn't sure how much time had passed since Angela and Jakob left. They couldn't have been to town, spoken with the sheriff, and returned in that amount of time. What was she going to say if they found her snooping around Henry's office?

"Angela!" A loud voice echoed from within the machine shop.

That answered her question about whether Angela and 'Jakob-with-a-K' had returned. However, it has now only raised more questions. Lilly grabbed the list and shoved it into her back jeans pocket. She then made her way slowly to the office door and snuck a quick peek around the doorframe. She couldn't see anyone in the shop area, though she certainly heard the man's heavy footsteps on the concrete. As quietly as she could, Lilly snuck from the office and stayed close to one of the work-in-progress trucks, only a few yards to the open garage door, and then her car.

"Hey! What are you doing?" The loud voice found her.

She screwed her eyes shut and winced. When she finally opened her eyes again, a tall man with a barrel chest dressed in a plaid shirt and Carhartt overalls stood in front of her. Lilly had to tilt her head back to meet his untrusting gaze. "Uh... hi?" Lilly offered.

"What are you doing in Henry's workspace?" the man asked.

"Oh, I was... well..." Lilly swallowed hard. "I was here visiting with Angela and, uh, Jakob—*with a K*—and they had to leave."

The man leaned down closer. Lilly's senses were assaulted by the strong smell of animal waste that overpowered the dominant aroma of metal and grease in the shed. "But that doesn't explain why you're here and they're not."

"Well... they had to go to the sheriff's office? And I had to, uh, well, I came here to get the registration information from Angela for next year's farmers' market." The words left Lilly's mouth before she could catch them. For a long moment, the man stared down at her, and she prayed that he believed even an ounce of what she had just said.

"Why would Angela's information be in Henry's shed?" The man asked. "She'd have that either in the barn or the house."

"Oh, that makes sense. They were in such a hurry to leave, Angela just said office, so I figured it'd be out here... I guess I have to wait until they get back."

The tall man scratched at the back of his head. "Jakob, huh?"

"Do you know him?" Lilly ventured.

"No, I don't make it a habit of knowing Angela's extracurricular men."

"And you are...?" Lilly held out a hand. She hoped he couldn't detect the tremor.

"Will Lueke." His hand swallowed up Lilly's in a firm, quick handshake.

"And why are you in Henry's workspace?" What was good for the goose was also good for the gander, at least that's what her grandmother always said.

"I was, well..."

"Well?"

"I planned to snoop in Henry's office like you were—"

"Snoop?!" Lilly cried.

"—as he's been holding my feed truck hostage for months. Always claiming to be ordering new parts for it, sending me new invoices for these parts that never seem to come." Heat crept up Will's neck. "I came here to look for evidence of those parts, and if I couldn't find them, I was going to take my truck back."

"What about the invoices for services rendered?"

Will barked out a derisive laugh. "Services rendered? Lady, you're hilarious. He hasn't touched my truck in months, and I can prove it. I told him about it last night at the dumb apple festival."

Lilly's brow arched. "You saw Henry at the festival last night?"

"Yeah, I caught him before he and his so-called wife went into the dance tent." Will rolled his shoulders back. "I told him I wanted my truck back today. And that he was going to make all those bogus invoices disappear, 'cause he can't charge for, as you said, 'services rendered' if there's no proof of anything done to my truck."

"And that's why you're here, to just... steal your truck back?"

"I'm not stealing my truck!" Will pinched the bridge of his nose. "I came here to talk to Angela about letting me have my truck back, and when the time came to go through all Henry's business dealings, just to ignore anything with my name on them."

"She'd back up your claim that he didn't fix your truck?"

Will snorted a laugh again. "Yeah, she knew. She was the only one who believed us when we complained about the time it took to 'fix' our trucks."

"Us?" Lilly asked. "How many more of you are there?"

Will jerked his thumb over at the two trucks in the shed. "One of these trucks is mine, another one is Johnny Burke's, and I think Rick Olsen finally got his back from Henry last month. No work done on it, so he's been fighting the seventy-five-hundred-dollar bill Henry was trying to stick to him."

Lilly bit her lower lip. That's a lot of new suspects to add to her mental murder board. She might have to start constructing a physical one to keep track of all the latest information. "What about Gregory Fitz? Did Henry do any work on his trucks?"

"Only a couple trailers," Will replied. "He does good work on trailers an' hitches. But with trucks, he'd claim inventory or delivery troubles, send bogus invoices, and say the truck was almost ready, while I've been missin' dates and money 'cuz I can't make as many feed runs with only one truck. He's just been sitting here with daddy's money and daddy's farm while becoming the town cuckold with his thumb up his bu—"

"I get the picture," Lilly forcefully interrupted.

Will turned his attention to the office door behind Lilly. "Did you find anything in there with my name on it, while you were snooping?"

"I didn't know where to start..." *Stupid.* Lilly's eyes narrowed. "I wasn't snooping."

"Sure, you weren't," Will grinned, showing a row of teeth the color of tobacco. "Like you don't have anything riding on what the police will eventually find in this place."

"What do you mean?"

"Everyone's heard what Cecilia Baxter has been saying about you." Will took a step closer to her. "You and Angela are pretty chummy, no? Maybe I'll find something interesting while I dig through Henry's stacks."

"We're not that chummy. And whatever Cecilia Baxter has said or will say is a flat-out lie. I had nothing to do with Henry's death." Lilly poked a finger at the man's chest.

His dark eyes twinkled, and his tobacco-stained grin came back. "Then that makes two of us, don't it?"

Lilly's throat went dry. She took a wide step around Will. "Well, I'd better get going. I should let you get to your digging."

"Heh," he chuckled. "And when Angela and Jakob come back, I'll be sure to tell them you were just leaving when I pulled up."

His laugh slithered down her spine as she hurried out of the machine shed to her car. Even the crunching of the gravel couldn't erase the sound of his laugh from her ears.

Chapter Fifteen

"You ran into Will Lueke?" From the sound of Faith's voice over the phone, Lilly could tell her eyes grew as large as one of her diner's dinner plates. "He's not right in the head. Never since playing football in high school."

"Too many concussions?" Lilly asked.

"And parties."

"Let me guess, he frequented the same parties that Henry, Owen, Cecilia, and Abigail did?"

"Of course he did, he was the hotshot high school football player. He had to go to all the parties."

Lilly sighed and let her head fall back on the couch. She didn't want to think any more about Will Lueke that night. Or ever, to the honest, he was a bit of a creep. She could still feel his eyes lingering up and down her body in the machine shed. She also hadn't heard anything from Angela concerning her phony farmers' market registration story. So, either Will didn't say anything to Angela and Jakob when they got back, or he left the farm before their return.

"Has Ryan decided to talk to you again?" Faith asked, a chuckle in her voice.

"Barely," Lilly groaned. "I forgot my phone in the car when I was at Angela's! I didn't get his messages about the chickens! How many times do I have to apologize?"

"Apparently, a lot more than what you have already done," Faith snickered.

When Lilly returned to the farm from her strange encounter at the Stilners', Ryan was in a mood. He was often in a good mood in the late afternoon after a long day of chores, but this was a completely different mood. None of the 4-H families wanted to take their chickens home after the cancellation of the Apple Dapple Day poultry contest. Which meant the hosting farms had to take them back. The chickens hosted by Lilly's farm were the last ones to leave the poultry tent before the festival committee started tearing it down.

And unbeknownst to Lilly, Ryan had left her three messages and ten total missed calls about the situation, explaining that he had to go to town to rescue the chickens. To try and heal the rift, Lilly did all the chores surrounding the chickens that evening after getting them safely into the coop.

The Colonel was undoubtedly happy to have all his ladies back in one spot.

Now, after a late supper, Lilly dared to rest in the living room in front of the television. The local news was on; naturally, the main story was Henry's and Owen's deaths, along with any new information that may have come from the sheriff's department. Then Faith called to see how the murder theories were panning out.

"Do I dare talk to the other truckers who were stiffed by Henry?" Lilly asked as she grabbed for the remote control. She was tired of hearing the same recycled information from the news. Nothing she hadn't already heard before. "Perhaps I should tell Michael about the list I found? It definitely ties Owen to Henry."

She heard the back kitchen porch door slam, and she rolled her eyes.

"It wouldn't hurt?" Faith responded. Lilly could see Faith shrug through the phone as clear as day. "I'm surprised they didn't have the whole machine shed cordoned off with yellow tape."

"I know, it's weird," Lilly tapped the remote on her chin. "You'd think the police would be looking into his finances by now, and looking into any business associates, and would have found it."

Ryan's heavy boots announced his presence before he entered the living room. "Look at you, you sound like you've just binge-watched a whole season of *Law and Order.*"

"Shut up, Ryan."

"Hi, Ryan," Faith called loudly from the phone.

"Hey, Faith," Ryan called back as he sank hard into a recliner and threw back the lever for the footrest. "You're seriously doing the amateur sleuth thing?"

"Get your boots off my furniture," Lilly hissed.

Ryan glanced down at them. "They're clean. They're my fancy indoor boots."

"Get them off."

He stuck out his tongue as he kicked the boots off and let them fall to the hardwood floor.

Lilly shook her head and turned her attention back to her phone conversation with Faith. The last thing she needed was to be distracted by Ryan. Or to have his unwanted commentary about her current theories about Henry's and Owen's deaths. Which were... what?

An ear-splitting scream suddenly erupted from the other side of the phone. It was so loud that it caught Ryan's attention. His brows arched sharply as he leaned forward in the chair. He mouthed something to Lilly, but she couldn't place his words. She waved him off.

"Faith, is everything okay over there?"

More chaos came from the other side of the phone before Faith finally answered. "The kids are fighting over one of the new kittens from the barn cats," she replied, her tone breathlessly annoyed. "Morgan brought the kitten in thinking we could make it an indoor cat, and now all the kids want their own indoor cat."

"That sounds exciting," Lilly smirked.

"I need to call you back, Lilly. I have to stop World War III in my living room and prevent a kitten from being torn apart." Faith rushed out before the call ended.

Lilly stared at her cell phone's blank screen, then turned to Ryan. He looked at her for a long moment, apparently expecting some sort of explanation for his sister's hurried departure. "One of the barn cats had kittens, and Morgan brought one in to be his indoor cat. Now the other two are fighting over the kitten," Lilly summarized.

Ryan nodded sagely, as if it made all the sense in the world. "Those three are obsessed with having an indoor pet, a cat, especially." Ryan chuckled. "Tobiah doesn't want an animal in the house."

"Poor kids."

Ryan scoffed, crossing his ankles in the recliner. "They have a farm dog and a herd of barn cats. What more do they need?"

"Something of their own," Lilly ventured.

"I know my nephews and niece," Ryan shook his head. "They'll promise to take care of it forever, and after two weeks, Faith will be in charge of everything. It's happened before, and it'll happen again. Which is why Tobiah put an end to it years ago."

Lilly put her phone on the couch cushion next to the remote, which she used to turn off the television. The local news had switched to one of the national news organizations, and she wasn't interested in learning about murders in faraway places. Dealing with the local ones was enough for her, thank you.

"Do you have any barn cats?" Ryan suddenly asked.

"I... think so?" Lilly's death-occupied brain had to switch gears quickly with his new line of questioning. "I've seen signs of them in the outbuildings, but I haven't seen any specific cats."

"You need a barn dog, too."

Lilly smiled. "Oh, I do, do I?"

"Yeah, every decent farm needs a farm dog," he continued. "Your grandparents' old dog died before they passed, so we never got around to replacing him."

"Hmm."

"What? You should get a farm dog."

"Why are you so adamant about me getting a dog all of a sudden?"

Ryan's mouth clamped shut. She could have sworn that his cheeks went a few shades darker. "Every farm needs a farm dog, that's all."

"Is that right?" Lilly pressed.

His eyes darted away from her gaze for a moment. "I heard you had a conversation with Will Lueke today."

"So what if I did?"

"And Angela Stilner and some guy named Jakob."

"With a K," Lilly added with a smirk.

Ryan narrowed his eyes on her. "You shouldn't be doing that, Lilly."

"Stop changing the subject."

"I'm not changing the subject," he countered. "You shouldn't be snooping around asking questions about murder cases again."

"What's wrong with going to check in on a fellow farmers' market vendor?" Lilly asked.

"Keep telling yourself that's all you went there for; if it helps you sleep at night," Ryan's eyes finally met hers, and now it was her turn to look away. "If you haven't forgotten, there is a murderer out there. You keep getting your nose stuck in other people's business, and you're going to—"

Lilly waited for him to finish, but he remained silent. She looked at him, and he lowered his eyes. "I'm going to what, Ryan?"

Ryan let out an aggravated breath before sitting up in the recliner, eyes locked on hers. "You're going to get yourself into a situation again, and I might not be around to help you."

Lilly remained quiet as he held her gaze. Had it only been six short months ago that Lone Tree experienced its first murder? And hadn't she gotten herself mixed up with the criminal, alone on this very farm? Thankfully, the felon had been taken care of by the fifteen-hundred-pound Dandelion lying down on them. Ryan had shown up on the scene unknowingly. If he had come to start chores any later... Lilly didn't like to think about what would have happened.

"So you're saying I need a farm dog to keep me safe," Lilly offered, the fight finally out of her voice.

"If you keep up this Nancy Drew schtick, yes," Ryan nodded.

Lilly bit her lower lip. "Do you know of anyone who has farm dogs for sale?"

Ryan's body finally eased back into the recliner once more, his feet crossed again at the ankles. "I can ask around to see if anyone has any puppies or a young dog to spare."

"Thanks."

He looked down at his wrist and lowered the footrest of the recliner. "Well, looks like I should get going."

"Ryan—"

"There's still some evening chores I have to finish up before I head home."

"I could help you," Lilly offered.

"Don't worry about it, it won't take me that long," Ryan shrugged as he climbed out of the recliner. "You just stay in the house, okay?"

He grabbed his boots as he left the living room. She allowed him to go and listened to his footsteps as he made his way to the kitchen, then went out the back door once more. Lilly sat in the eerie quiet of the farmhouse, with only the solemn tick-tock of the grandfather clock from down the hall.

Chapter Sixteen

Monday morning started as any other Monday morning, the Colonel crowed with the sunrise, and the cows followed suit, each animal on the farm slowly joining the chorus demanding their breakfast. Lilly lay in her bed and stared at the ceiling. She hadn't gotten much sleep the night before, her brain running through her theories of Owen's and Henry's murders, who exactly Jakob-with-a-k is to Angela Stilner, and why Ryan continued to be so difficult.

At one moment, he acted as if she were an equal with the running of the farm and chores, then the next, he treated her like a child, incapable of functioning in the outside world. True, it had been fifteen years since she was last on the farm, so she was a little rusty in getting her so-called 'groove' back when it came to chores. She did have to ask more than her fair share of questions when it came to specific pieces of equipment or animal protocols, but didn't that show she was willing to learn?

It also didn't help that, yes, Lilly was getting her nose stuck in other people's business as she admittedly snooped in places she wasn't welcome.

Lilly began her Monday, as she had many Mondays before, getting ready for battle with the chickens. Namely, the Colonel. Although today she skipped most of the more cumbersome pads and kept to the heavy-duty boots, shin guards, Carhartt jacket, and leather gloves. In a preoccupied daze, she wandered out to the farmyard with her egg basket and feed bucket. The chickens and ornery rooster met her at the gate, clucking and chirping their displeasure over waiting for their food. She threw a handful of feed through the wire fence, causing the poultry to scurry over to the other side of the enclosure, allowing her an easy entrance into the chicken's domain.

As she scattered feed along the ground on her way to the chicken coop, Lilly tried to piece together the trail of clues and possible suspects in the murders. Even the cantankerous chirps and bawks from the fowl couldn't distract her from her thoughts. She mentally went through her list of suspects, trying to determine who had the most to gain from Owen and Henry being out of the way.

The name that kept popping up first was Angela Stilner, the unfortunate wife. All she had to go on with motives for the former spouse was an unhappy marriage and rumored infidelity on Angela's part. The appearance of Jakob-with-a-k at the Stilner farmstead certainly didn't help to squash those rumors. Lilly had to figure out who that Jakob fellow was and how he fit into the rumors. For all she knew, he was a friend who came in Angela's time of need. If the rumors of Angela cheating on Henry were true, what was the motive to kill him? Why not just get a divorce or leave him? There had to be more to their relationship to keep Angela married to him for this long. Perhaps he didn't want to give her a divorce for whatever reason, rumors be damned?

Even Lilly couldn't see an apparent motive; the presence of Angela's pineapple scarf at the scene of the crime didn't help matters.

Speaking of evidence, the photo of the EpiPen she caught a glimpse of at the sheriff's office came to mind. Lilly had no way of knowing now if Henry had an allergy or a condition that required him to carry an EpiPen. Maybe he had a reaction to something at the festival and attempted to administer the drug, and failed to do so in time?

But Cecilia Baxter always carried an EpiPen for her son's allergy. And she confessed to being in the poultry tent that night. Her long grudge against Henry for being the alleged cause of her sister's death certainly put Cecilia among the forerunners of suspects. Never mind how she was so quick to divert attention from her to Lilly with that horrid text message fiasco.

Owen seemed to be connected to Henry through their drug operation. Still in business all these years after high school. Perhaps Angela found out about the drugs and killed them both. But that felt more like a Cecilia motive due to her sister's death. Maybe Angela killed Owen to shift suspicion to Cecilia?

Were there only those two women as suspects?

Lilly entered the chicken coop as the poultry pecked happily at the ground for their feed. She checked their water sources to ensure the animals were getting enough while they were in the coop. After confirming the chickens weren't going to dehydrate any time soon, Lilly went to check the eggs.

She was startled to see Mrs. Patmore nestled in one of the brooding boxes. Lilly figured she was so preoccupied with her mental murder board that she forgot to count the hens to make sure they all came out for breakfast.

"Mrs. Patmore, you're going to miss breakfast if you don't get out there," Lilly informed the brown mottled Sussex hen. "C'mon, out you go." She reached under the hen to gently lift her from the brooding box and coax her out to the yard.

A soft nip to the tip of her finger caused her to cry out. Lilly whipped her hand out from under the hen and shook her smarting finger. "What was... oh no..."

Lilly lifted Mrs. Patmore's wings with both hands and stared dumbfounded at three little tan and white balls of fluff under the hen.

"What the..." Lilly stared at the three little chicks, each trying to nestle further under their mother than the other siblings. "Oh no, Mrs. Patmore! You weren't supposed to be a mama! How did you get three eggs by me?"

The brown hen chirped and cooed in response, wriggling in Lilly's grasp to get back to her little brood. She sighed and lowered the chicken onto her children. What was she going to do with chicks? How was the Colonel going to handle the three new ones? He proved to be a territorial jerk on his best days, an absolute horror on his worst. Although the rooster appears to tolerate the other hens well enough, perhaps he'll accept the chicks as they are his progeny.

Lilly put a pile of feed in the brooder box next to Mrs. Patmore and continued her check for eggs. The day's haul produced eight eggs, a colorful combination of brown and white. Thankfully, no other boxes produced any more surprises.

She left the coop and tossed the remaining feed on the ground around the chicken's enclosure. Brown and white Marta, along with the over-down marshmallows Fancy Pants and Francesa, scurried around the chicken pen, cooing and chirping happily as they pecked and scratched at the ground. The Colonel strutted around the area, talking quietly with his ladies as he casually pecked at the blades of grass. Lilly watched the Colonel, waiting for him to turn on her as he was known to do.

One never lets one's guard down around that blasted bird. For the first time in a long time, Lilly was able to get in and out of the chicken enclosure without a hassle from the Colonel. Perhaps fatherhood had mellowed the old man.

Though she wasn't going to put those three chicks' lives at risk over an assumption, Lilly knew she needed to talk to a chicken expert about ensuring the safety of her not-so-little flock.

Nathan.

Of course, she'd pick the brain of their veterinarian over the care and keeping of her livestock, even if these weren't of the bovine variety. He'd have to know something about chickens, or at least know someone who did.

As she left the chicken enclosure and made her way up to the farmhouse, Lilly's mind began to wander once more back to her mental murder board. Nathan and Cecilia were in the poultry tent the night that Henry died. And had been suspiciously absent ever since.

Why did he disappear after their dance? Cecilia's 'urgent business' didn't take that much time. Otherwise, Cecilia and Nathan would have seen the murder take place if Cecilia were to be believed. Why didn't he come back to the tent after he was done checking on the pressing needs of Cecilia's bird? Why couldn't he at least call to apologize for ditching her on their date?

And hadn't he been connected to the infamous high school party that caused the death of Cecilia's sister?

Lilly stopped as she ascended the back porch stairs, her brain running at a frenzied pace.

Now he owed her more than one explanation.

Chapter Seventeen

After lunch, Lilly sat on a straw bale in the lower level of the barn, listening absently to the low *mrrroowing* of the cows as they lazily chewed their cuds and lay in their stalls. She watched Ryan leading certain cows out from the barn to the back pasture, trying in vain to figure out the method to his choices. It seemed random to her why one cow went out yesterday but not today.

Whenever she asked him about why certain cows went out and others stayed in the barn, his only reply was, "Reasons."

Reasons.

She was never going to succeed at the business of farming if the little nuances of the day-to-day care of the livestock—her livestock, to be exact—were kept from her. Maybe Ryan's grudge against her for breaking up with him and ghosting him for fifteen years ran too deep. It was larger than his prior devotion to her grandparents, as they had been his former employers. Maybe he wanted to see her fail and lose the farm as the ultimate payback for how she unwittingly shattered his heart all those years ago.

What?

Lilly shook her head to chase that horrible thought from her mind. She had other things to worry about than the beleaguered heart of her high school boyfriend.

Nathan was coming soon to look at her sick cows and give chicken advice.

Well. That was what Lilly had texted him to get him to come to the farm. True, the cows she claimed were sick, that he had checked on a few days ago, were doing fine. Their treatments were doing what was expected, and she couldn't be happier that her herd was on the mend once more. Summer pneumonia was nothing to mess with, and having an inexperienced, urbanite owner only meant that she was more worried than the average farmer.

Not that Lilly wanted to exploit her 'city girl' persona. She was actually trying to live it down around town. She even toned down her 'extravagant' clothing and seldom wore three-hundred-dollar outfits out into the barn anymore. But sometimes it helped the cause to play the ditzy-city-girl card occasionally.

"What is the vet doing here?" Ryan barked as he unhooked Dandelion from her stall harness.

Lilly jumped to her feet and bolted toward the door. She had heard the growl of the diesel engine and the crunch of gravel under tires before Ryan's announcement, but her nerves got the better of her. What should she ask him first? What was he doing with Cecilia in the poultry tent Saturday night? Did he see anything suspicious? Did he even see Henry while in the tent?

"Why don't you ask him about the cows first, then the ditched dance?" Ryan's low voice brushed past her ear.

She couldn't help but shiver as she spun around. "What?" Lilly snapped.

"You're like an open book, Lilly," Ryan smirked as he crossed his arms over his chest. "You asked Nate the Vet here about your botched dance."

Well, you're almost right. Lilly hated how her neck and face flushed hot under his amused gaze. "And what if I did?"

"It screams of desperation and, frankly, is a bit juvenile," he answered. "But hey, some guys go for that type of stuff. If it floats your boat, then..." he let his words die away with a shrug.

"I think I'm owed an apology at least," Lilly defended.

"Why didn't you ask him when he was here last for the stomach surgery?"

"You two were a little busy," Lilly shrugged. It was true, to a point, that the imminent thought of surgery and blood had chased the demand for an explanation right out of her.

"Mm-hmm."

Lilly glared at him, almost telling him the real reason she had asked Nathan to the farm, but feared the admonishment she'd get from Ryan. He was already unhappy with her poking her nose around the deaths. How would he react if he knew she suspected the vet had something to do with a death? Maybe not Henry's, but one from a long time ago.

And she wanted Ryan to trust her enough to share his apparent secrets about farming. If that meant he thought her a little desperate when it came to Nathan and their date instead of investigating a man's death, then so be it. She couldn't get rid of Ryan for good, at any rate. Lilly had no idea how to run a farm and knew nothing of the intricate ins and outs of animal husbandry. If she got another farm hand, then she'd be relying on their knowledge instead of her own, and she'd be back to where she had started. At the moment, she was stuck with Ryan until she cracked that protective shell of his.

The heat in her glare intensified as she heard Nathan's boots thump toward the barn.

"What's going on with these animals, Lilly?" Nathan asked as he entered the barn.

Lilly caught herself staring at Nathan, backlit by the afternoon sun and framed in the barn doors. If he didn't look like the romantic lead in some Hallmark movie –- she had to shake her head quickly to get back into the proper frame of mind. Just because he was attractive didn't mean she had to lose all her senses around him.

"Yeah, Lilly, what's going on with the animals?" Ryan mimicked from behind her.

"I just wanted you to check on the ones you gave the treatment to." Lilly shot a burning look at Ryan, "just to make sure that things are progressing as they should. And I was worried about 346... with the surgery and all,"

Nathan looked from Ryan to Lilly, back to Ryan. The latter only gave a helpless shrug. "I suppose I can take a look, it is a bit early in the treatment, though."

"Please, I don't want to lose my herd." Lilly knew she was laying on the ditzy-city-girl act a little thick, but it seemed to work.

Nathan let out a short sigh and nodded. "Fine, let's take a look at them."

"Oh, thank you!" Lilly gave him her best, if not a genuinely relieved, smile.

"Unbelievable," Ryan muttered as he brushed past the two of them and exited the barn.

Nathan watched as he left. "What's up with him?"

"I don't know most days," Lilly shrugged. A knot started to form in her stomach as she watched Ryan leave. She had hoped to ask him which cows had been treated, as she honestly couldn't remember their names. However, that lapse in knowledge helped the bumbling farm owner act. "But I should go get him, I don't know which cows were treated."

"Don't worry him about that. I have it written down in my truck," Nathan jerked his thumb over his shoulder. "Give me a sec and I'll grab it."

He jogged quickly back to the cab of his truck and dug around for the information. Lilly's stomach settled a little. She still didn't know how she was going to break into the heavy questions with Nathan. As much as she wanted him to have nothing to do with Henry's death, or Abigail's, the slim chance of that becoming a reality was too close for her liking.

Nathan soon returned with his metallic clipboard, listing all the cows in her small herd. He motioned for her to follow him, and he led the way down the main walk between the two aisles of cows. Most of the stalls were empty at the moment, with most of the herd taking a much-needed break in the pasture.

Lilly bit her lip, not knowing what question to ask Nathan first. What was the proper wait time for asking about ditching on a date or being a possible accessory to murder? Her mouth opened before she formulated a plan.

"Could I see the list of the cows?" Lilly blurted out.

Whew. Dodged that bullet.

Nathan glanced at her, a puzzled expression on his face. "Uh, sure." He handed her the clipboard.

It was as if he had handed her the Holy Grail. Lilly stared at the master list of the cows. Some names rang familiar, like Dandelion and her two daughters, Daisy and Daffodil, as well as Peony and her sister, Poppy. The names Rose and Peony had black pen stars drawn next to them, with "TRTMNT" scrawled next to their names. Other names were painfully foreign to her, like Magnolia and Pansy, and a sub-list of calf names. All the calves, except Envy, were not known to her.

Curse you, Ryan.

"Do you not get to look at the herd roster much?" Nathan asked.

"Not really, no." Lilly's voice stuck in her throat as she tried to answer. "I've been trying to learn their names, but since they don't have collars with name tags, I've been left to learn by hearing their names being used. Ryan likes to keep the main list of the herd hidden from me."

Nathan stopped walking as he approached Cow 346. Lilly remembered her from the long scar along her flank, as well as the yellow numbered tag in her ear. "I'm glad you messaged me to come over, I also wanted to check on our twisted stomach here," Nathan said with a grin. "You're not going to faint on me, are you?"

"Are you going to open her up again?" Lilly asked.

"Nope. Just check her incision for infection and that it's healing right."

"Then we should be fine."

"Hmm." Nathan turned to the cow and ducked under the stall stanchion and her restraining chain. He grabbed a pair of blue medical gloves from his back jeans pocket and put them on before he started inspecting 346's side. "So, Ryan doesn't allow you to see much of the cows, does he?"

"He's pretty protective of them, I guess," Lilly found herself defending her hired man. "He likes to keep how he runs the farm close to the chest. I try to help, feed the calves and such, but he won't let me mix the milk replacer for the calves, or even try to mix the specialty TMR feed."

"Hmm," Nathan continued to prod at the incision along 346's side. "Why is that?"

"I have no idea," Lilly huffed, her shoulders slumping. "He was close to my grandparents for the last few years of their lives, and he could be keeping their secrets safe in a weird loyalty to them?"

"But you're their granddaughter," the vet pointed out, gesturing to her with a blue-gloved hand.

"You'd think that'd give me an all-access pass to this place, but it doesn't," she sighed. Nathan poked an apparent tender spot on 346's side as her head came up from nosing through the feed in front of her to bellow at Lilly's stomach.

"Sorry, old girl," Nathan apologized.

"Is she okay?"

"Just a tender part near the stitches," Nathan informed her. "I don't see any sign of infection. The incision is healing nicely. Just some run-of-the-mill post-operative pain."

"That's good to hear."

"So, what else is keeping Ryan from giving you full rein of your grandparents' farm?" Nathan ducked under the stanchion once more and stood next to her. Almost too close to her. She caught hints of leather and smoke under the stronger aromas of the barn.

She swallowed hard and took a step back. "It might be that he's still hurt over what happened fifteen years ago."

"Your family left in the middle of the night without a goodbye?" Nathan's brow arched as he smirked.

"How did you know...?"

"Oh, everyone in town knows about your dad's sudden departure from town," he answered. "What the town didn't know was why, and that just drove the busybodies crazy."

"So you know that Ryan and I—"

"Dated once in high school? Yeah." Nathan nodded. "I went to the same high school as you, though I was a year ahead of you two."

"Oh."

"And really, if he missed you that much to be still harboring a grudge all these years later, then why didn't he try to track you down? Fifteen years is a long time to go without getting some answers." Nathan led them back to the front of the barn. "Looks like Rose and Peony are outside. Care to walk with me in the pasture?"

"Sure," Lilly replied.

What Nathan had said about Ryan not trying to contact her sometime over those fifteen years struck her in the gut. If that was true for Ryan, why not her? Why didn't she try to reach out to Ryan or any of her friends in Lone Tree after her father uprooted them? Because her father forbade any contact with anyone from Lone Tree. At the time, she didn't dare disobey her father by trying to contact anyone. He had kept a close track of her calls and online interactions at the dawn of the social media age. All because he had been hurt by someone close and chose to run away rather than face that hurt. And his hurt had spread to so many others.

Their walk out to the pasture was short and quiet. Lilly appreciated the time to think and clear her head. Although being this close to him, alone and undisturbed, was proving to be a distraction. How did a man as attractive as him even want to go on a date with her? She didn't think they were in the same league. Maybe that was why he took advantage of Cecilia's interruption and ducked out of their date early.

"So, since we're talking about a long time without answers..." Lilly began. "About Saturday night..."

"That was wild, wasn't it?" Nathan stood in front of the pasture gate and started to undo the locking bolt. "Town's been buzzing about Henry and Angela all weekend..." He turned and saw her face. His eyes immediately lowered, and his cheeks flushed pink. "But that's not what you're talking about, is it?"

"No, not really." Lilly's voice came out more forceful, almost hurt. She wasn't sure how she felt about their short date. It wasn't like they had a lot of history together. "You didn't come back after Cecilia took you away."

"Yeah, I know, and I'm sorry, really," Nathan replied. "Cecilia swept me away with her sob story about her daughter's chicken. When I finally could pull myself away from that farce, I ran into some old friends on the way back to the dance tent. Then everything just went sideways with Henry."

Lilly let his explanation sit for a while. Plausible. But short. What was the saying, too much detail was the sign of a well-thought-out lie? The two walked carefully through the hoof-pocked pasture. The cows had congregated toward the far corner, closest to the shade given by the surrounding grove of trees.

"Did you and Cecilia talk about anything other than chickens?" She heard a hitch in his breath. She turned to him, his face stoic. "Nathan?"

"You've heard about it too, then." It was more a statement than a question.

"Stories have a way of following people, no matter how much time has passed." Lilly stood and walked as close to him as she could as they crossed the uneven ground. "Cecilia told me about the party that Henry Stilner held back in high school. Her sister died of a drug overdose. I know that the party was held at your house. She blames both of you for her sister's death, mainly Henry, though."

Nathan stopped walking. They were halfway to the cows. Some of the bovines turned toward them and bellowed, either in welcome or in annoyance at being disturbed. He sighed and tapped the metal clipboard against his leg. "The party in question was held at my house. Henry insisted on his parties being held at different houses each time. We thought it made it harder for the parents to keep track of which were the 'bad houses.'"

"Were you close with Henry or Owen?"

"No, not really." Nathan shrugged. "He was popular because his dad was loaded. Our parents ran in the same crowds, being founding fathers and all that garbage. But we weren't really friends. They'd just ask to use my house for a party when they knew my parents would be out of town, like they asked all the other kids."

"What happened that night?"

"Henry was known for bringing drugs to his parties. Normally, it was just alcohol we'd swipe from the parents' cabinets, all those cliché things. But sometimes Owen would bring the harder stuff, pills and injectables. Things we had no idea what they were or where they came from. We just trusted him when he said it was legit. We were kids, we didn't know any better."

Nathan let out another sigh and ran a hand through his hair. "Abigail and Cecilia came to a few parties. They weren't regulars, at least not Cecilia. Abigail started to use the drugs more when they became available. I don't think Cecilia quite knew how much of a problem her sister had."

"It wasn't her first time doing drugs, the night she died?"

"No, it wasn't. She wasn't a pro or anything, but it wasn't her first time." Nathan shook his head. "I'm betting the family told themselves it was her first time, because that's all they knew."

"I was told no one was arrested for the party, for the drugs, and what happened to Abigail," Lilly pressed.

He looked at her for a long moment. "All the kids were freaked out when she died. So to save our hides, we kept quiet on who brought the drugs. And for the most part, the kids were right. There was only a small handful of us who knew for sure who supplied the parties. Henry's and Owen's friends from Mankato. Older kids, friends of his older brothers. That's who he got his drugs from."

"Why not tell the police?" Lilly asked. "Why not say something now if you knew about it?"

A darkness settled over his eyes. "Because I was the scapegoat. Because the party was held at my house, I was ultimately responsible for the safety of the people there. I got in trouble for the party, the underage drinking, and the drug use. Back then, the laws were different; I wasn't charged with Abigail's death. It was ruled an accidental overdose, but the damage was done."

"What happened?"

"I did community service for disorderly house violation. Since no one was able, or willing, to identify the one who supplied the drugs, criminal charges were hard to file, so we got a lesser charge of a disorderly house party. My parents settled the matter out of court with Abigail's parents, and I don't remember much about that side of things. I think my parents kept that information away from me," Nathan answered, his voice low. "And then I left Lone Tree. Much like you did."

Lilly allowed his words to sink into the ground between them. She suddenly wished she had her phone with her again. This conversation was not going the way she had envisioned. A knot started to form in the pit of her stomach.

Nathan turned and caught her gaze. "I know what you're thinking, Lilly."

"Which is?"

"I had something to do with Owen's and Henry's deaths."

She swallowed, her throat unexpectedly parched. "Well, after that story you told me, it's hard not to think that."

"So, that friend I ran into after Cecilia's chicken fiasco? It was Henry."

"You saw him in the poultry tent?" Lilly gasped.

"Yes, and I'll tell you what I told the police. I saw him in the tent, said "hey" to him, and told him we should get together for a drink sometime to catch up about old times. Then I left the tent. Angela came in and was trying to collect Henry. He was a few sheets to the wind and had wandered out of the dance tent." Nathan's voice was calm, his eyes losing their dark intensity. "After she showed up, I left the tent and was on my way back to the dance, and you ran into another... friend... and were dancing when the screaming started. Then all hell broke loose, and the police questioned me, as I suspect you were questioned as well."

"Yes," Lilly nodded, her eyes lowering.

"I get it, I really do." Nathan put a hand on her shoulder. "Everyone's freaked out about the murder and trying to figure it out themselves. And you just happen to be close with some of the people who were sadly in the wrong place at the wrong time."

"True," Lilly had to agree. "But what happened that night—"

"It was strangely a blessing in disguise." Nathan's tone grew lighter. "I got my act together. Got away from the parties and the alcohol. I had a better life at Sleepy Eye High than I did in Lone Tree. Without that hiccup in the road, I wouldn't have gone off to vet school and continued my family business. Who knows where I would have ended up? Probably drunk at every town festival, riding the coattails of my father like Henry did. And look where that got him."

"I suppose."

"Trust me, if we had had this conversation right after that night, I would have wanted every sort of evil to befall Henry for throwing me under the bus." Nathan gave her shoulder a little squeeze, then released her. "But I'm over that now. I'm a better man after all I had to go through. I wanted to tell Henry that when we got together next. But I guess he'll just have to hear about it later."

Lilly nodded. "Nathan, I'm sorry..."

"Don't worry about it," Nathan gave her a smile that melted the twists in her gut. "Come on, let's check on Rose and Peony, and maybe we can go grab a bite to eat?"

"Really?" She almost stopped in her tracks.

He glanced down at the watch on his wrist. "I haven't had lunch yet, spent most of my morning herd-checking over at the Grisbys." Nathan grinned as he continued his way to the group of cows. "Call it a make-up date for the one I stupidly let fall into the hands of Ryan Swenson."

Chapter Eighteen

Even though no one was overtly looking in their direction, Lilly felt the eyes of every patron in Grandma's Attic rest on their booth.

Nathan was true to his word. After he had checked on Peony and Rose, he drove her to a late lunch at the Attic. Lilly fought the urge to apologize for the needless bovine health check; the guilt over summoning him to her farm under false pretenses gnawed at her stomach. She had a light lunch earlier and wasn't sure how much of an appetite she'd have when they arrived at the café. But now back in the public eye after such an eventful weekend, Lilly felt the last bit of hunger leave her twisted belly.

He sat across from her in her usual booth at the back of the café, which offered some level of protection from prying eyes. At the moment, Lilly was more concerned about Faith's ever-present gaze. From the moment she and the veterinarian stepped foot in the restaurant, Faith had kept the pair in her sights.

"What do you normally get here?" Nathan asked as he looked over the laminated menu. Lilly blinked, almost stupidly, as she watched him use the menu. Since she'd arrived back in Lone Tree, Lilly had never bothered to pick up the menu. She trusted Faith to bring her the best on the menu each time, or her usual bacon cheeseburger, fries, and iced tea.

"I normally let Faith pick for me," Lilly admitted as a sheepish look crossed her face.

"Really?" Nathan glanced up from the menu and over to the back counter and register area. "That takes a lot of... faith in the staff, doesn't it?"

Lilly allowed herself to chuckle at the terrible joke. "She hasn't steered me wrong yet."

"Maybe I'll follow suit and let Faith pick my food as well," Nathan lowered the menu.

Faith appeared from behind the counter as if hearing a subconscious signal and made her way over to their booth. "Hey, you two," she said with a pointed look at Lilly. "What can I get you?"

"I'll get my usual," Lilly said.

"What's that?" Nathan asked.

"Bacon cheeseburger, fries, and iced tea," Faith and Lilly answered as one.

His eyes danced from one woman's face to the other. "Well, I guess I'll have the Lilly Special as well."

Faith's lips pressed into a tight line as she gathered the menus from the tabletop. "Two Lilly Specials coming right up!" She announced brightly to the rising flush in Lilly's face.

After Faith disappeared back into the kitchen once more, Nathan turned to Lilly with what she thought appeared to be almost a predatory smile. She sank back into the booth cushion. "So if you're not going to ask me about chickens," he began, "which elephant in the room should we talk about first?"

"I don't know what you mean..." Lilly's voice trailed off.

"Come on, you know," he purred. "Less than an hour ago, you had me as a suspect in Henry's murder. You have a reputation for asking around after murders—"

"Only once before," Lilly defended.

"—and now there are two murders about which you're asking around again, aren't you?" Nathan continued. "Do you want to talk about your theories, which include me, or do you want to talk about your failing tourism business?"

"How do you know—" Lilly began, but bit back her words. She cleared her throat and tried once more. "What do you know about the Accidental Farmer Experience finances? Has Ryan been talking to you?"

"He hasn't said a word to me about it," Nathan raised a hand to deflect her accusations. "It's not hard to figure out, Lilly. The farm is behind on its veterinary bills. As veterinarians, we often overhear conversations when we visit other farms and even at the feed mill. It's obvious. Your little venture isn't bringing in tourists as much as you hoped."

Lilly lowered her eyes as her face flushed with heat. "It's only been six months, less than that. It'll take time for the business to get its feet on the ground, that's all."

"True, true," he nodded.

Fatih came with their iced teas. "Burgers will be up in a few minutes, you guys." She looked at each face and frowned. "Are you guys okay?"

Lilly looked up when Faith nudged her leg under the table with her foot. "Yeah, we're just discussing self-starting businesses."

"Oof, that's a heavy topic for a first date," Faith shook her head. "Lighten things up, Wilhelm, seriously."

Both watched as she moved to check on another table in the café.

"I suppose that was ungentlemanly of me to bring up such a delicate subject," Nathan turned back to Lilly. He reached out and took hold of her hand on the tabletop. "I apologize for bringing that up. We can talk about whatever you want, Lilly."

She eyed him for a long moment. "Even if it's my amateur murder theories that you were a part of?"

"Even if it's that."

Lilly shook her head and gave a small smile. "I've had enough talk of murder and suspects. I just want to have a normal date, is that too much to ask?"

He mirrored her smile. "What does a normal date look like?"

"I'm not sure, it's been so long since I've been on one," Lilly admitted.

"Same here."

"Oh, were you married previously?"

"No, never married. I recently got out of a long-term relationship," Nathan replied.

"So that makes me the rebound date then?" Lilly asked.

He laughed. "You are far from a rebound date, Lilly."

One of the kitchen staff delivered their burgers and fries, breaking the flirtatious spell momentarily. The two fell into an easy silence as they worked on their meals, asking the occasional first-date staple questions. Eventually, conversation bubbled naturally between them while they ate. Lilly finally felt a true sense of normalcy for the first time in a long time.

"I'm so happy to bump into you, Lilly!" So lost in her conversation with Nathan, Cecilia Baxter's voice took a few moments to register with Lilly. Instantly, the burger in her mouth turned sour, and she made an effort to swallow it before addressing Cecilia.

"Hello, Cecilia, nice to see you again," Lilly said, giving her her best pleasant smile. Just because the woman tried to tie her to a murder publicly, she had nothing to do with didn't mean she couldn't attempt to be civil towards her. "Have you decided if you will join us for next summer's farmers' market?"

A tight smile crossed Cecilia's too-perfect face. "No, no, I haven't finalized my decision yet. Too many loose ends right now. But I did want to give you my condolences about your bookings."

"My bookings...?" Lilly turned in the booth to face the woman, her stomach sinking to her feet. "My Accidental Farmer Experience..."

"I'm surprised you haven't been checking your emails, Lilly. They must be absolutely blowing up about now."

Lilly frantically dug through her purse and retrieved her phone. She had been so busy with chicken chores and spending time with Nathan that the thought of checking her emails, personal or otherwise, hadn't crossed her mind. Lilly brought up her email app and began scrolling through it. "What is..." she said.

"What's wrong, Lilly?" Nathan asked quietly.

"Yes, Lilly, what's wrong?" Cecilia mocked.

Lilly's vision focused on the four new emails sitting at the top of her inbox, all from earlier that morning. The emails had been forwarded to her personal inbox from the Accidental Farmer Experience website's Contact Us page. All four were emails from the few AFE bookings she could get from a whole summer's worth of farmers' markets and vendor fairs.

Dear Lillian, we regret to inform you that we must unfortunately cancel our reservation for later this fall at The Accidental Farmer Experience, due to the unsafe conditions in Lone Tree.

Three other variations of that email stared back at her as she paged through them. Lilly's vision blurred as she skimmed each message. She didn't need to read through each one to know what they said; that they

were canceling their reservations and requesting a refund of their down payment. Lilly looked up from her phone to Nathan's concerned face. He sat back into the booth at the intensity in her eyes. "Lilly?"

The woman dug into her purse and pulled out a crumpled piece of paper. She laid it on the table between their plates, manicured fingers digging into the paper. "You didn't do an excellent job picking up after yourself on the last day of the farmers' market," she said.

Lilly stared open-mouthed at the paper. She grabbed it from under Cecilia's grasp. "My mailing list!?"

"Found its way into my booth after yours unfortunately blew over," Cecilia feigned concern. "I'm glad I could get it back to you before something bad happened with those poor people's emails."

"What did you do?" she whirled to stare at Cecilia, each word ground out from between her teeth. The fierceness of Lilly's gaze caused even Cecilia to take a step back.

"I only did what any good, concerned citizen would do if there were an unsafe situation in their community." Cecilia crossed her arms over her stomach. "Can't be bringing more innocent victims into the clutches of an alleged killer."

Lilly's vision blurred again as she glanced from the crumpled email list to Cecilia. Suddenly, her gaze focused on an orange and blue cylinder sticking out from Cecilia's purse. "You better get home, Cecilia, before the police want to see if that's a matching EpiPen."

"What?" Cecilia gasped. She looked down at her half-open purse and snapped it shut. "You're just as bad as Angela. I hope you both get what's coming to you."

"Cecilia, leave," Nathan snapped.

"Are you threatening me, Nathan?"

"No, but I can call Faith over here." He gestured over to the back counter. "I know she gets awfully protective of her patrons and isn't afraid to kick people out."

"Fine." Cecilia snapped her red-bottomed heels together and took one step away from the booth. She turned back slightly, a rueful smirk on her face. "You two have a good afternoon."

Lilly waited until the chimes above the café door sounded, signaling Cecilia's final departure, before she buried her face in the email list and cried.

Chapter Nineteen

Sleep escaped Lilly that night. Her mind was stuck in a cycle that replayed the day's events and considered unlikely, yet believable, scenarios of what would happen in the coming days. Flashes of the horrible scene in the café continued to turn in her mind every time she closed her eyes. The list of emails taunted her, along with Cecilia's smug face.

She lay in bed and stared at the ceiling in silence. The dark bedroom offered her little comfort. The leftover knick-knacks from her grandparents were dimly lit by the faint green light of her bedside clock, nothing but darker shapes within the established shadows of the night.

The Accidental Farmer Experience, as far as she was concerned, was dead in the water after that day. Lilly struggled to find a scenario where she could salvage her business from Cecilia's horrible sabotage. What was the old saying? a customer with a good experience tells three friends, while a customer with a bad experience tells ten? Negative will always outweigh the positive. Without knowing what exactly Cecilia said to the customers, Lilly had no idea how to combat the emails and salvage the reservations. She was going to have to cancel them with barely a fight.

Did Cecilia merely mention the murders in town and paint Lone Tree as an unsafe community to visit? Lilly could concoct a rebuttal to those claims. Lone Tree's crime rate was drastically lower than that of many other places in Minnesota. But if Cecilia had insinuated in her emails that Lilly was somehow involved in the murders, that would prove harder to recover from. Without having any hard evidence, it was, at least at the moment, Cecilia's word against Lilly's. Why wouldn't the recipients of those emails give some credence to a woman of standing in the community like Cecilia, who they believed to be a well-intentioned Good Samaritan, not someone who had an outlandish vendetta against Lilly?

Perhaps Mike was on to something when he suggested suing Cecilia for libel. She certainly crossed a line when she contacted the four reservations, Lilly's potential future sources of income. That definitely caused her hardship due to her continual lies. As tempting as it was to see Cecilia lose credibility and clout about town, not to mention pay out a monetary settlement, in a court of law, Lilly doubted she'd have the energy to fight that woman legally.

And not to mention it'd be impossible to find an impartial jury anywhere within rock-throwing distance of Lone Tree.

"Why is that woman such a horrible person?" Lilly asked the shadowy room. Only silence responded. "Is she so bitter toward the world because her sister died? I get it, your sister died, but why take it out on other people?"

Instantly, Lilly felt horrible for having thought that way. Everyone handled grief in different ways. And with the sudden manner in which she lost her sister, both being so young, an event like that would alter one's way of interacting with the world. Some people just never recover after a trauma like that.

She needed more background on Cecilia Baxter. Unfortunately, it was the middle of the night, and her usual sources would be fast asleep. Being awakened to discuss the town's bitter busybody would not win her any friendship points.

Her grandmother's journals suddenly crossed her mind. As long as her grandparents were married, her Grandma Beverly kept a journal documenting everything that happened around town—the good and the bad. Perhaps Grandma Bev wrote about Abigail's death. If her grandparents had been reasonably close to Cecilia's family back then, there might be more insight into the family dynamics after the untimely passing of their daughter, and if Cecilia's current disposition was always this way, or if it changed.

Lilly pulled herself from the warm cocoon of her bed and padded barefoot down the second-floor hall to the top of the main stairs. The entrance to the attic was at the top of the stairs, up on the ceiling. She sighed, knowing she'd had to make a detour down to the kitchen to grab a step stool to reach the cord that opened the collapsible staircase. After a quick trip to the kitchen, Lilly set up the step stool below the doorway.

She climbed the stool and reached for the cord. It was a heavy-duty nylon cord, unlike the old string that snapped in half the last time she tried to enter the attic. This time, the door slid open easily, the collapsible stairs sliding down to the floor with a whisper. Lilly climbed up the stairs carefully and entered the attic. She was thankful she had spent a couple of days in the summer organizing the piles of boxes that were immediately stacked by the attic entrance. Many of the boxes held old holiday decorations or clothes from her grandparents' years living in the farmhouse. Her grandmother's years' worth of journals were among the boxes she organized. Lilly had organized the journals in a better chronological order. She labeled each box with the year inside, to make it easier to locate the selection in case she ever needed to seek her grandmother's words and wisdom. She mentally patted herself on the back as she quickly found the box labeled with the appropriate time frame, 2005-2012, and sat with it next to the attic entrance.

Fifteen years ago, her family left Lone Tree. Two years after that, the infamous party took place. That would put the journal needed sometime in 2007. Lilly opened the box and began digging through the leather-bound tomes until she found the two marked with 2007 in her grandmother's tight script.

Lilly skimmed through the journal entries from the beginning of 2007, her eyes scanning for any mention of Henry, Abigail, Cecilia, or a party death. She finally found a mention of the party in February.

February 5
Tragedy struck the high school over the weekend. A young girl died at a party over at the Wilhelm's farm. Community devastated. The Schimmels are shattered. I'm glad my Lillian wasn't around to get caught up in that.

That entry gave Lilly a good sense of when the party occurred, the weekend of February 2nd through 4th. If she had to make an educated guess, she'd place the party happening most likely on that Friday or Saturday night. However, the entry didn't provide her with any additional information about the death or the other players involved. Save Nathan Wilhelm. Lilly frowned, wondering what other information she'd find and what would be revealed about his involvement. She paged through the journal until a couple of months later.

April 27

The town is still a buzz about Abigail's death in February. No one has been charged with her death, and it was ruled an accident. The Schimmels are uncertain about the findings and believe someone needs to be held accountable. The eldest daughter blames the Stilner boy. All the rumors about town say that "everyone knows Henry did it". Why the police haven't taken him in isn't surprising, probably because Oscar Stilner has the police chief in his back pocket.

Lilly stared at the journal and reread that passage a few more times. The whole town knew, or at least believed, Henry was involved in Abigail's murder. It was common knowledge, it seemed. Abigail and Cecilia's parents knew someone had to be responsible for their daughter's death. Although her grandmother didn't explicitly say he supplied the drugs at the party that Abigail overdosed on, it does seem pretty clear that he was involved.

That was it. That entry held proof that people knew Henry and Owen were involved in Abigail's death, and the police at the time did nothing about that information. Cecilia and her family held a grudge against Henry Stilner for thirteen years. And knowing the town knew the truth and yet did nothing about it? That'd turn anyone bitter toward the world as a whole, especially the police. If the police force had somehow been corrupted back then, as Grandma Beverly speculated, then the justice the Schimmels sought would never have come until those crooked cops had been gone. By the time those officers had left the force, the accidental death case would be long closed and never cross anyone's mind again. It was found to be accidental. Why bother to open it up after all this time?

Thirteen years is a long time to hold a grudge and harbor a sense of misplaced justice.

Lilly reread the passage once more. This may have been enough to get Cecilia looked at for more than just a person of interest in this case; it was more like The Person of Interest. This historical proof of a long-harbored hatred of Henry Stilner, coupled with the dropped EpiPen in the crime photo, definitely puts Cecilia at the scene of his death. How easy would it be to connect the dots to Owen's death? He supplied the harder drugs for Henry's party. The shopping list proved he was the one with the means of obtaining. And how has Cecilia been trying to deflect attention from herself? It seemed surprising how quickly Cecilia named Lilly an accomplice for merely being associated with Angela.

It felt to Lilly that Cecilia was trying too hard to shift attention to anyone, specifically her.

As swiftly as she dared, Lilly descended the attic stairs with her journal in hand. Her excitement over a new development in the case burned away any lingering remnants of sleep. She wanted to discuss these changes with someone, and she wanted to talk with someone now.

But the grandfather clock downstairs chimed out at three o'clock in the morning. It was way too early to be bugging Faith about the case. She'd most likely lose her friend over a stunt like that. And the same could be said if she had contacted Sheriff Branford this early without a genuine emergency. He'd have more than a few choice words for her when he picked up his phone.

Lilly made her way back to her bedroom and the soft embrace of the sheets. She held the journal against her stomach, a hand lay protectively over it. And she listened to the grandfather clock in silence as the old clock ticked time away.

As soon as the clock struck a reasonable hour on Tuesday morning, Lilly reached for her phone and texted Faith, stating she had a new source that tilted the pendulum of guilt onto Cecilia. While she waited for her friend to respond to that message, she hurried out to the chicken run and checked for eggs. Thankfully, there were no more chick surprises, though Marta displayed some concerning brooding behavior. She quickly removed the eggs before anyone else had crazy ideas about becoming a mother.

Despite getting less than her usual amount of sleep, Lilly bounded about the house with unusual vigor. She waited until eight o'clock, the start of typical business hours, before contacting her cousin, Sheriff Michael Branford. She sent him a quick text, a brief note stating that she had a possible lead on the Stilner case.

The Sheriff called back in less than five minutes.

"Good morning, Sheriff," Lilly said pleasantly into the phone.

"I told you to knock off the sleuthing stuff, didn't I?" Mike Branford asked.

"Yes, you did."

He sighed. She knew by that sound he was rubbing the bridge of his nose with his eyes closed. "Then why did I get a text that you have a lead for me and my men to look into?"

"Because I do," Lilly replied matter-of-factly. "I think you need to look at Cecilia Baxter."

"Has she been harassing you again via group chat?" the sheriff asked.

"No, not that. You need to look into her for the Stilner and Perkins cases. I think she killed them to avenge her sister."

"Her sister?"

Lilly explained the high school party from thirteen years ago and how the police were never able to find who supplied the drugs, although the whole town suspected Henry and Owen of being the sources. As she presented the facts of the case, she could hear him sigh and groan on the other end of the phone.

"Cecilia killed Owen and Henry for supplying the drugs that her sister OD'd on," Lilly concluded.

"Why would she kill him now?"

Lilly shrugged, even though the sheriff couldn't see it. "After all this time, she finally snapped. The police weren't doing their jobs—"

"Hey!" the sheriff exclaimed.

"The police back then," Lilly clarified. "Grandma Beverly said that the police chief back then was somehow connected to an Oscar Stilner, which probably slanted the investigation away from Henry."

A sharp exhale of breath came from the other side of the phone. "Chief Klein is still the chief of police, Lilly. And I don't think he'd take very kindly to accusations of being a crooked cop, or having any corruption in his force, then or now."

"I'm not saying all of this is one hundred percent true," Lilly swallowed.

"And Grandma Beverly said… how did she say anything, she's been dead for six months," Sheriff Branford said.

"Super tactful," Lilly snapped. "I found entries in her journals around the time of Abigail Schimmel's death. There's probably more if I looked through it more carefully."

"Your grandma's journals?" The sheriff asked. "You want me to base my investigation on fifteen-year-old writings of a woman who wasn't even directly involved in the case?"

"Thirteen-year-old writings," Lilly corrected. "It's something to help back up the EpiPen." Silence flowed from the other end of the phone. Lilly glanced at her phone screen to ensure the call was still connected. "Mike?"

"How do you know about the EpiPen?" He asked, his voice low and serious.

A chill spilled down Lilly's spine. Oops. "I, uh, when I was in your office before and knocked the file on the ground, I saw some of the crime scene photos. And I saw the EpiPen."

"Lillian..."

"I haven't said anything to anyone!" Lilly cried. "But Cecilia has an EpiPen just like that one in her purse; her kid needs it for his allergy. So the long family history against Henry Stilner, with Cecilia and Henry being in the poultry tent together, and the EpiPen next to him? I mean, come on! There's enough there for probable cause! Was there anything funny on a toxicology report for Owen or Henry? Would epinephrine show up on a report like that?"

Silence greeted her once more.

"Lillian, I'm going to say this to you again, and I don't want to repeat myself, is that clear?" Mike asked, each word clipped and measured. "Stop asking around about the Stilner case. Stop trying to play detective. Just. Stop."

"But it wouldn't hurt to look into—"

"Lillian. Stop." Mike's voice softened a degree. "If I hear of you asking questions of people or even talking to people about your theories, I may have to bring you in."

"You can't do that—"

"Goodbye, Lillian. Stay out of trouble." Sheriff Mike ended the call.

Chapter Twenty

The rest of Tuesday, overall, was particularly difficult for Lilly and the Accidental Farmer Experience.

The grandfather clock in the main hallway chimed away the hours as she sat in her office. It once was her grandfather's study, though she finally organized it over the summer to suit her needs. Most of his old books on the wall shelves had been boxed away and stored in the attic for safekeeping. She hadn't quite felt it was time to get rid of any of the books, though many of them were slated to be donated to the library or the Brown County Historical Society. Grandpa Harold's old desk had been cleared and retrofitted for her desktop computer and filing system. Despite having her desktop system set up, she still used her laptop while sitting in Grandpa Harold's overstuffed leather chair.

Softened by decades of use, the leather chair was one of her only sources of comfort that day. Thanks to Cecilia and her back-stabbing interference, Lilly spent her morning replying to the four cancellation emails and issuing refunds for AFE deposits. Her stomach sank, as did the bank account, with each correspondence. She wasn't sure what she could say to make the former guests change their minds and reconsider canceling, so they could reschedule for another date. It was pretty clear from each email that cancellation and refunds were all they expected from any future communication.

Once the last email was sent, refunds were scheduled to be processed within the next three to four business days. Lilly sank into the plush back of the chair and felt about as low as she could possibly go. She knew she'd eventually have to break the news to Ryan about her most recent failure. Though she had an idea he had already heard about Cecilia's latest stunt. She'd even received another sympathy text from Nathan. He had promised that this would all blow over in a couple of months, and she could try again for the spring.

That was in another six months. It was only the beginning part of September, the start of the prime autumn adventure season. Apple picking, pumpkin patches, and corn mazes had already started advertising, and she was hoping to capitalize on the local orchards and maze farms to snag some of their patrons while they were still in the area. But now that she was erroneously linked to an open murder case, Lilly knew there was no way to come back from this quickly.

Lilly propped her feet on the large, matching leather ottoman and fought the urge to hop over to an online shopping site to drown her sorrows. The last thing she needed was to be tempted by pretty heels and dresses she knew she'd never be able to afford. Ever again.

Heavy boots *thunked* along the hardwood floors of the farmhouse. Lilly blew out a frustrated breath, not looking forward to any type of conversation with Ryan. No matter how hard they try, one of them always seems to put their foot in their mouth and ruin what could be a decent interaction.

"There you are," Ryan popped his head into the office. "I missed you with the calf chores."

"So, now you want help with calf chores?" Lilly asked. Lilly asked. "The one day I don't ask you is the day you decide to say 'yes'?"

His eyes lowered to the floor as his jaw worked to form a follow-up. "Sorry."

"Sorry," she echoed as she snapped her laptop closed.

"Rough morning?"

"You could say that," Lilly hugged her arms tight to her stomach. She couldn't meet his gaze, though she knew his eyes were fixed on her. She took a long breath and let it out slowly. "That was a lot of money, Ryan. Gone. Lost. All because of that... because of..." her voice wavered off.

"I'm sorry," Ryan said.

Lilly finally turned her eyes to him. "That's it?"

"That's it. I don't know what else to say, Lilly," Ryan returned.

"No..." Lilly shook her head. "That's it. For the farm. For me. All the money I put into the place to get it ready for this stupid dream of mine, all wasted. I don't know how I will bounce back from this, Ryan."

"Don't say that," Ryan walked into the office and sat on the ottoman next to her feet. "You still have the cows and the chickens. We're making enough with milk and meat sales."

Lilly made a face when he mentioned the latter. She still didn't like the idea of sending the older cows to the processing plant when their milk production hit a particular low. Even when she spent most of her childhood on the farm, she wanted all the older cows to stay there and live out their days in the pasture. Her grandparents, and even now Ryan, told her many times that it was part of a dairy cow's life cycle: after being born they were to have babies and give milk, and when unable to do either of the prior requirements, they went on to the next stage in the food production process as meat. People needed their hamburgers and steaks.

"We're going to have to get rid of many cows to make up for my over-spending," Lilly said. She swallowed hard and stopped herself from saying anything else, lest the tears she fought would start falling.

"We'll make it through the winter." Ryan wrapped a hand around one of her ankles and gave a squeeze. "Earl Graves will give us the second half of his land rent check in a month or so, and we'll be sitting pretty good, money-wise. It's not as dire as you think."

"Really?" Lilly sniffled and rubbed a hand across her cheek as an errant tear escaped her lashes. She had forgotten about their renter, Earl Graves, the crotchety old man who lived on a farm bordering hers. He had struck up a deal with her grandparents many years ago to run their cropland when it was determined Grandpa Harold couldn't handle the planting and harvesting.

"We're going to be fine," Ryan said, giving her ankle another squeeze. "Please don't put the farm up for sale or anything drastic, okay?"

Lilly stuck her tongue out at him and wiped at her tears. "Fine. I won't put the farm up for sale."

Ryan returned the gesture. "Good."

"Can I put the Colonel up for sale, though?" Lilly asked. "He gave Mrs. Patmore three unexpected chicks."

He shook his head. "I thought I saw small yellow things in the chicken run today."

"What are we going to do with them?"

"Let them get bigger and either have more brooder hens, or we can offer farm-fresh chickens at the farmers' market, " Ryan suggested.

"Why do we always have to go back to killing the animals?" Lilly whined, thumping her foot against Ryan's thigh.

"Because that's what the animals are meant to do," Ryan reminded her. "Be born, get big and make babies, or become dinner."

"You're so gross."

"It's true!" He grinned. "How many times have I told you not to have any H names for the cows?"

She rolled her eyes. "Because the H names are saved for the males, 'cause they're all *hamburger.*"

"I think we should name Magnolia's next male calf McDouble. She always makes her bulls extra big."

"Stop it!" Lilly said.

Ryan bounced his leg against Lilly's foot. "But it worked on getting your mind off the money problems, right?"

She shook her head again, letting out a small breath. "Yes, I suppose."

He looked down at his wrist and checked the time. "I have to go into town and get ball bearings and more grease for the skid steer. Do you want to come with me?"

Lilly opened her mouth to respond when her phone pinged. "Oh, hang on, I got a text..."

"Be careful, your track record with texts lately hasn't been the greatest," Ryan warned.

"It might be Nathan."

Ryan groaned. "I rest my case."

Lilly ignored him and opened her messages. She was expecting another text from Nathan or even Faith to check in on how she was handling the financial situation—any sort of distraction from her current economic woes. However, the name attached to the message shocked her into a prolonged silence.

> Angela Stilner
>
> **Can we meet today? ASAP**

> **Lilly Schmidt**
>
> Sure, when/where?

"Earth to Lilly," Ryan snapped his fingers. "You want to come to town with me?"

Lilly narrowed her eyes at him. "You did not just snap at me."

"Town? Yes or no?"

"Give me a moment..."

> **Angela Stilner**
>
> Library at 1 pm

> **Lilly Schmidt**
>
> Perfect. I'll be in the computer lab.

Ryan leaned over her shoulder. "Who are you texting?"

Lilly tilted her phone screen away from him. With one hand, she swatted at his stomach while hissing, "Shhh!"

> **Angela Stilner**
>
> OK. See u there

Lilly checked her phone's clock. It was just about twelve-thirty. That didn't give her much time to get from the auto store to the library. "To answer your crudely asked question, yes, I will go to town with you. Only if you promise to drop me off at the library by one."

Ryan's face crinkled with confusion. "Why the library?"

"I found my perfect distraction from my monetary woes."

Lilly ascended the steps to the Lone Tree Library, nestled within a refurbished Victorian home. Its three-story, yellow façade made it stand out amongst the mid-century homes of the surrounding neighborhood. She glanced at her phone's clock and quickened her pace up the stairs. Ryan had proven to be a nagging chauffeur, demanding to know why she wanted to go to the library and if she was meeting someone. Naturally, his thoughts went to Nathan, and that swiftly soured his mood even more than when Lilly refused to answer his questions. He fought to go to the auto supply store before he dropped her off at the library. But her one o'clock deadline was approaching fast, and she wouldn't budge on being dropped off first.

The library was quiet for a Monday afternoon. As Lilly made her way through the stacks on the main floor toward the staircase, she heard muffled voices from fellow patrons and the tell-tale *thump-twack* of Mrs. Krzmarzick, the librarian, stamping returned books. Even with the advent of the technological age, which brought electronic check-in and check-out systems for libraries to track the comings and goings of books, the Lone Tree Library clung desperately to the old ways of using check-out cards and date stamps. The word around town was that the city council and library board were waiting for one roadblock, Mrs. Krzmarzick, to retire, so the library could finally enter the twenty-first century.

Given how stubborn the librarian was, the board and council would have to wait a long while before she finally gave up her rubber stamps.

Lilly walked through an open area of the library's main floor that held mostly long tables and chairs, meant to be an open meeting space for patrons to sit and read, put together a puzzle from the library's small collection, or for the local card clubs to come and host their weekly get-togethers. Today, the tables were full of elderly card players, each table comprised of two men and two women, although every table played the same game.

She walked around the tables and stood momentarily, trying to determine what game the group was playing that day. Lilly had learned that the group came to the library on different days, at least three times a week, and played a different game each day.

"Good afternoon, Lilly, dear," Mrs. Elvira Robertson called from her table.

Lilly focused on the diminutive woman, dressed head to toe in a kelly-green tracksuit with white lining. A matching faux flower adorned the left side of her midnight black bouffant hairdo. Every day, Elvira came to the farmers' market and invited Lilly to join the card club, bemoaning that the 'youngsters' didn't want to learn the classic games anymore. Lilly would politely decline each time, too ashamed to admit she feared the ferocity of how the card club played their games.

She believed a Call of Duty live stream didn't have the caliber of insults these elder players had.

"Afternoon, Elvira," Lilly waved to the woman as she scanned the card layout on the table. "What's the game today?"

"Five hundred," Elvira's female partner, a woman Lilly learned was named Betty. The card group had its core players, the diehards who came every day without fail, players like Elvira, while others came and played occasionally. Those players were the ones who often lost. Unless it was Eddie, he was one of the only diehard players who lost religiously, no matter the game.

"You should come play," Eddie chimed in.

"You only want someone worse at this game than you," a man from another table cut off Lilly's response. The gathering of players erupted in laughter. This only caused a hissing *sshhhhhh!* from the main desk area beyond the shelves.

"Oops, we ticked off the warden," Elvira smirked, shooting Lilly a wink. "We'll let you get to your meeting. You're running late."

"My meeting..." Lilly narrowed her eyes at Elvira. She had already returned to dealing out the hands for the next round of five hundred.

Lilly shook her head and made her way to the stairs. However, Elvira knew that she was meeting someone here, although she had no idea who it was. But the elder woman was right. She was late meeting Angela in the computer lab by one o'clock. She hurried up the main stairs to the second floor, where most of the non-fiction and reference sections were, including the modest selection of computers for patron use. The second floor saw less traffic than the main floor, where the children's and teen sections resided—a perfect spot for a clandestine meeting.

She turned to the left and made her way to the computer room. The room was silent, save for the gentle humming of the computers. Sitting at a computer, the farthest from the door, Angela Stilner looked up from her phone, alarm sneaking into her eyes.

"You're late," the woman said, fighting the shaking in her voice.

"I'm sorry, I got a ride into town and then I got sidetracked by the card group downstairs," Lilly sat at the computer next to Angela's. "I got here as soon as I could."

Angela looked her over, sitting a little straighter in the chair. "Thanks for coming, I guess."

"Why did you ask to meet with me?"

Sharp eyes caught Lilly's gaze. "I heard you were sneaking around my farm after I left the other day."

Lilly wasn't the only one getting straight to the point. Lilly cleared her throat. "Yeah, about that," she sighed. "I guess I was looking for proof."

"Proof that I killed my husband?" Angela's face paled under the fluorescent lights of the library.

"No, not that, proof of..." Lilly's voice failed her. "I'm not sure why I was looking around the shed, Angela. I'm sorry. There's been so much going on with this whole thing, and then Cecilia—"

"I heard she tried to implicate us in conspiring to kill Henry," Angela interrupted. "I can imagine you were looking for something to clear your name."

"And yours."

Angela scoffed and moved the chair away from the table, making to leave.

"No, Angela, really." Lilly reached for Angela's arm but withdrew it before they touched. "I don't believe you killed Henry. I was trying to find evidence for... I'm not even sure what I was looking for. I was hoping it would jump out at me."

The other woman stared at Lilly for a few long moments. "Were you hoping to see if the rumors are true? That I've been cheating on my husband?"

"Well... that did cross my mind," Lilly admitted. "Especially with Jakob-with-a-K there with you."

Angela scoffed once more, a tired, exasperated laugh that spoke volumes. "Jakob is my cousin."

"Cousin?"

"He came into town to help me; he arrived Saturday morning. I called him immediately after Henry's death."

"That's awfully nice," Lilly nodded. "What about your parents?"

"He's the only family I have."

"Oh, I'm sorry, Angela."

Angela eyed Lilly, then shook her head. "I forget you'd been gone for a few years. You're not up on all the drama that happened after you left."

Lilly smiled, "Which is surprising, given how much drama I've been caught up in since I got back."

Angela matched her smile, though there was pain behind it. "You're probably wondering where all the rumors came from."

"It has crossed my mind a few times - that old saying, if there's smoke, there's typically fire." Lilly shrugged. "I mean, Angela, you're a little out of Henry's league."

She smirked. "Henry and I got married almost immediately after high school. And yes, I guess I was out of my league. But I was also desperate."

"Desperate?"

"To leave my family." Angela lowered her eyes and focused on fidgeting with her thumbnail. "While Henry had his founding family and wealth, in comparison, I grew up on the 'wrong side of the tracks'. My parents separated and were barely around when I was growing up. I had to take care of myself most of the time. And when my parents were around, things were... bad. Then Henry started showing interest in me; I wasn't going to discourage him."

Lilly narrowed her eyes when Angela grew quiet. "It was a marriage of convenience."

"In some ways, yes," Angela nodded. "He got a wife to appease his family, hoping he'd settle down and start taking things more seriously. You've most likely heard the stories of his parties during high school, right?" Lilly nodded. "Well, he needed to prove to his parents that he stopped his wild ways, and I needed to get away from my parents... so why not?"

"You must have cared for him at some point?"

"I suppose," Angela shrugged again.

A tense silence fell over the women. Lilly's mouth slowly gaped open. "The rumors are true!" she gasped.

Angela nodded. "I was cheating on Henry."

"What!"

"It wasn't like he wasn't either," Angela replied defensively. "He had his legion of women on the side."

Lilly gaped at Angela, her brain trying to process what she was being told. "Why stay together if you both weren't happy?"

"He wouldn't give me a divorce," Angela sighed. "After almost ten years of us respectively cheating on each other, I asked him for a divorce. He wouldn't sign the papers. Would hide them in his work shed or feed them to the goats. All sorts of crazy things until I stopped asking."

"But... why?"

"Something to do with his family and his inheritance. He tried to explain it to me, some clause in his father's will that stated each of his children must be married or naturally widowed at the time of his death to receive the majority of their inheritance."

"That makes no sense."

"The wealthy often don't do things that make a whole lot of sense," Angela shook her head.

"Why not leave without a divorce? Get a separation. You were okay with being branded as the cheating spouse?"

"I wasn't okay with it, I hated it!" Angela snapped. "To be the only one called out by the town when he was just as guilty, if not more so. He certainly had more women than I had men."

Lilly pressed her lips together and looked at her feet. "Wasn't there one man who was worth leaving Henry?" She asked gently.

"There was..." Angela's eyes glanced over Lilly's shoulder and gazed at something only she could see. "He wanted to get serious, I did too... but it was something I couldn't give him. Not until Henry agreed to let me go."

"That'd certainly make me pretty angry," Lilly said softly.

Angela's eyes flared dark. "I didn't kill Henry, if that's what you're thinking."

"It does sort of make sense, Angela." Lilly kept going. "What about Owen? He and Henry were selling drugs after all this time. Get that part of the problem out of the way."

"You sound like the police," she grumbled. "I didn't kill Henry or Owen."

"Your scarf..."

Angela suddenly stood, her chair clattering to the floor behind her. "I think we're done here."

"Angela, wait. Please..."

"What? You said you didn't think I killed Henry, and then you sound just like everyone else in the blasted town," Angela said.

Lilly remained seated and softened her voice. "Do you know how your scarf ended up with Henry?"

She stood in front of Lilly and took some deep breaths. "We left the dance tent after Cecilia made her scene about us arriving. I know you saw it, and you were dancing with that vet. Everyone saw it. I was done being the unwanted center of attention, so I made Henry leave. I followed him to the poultry tent. He was drunk, and I was trying to get him to come with me back to our car. We fought, he grabbed at me, and snatched my scarf from my neck. I was done dealing with him, so I went home."

"You left the festival?"

Tears brimmed in Angela's eyes. "I wasn't even there when he died. I was halfway home in our car. Someone killed him and I left him there alone!"

Chapter Twenty-one

The ride back to the farm was long and quiet. Well, mostly quiet. Quiet on Lilly's part.

"Are you not going to tell me what you were doing at the library?" Ryan asked Lilly for what felt like the thousandth time.

Lilly sat in the passenger seat of Ryan's old rusted-out Chevy truck, legs crossed and arms pressed to her stomach. She tried to get lost in the earthy smells of his vehicle, a heady combination of machine grease, animal feed, and barn aromas. Next to her feet was a brown paper bag full of what she suspected was his haul from the auto store: ball bearings and grease.

"I can tell you didn't pick up any books," Ryan continued, eyeing her lap. "I'm surprised you didn't come home with an armful of BookTok recommendations."

She rolled her head to look at him and sighed. "Ryan."

"Lillian."

"I don't like it when you use my full name."

"Don't make me bust out the middle name," Ryan grinned.

Lilly looked at him silently for a moment, then turned to face the passenger window.

"Seriously, Lilly. What happened at the library?" Ryan's voice lowered. She hated the concerned tone in his words.

"I don't want to talk about it now."

"When we get back to the farm?"

How was she supposed to tell him she met a suspected murderer at the library? Well, one of the top suspects in a murder case. He had warned her not to get caught up in the deaths of Owen and Henry, and here she had just met with the somewhat bereaved widow. Maybe if she told him what she'd been up to at the farm instead of the confines of the truck cab, she'd be able to get away from him and his constant "I told you so"s.

Outside the truck, the scenery had changed from town to cropland, the fields almost ready to be harvested. In a few short weeks, the tall golden corn stalks and browning beans will be mowed down by combines and whisked away to various processing plants for human or animal consumption. This is another signal of the changing seasons in Minnesota farm country and another sign of her failure to get her agri-tourism business up and running.

That prompted her to reflect on what she had learned from Angela. She freely admitted that she cheated on her husband with other men. And how he cheated on her with other women. An equally unhappy marriage of convenience that ultimately didn't fulfil the needs of either party. Suppose Angela truly married Henry to escape a difficult family situation and improve her circumstances. How dire was her home life that she chose to stay in such a poor arrangement?

Would she have stayed in such an arrangement if it meant a marginally better stance in the world? What would she do to change the situation of the farm?

Ryan's truck turned down the farm's gravel driveway as Lilly forced those thoughts from her mind. She needed to keep focused on the murder case, even though Ryan and her cousin, the Sheriff, wouldn't appreciate her further involvement. She needed more information.

Angela mentioned she recently had a boyfriend—would you call them boyfriends? —who wanted more from their relationship than what she could give. Could he have been the jealous type? The possessive type who didn't like being kept from the relationship he wanted?

"Lilly? Are you okay?" Ryan's words broke the silence in the truck.

Lilly waited until Ryan turned the truck off before undoing her seat belt and moving to face him. "I'm fine," she said.

"I'm sorry if I badgered you too much about the library," he pulled the keys from the ignition and held them, the metal clinking together gently. He looked as if he was trying to form his next words carefully. "I... I am just worried about you, okay? With the murders and the state of the farm, I just want you to know that you can... You can always talk to me, all right?"

"Talk to you," Lilly echoed.

"Yeah, I know, a lot has happened between us, and you might not think we're back to what we used to be in high school, but I want you to know you can talk to me." The words rushed out of Ryan's mouth. "I know you don't have a lot of friends to talk to, besides my sister, so yeah. You can always talk to me."

"Not a lot of friends..." Lilly repeated, suddenly looking down at the stick shift in between the two, her mental gears steadily grinding to life.

He aggressively groaned, raking a hand through his hair under his John Deere cap. "I'm not saying this right, I'm sorry—"

Lilly lunged across the truck's center console and wrapped her arms around Ryan's shoulders in an awkward yet tight hug. "She doesn't have a lot of friends!" Lilly exclaimed as she pulled back from Ryan enough to look at his face.

"What?" Ryan sputtered. "Who doesn't have friends?"

"Thank you!"

"For what?"

His answer came as a quick kiss from Lilly on his stubbled cheek.

Both leaned back and stared at each other, unsure how to proceed after the spontaneous kiss. Lilly knew her face had flushed as dark pink as Ryan's in the dim lighting of the truck cab. "You just, uh, gave me, uh, a good idea," Lilly stammered as she hurried back across the center console to her seat.

"Uh-huh," was Ryan's only reply.

Lilly scrambled for the door handle and opened it before anything else unexpected could happen. "Thanks for the ride into town."

She scurried out of the truck cab, shut the door, and hurried up to the farmhouse. Lilly dared not look back at the truck, lest she get sidetracked from her new mission. Lilly was sure that Angela didn't have many friends in town, thanks to the now-founded rumors of her infidelity. Not very many Lone Tree citizens would want to be the sounding board to a known adulterer complaining about an unending situation. Who else did Angela have to talk to but one of the few decent family members she had left?

Lilly needed to find a way to track down Jakob-with-a-K.

Chapter Twenty-two

Monday afternoon went by slowly as Lilly struggled to find a legit reason to talk to Jakob-with-a-K. She went out to the chicken run to check on Mrs. Patmore's chicks and the rest of her little flock, hoping the mundane task would spark some great ideas. All she seemed to spark was more chicken droppings on her boots and an uneasy truce with the Colonel. Fatherhood suited him well. He appeared to have taken his new offspring under his wing, following the three yellow puffs around the enclosure when Mrs. Patmore was off eating with the other hens.

Thoughts of that kiss in Ryan's truck became unwanted in her mind as she tended to the chickens. Lilly told herself not to read too much into it. She was merely excited over her idea of how to track down who Angela's most recent paramour was. Nothing more, nothing less.

Though it was hard to ignore the memory and all the long-forgotten feelings that a quick peck on the cheek stirred up.

Lilly entered the kitchen through the back porch entrance, carrying the chicken feed pail and a handful of three eggs from the feathery ladies. No need to wait for tomorrow morning's egg run for those, lest they turn into another little brood of Colonel progeny. However, Lilly didn't know what to do with her surplus of eggs now that the farmers' market was done for the season. She'd have to stop by the library and see if any card club members would like to buy eggs until market season opened up in the spring.

Her cell phone rang from the center of the kitchen island. Lilly hurried to answer the phone as quickly as she could without dropping an egg. She wasn't expecting a call. It was doubtful that Angela would contact her with any follow-ups to their tense conversation earlier at the library. Perhaps it was her parents finally calling her back.

After taking over the farm six months prior, Lilly had held off on telling her parents what happened to her after her divorce. They had inquired about where she was staying since Alec and his mistress had acquired their Lowry loft during the divorce proceedings. Given her father's lingering sour feelings towards Lone Tree and her grandparents due to decades' worth of family secrets, Lilly toiled to find the right time to break the news that she had moved back to the one place her family loathed. Now she has been waiting for a reply to her voicemail about the move for two months.

Lilly grabbed her phone and answered at the last ring before it switched to voicemail. "Hello?"

"Lillian."

The use of her full name never boded well. She grimaced and sat on an island stool, awaiting the verbal reprimand. "Hey, Cousin Sheriff Mike."

"Lillian, just call me Mike," Sheriff Branford sighed. "What have you been doing?"

"Collecting eggs, why? Do you and Katie need some?" Lilly bit her lower lip.

"Stop stalling," Mike snapped through the phone. "I've been hearing some disturbing rumors about you."

Lilly gnawed on her lip more. "I told you Cecilia made that all up. I thought we talked about her group chat lies."

"You've been asking questions about Owen and Henry's death," Mike said.

"Yeah..."

"After I told you not to get involved?"

"Sorry," she apologized softly. "But since I have you on the phone, can I pick your brain?"

"Lill—"

"Have you checked Henry's finances? I heard from Will—well, you probably already know that Henry was demanding money from clients even when he wasn't doing any work! And don't get me started about that list of drugs Henry wanted Owen to buy. That just shows they were up to no good all this time."

"Yes, Lillian, I heard you went snooping around the Stilner business," Mike's words ground out in exasperation. "And if we've checked his financials, it's none of your business. None of this is your—*what list?*"

"And did you know that Angela was cheating on Henry? Multiple times!" The words continued to flow from Lilly without any hint of stopping. Her mind needed someone to bounce her ideas off, and who better than the officer in charge of the case? "Well, Henry also cheated on Angela. They had a weird mutual cheating arrangement going on with their marriage. Would that make it an open marriage? Anyway, I heard from Angela that her recent extramarital affair ended. Have you looked into any of her recent beaus? Would it be possible to get—"

"Lillian!"

The words finally stopped, and the kitchen grew silent.

"Lillian," Mike's sigh betrayed how tired he was. Whether with her or the case, she didn't want to know the exact answer. "I appreciate how invested you are in figuring out who killed Owen and Henry. I do."

"Thank you."

"*However*, you are not part of the police force." Even if Lilly knew it was true, it still hurt to hear the words come from Mike. "You need to stop this."

"I have an idea, what if—"

"Stop, Lilly. Please. If you don't stop, I may have to arrest you for interfering with an ongoing police investigation."

"You wouldn't!" Lilly's grip on the phone slipped, and the phone almost fell.

"Do you want to try me?"

Lilly held her breath, trying to formulate a response that wouldn't get her in jail. "I'm sorry, Mike. I don't... I just don't believe Angela did it."

"And no one is saying she's the only suspect," Mike's tone softened. "The police are looking into various leads right now. Angela's not the be-all end-all suspect, no matter what the town rumor mill might be saying."

"Really?"

"Yes, really." She could hear the nod in his voice. "Now, will you please stop asking questions around town?"

"I suppose."

She heard another sigh escape through the phone. "If the thought of possible jail time doesn't deter you, how about the knowledge that there is still a murderer running around the area? If you go around asking the wrong people the right questions, you're going to end up hurt or worse, Lilly."

"Oh."

"Yeah, 'oh' is right," Mike said. "Leave this to the professionals, all right?"

It was her turn to sigh. "All right, Mike,"

"Thank you," the relief in his voice was palpable through the phone.

"But what about—"

"I'm hanging up now, Lilly."

And then the line went dead.

Lilly looked at the darkened cell phone screen and made a face, as if it would still transmit that to the departed sheriff.

She didn't even get to tell Mike about her theory that the overly jealous ex-lover came to kill Owen and Henry in a fit of rage over not divorcing Angela. Though he probably already knew about the Stilners' open relationship and any recent paramours, his or hers, who would have the slightest motive to make the marriage permanently open.

But that didn't answer her questions about who Angela's recent lover was. And if this unknown man acted alone in killing Owen and Henry, or if it was a joint venture between the beau and the unhappy spouse. The thought that Angela may have had a part in the killings soured Lilly's stomach. As much as she wanted to believe Angela was innocent, there was much about the woman that Lilly didn't know. It wasn't like they were close friends—just acquaintances from the farmers' market.

She needed someone else to discuss her theories with. Lilly picked up her phone again and dialed the best person in town who would have answers to her questions and theories to match her own.

"Hey, Faith. You busy?"

The largest basket of loaded cheese fries awaited Lilly when she entered Grandma's Attic. The café was in a key lull between the late lunch and early supper crowds. This meant there were fewer prying eyes and ears to overhear what the two friends planned to discuss over their unhealthy snack choices.

"Thanks for sneaking me into your busy schedule, Faith," Lilly grinned as she slid into their usual back booth.

Faith had already started on the fries, negotiating a fry with a large blob of yellow cheese into her mouth. Her medium-length brown hair was pulled back in a red gingham bandana, her face flushed from standing by the fryers recently. Faith's jeans and matching red gingham shirt were protected by a white apron adorned with various splatters.

"Anything for you, my friend," the restaurateur said as she chewed. "I always have time for your theories."

"No one wants to listen to me," Lilly whined as she pulled a fry from the gooey pile. She had to twirl the crispy stick multiple times to rein in the stretchy cheese.

"You mean your copper cousin or my brother?"

"Either."

Faith popped another fry in her mouth and wiped her mouth with a napkin. "Maybe they're on to something, Lills."

"Not you, too!"

"I just want to do my due diligence of looking out for my friend before we get into the juicy stuff, that's all," she said. "Plausible deniability and all that junk in case you go and do something stupid."

"When have I ever done something stupid?"

Faith's eyebrow arched sharply as she caught Lilly's gaze. "Do you want a list?"

"No."

"Good. Now, hit me with your latest."

Lilly filled Faith in on the previous theories. The first pertained to Cecilia Baxter finally seeking revenge after decades of no closure for her sister's overdose death, from the drugs that Henry and Owen, allegedly, brought to a high school party. Still, for some reason, they were never brought to justice. The accidentally viewed crime scene photo of the EpiPen next to Henry's body came up once more, now that Lilly had seen Cecilia with a similar EpiPen in her purse multiple times, the orange and blue cylinder could have been used to kill Henry with an unnecessary dose of epinephrine.

A similar mode of death was found at Owen's crime scene. However, she didn't know the substance that the syringe held. Lilly wouldn't be able to ask for the details from the sheriff. Maybe Faith had heard something.

"Have you heard anything about the other crime scene? Owen's? There was a syringe by the bench. It was empty." Lilly prompted, raising her brows in the hopes of a plausible, innocent expression.

Faith shook her head. "I haven't heard of anything. No, wait. One of the EMT crews came in last night and started talking shop. Said something about a syringe and an air embolism."

"Air embolism?" Lilly echoed. "What is that?"

To the Google machine!" Faith grinned.

Lilly grabbed her phone from her purse. After a few silent moments typing, Lilly made an affirmative grunt. "Air embolism. Air pocket in the blood vessel around the heart. It can cause confusion or trouble breathing. Depending on the amount of air, a patient could die within minutes or hours of the embolism forming."

"Given that the syringe was there at the scene, whoever poked old Owen made sure that the whole syringe was full for it to work so quickly," Faith said grimly.

"Wow." Lilly put the phone down and sat in silence for a moment, pondering who would inject air into someone as a means to kill them—such a diabolical and intimate way to die.

Lilly wasn't sure if that level of epinephrine would be enough to kill a man like Henry outright. However, he had been drinking the night of his death. Would that have made the perfect storm to cause the extra epinephrine in his system to cause him to die? Would Cecilia have known when she stuck him with the pen?

"Do you know what happens when someone is hit with an EpiPen and they don't need it?" Faith asked between fries.

"I was going to Google it and find out," Lilly admitted as she reached for her phone. After another quick internet search, the answer came. "Let's see... it says that normally the side effects are temporary."

"What side effects?"

"Increased heart rate, high blood pressure, sweating, nausea, increased anxiety, heightened fight or flight response..." Lilly scrolled further down the page. "It says that these effects would decrease quickly, and a normal person wouldn't have a dangerous reaction."

"But...?" Faith urged. "Sounds like there's a but at the end of that sentence."

"Unless they had pre-existing heart conditions, higher blood pressure and heart rate may be the only cause of concern," Lilly concluded.

"Did Henry have a heart condition?" Faith asked. "Did Owen?"

"Well, he was drinking that night," Lilly offered. "Angela said he was pretty drunk. Don't know much about Owen's physical state when he was poked."

"Angela said..." Faith's brows arched once more. "When did you talk to Angela?"

"Earlier today," Lilly bit her lip sheepishly.

"Why?"

"'Cause she found out that I was snooping around Henry's machine shed."

Faith flopped back into the booth cushion. "See, this is what I mean about doing something stupid."

"I had wanted to go out to Angela's to see if she was okay, but then she left with Jakob-with-a-K, and I thought I'd take the opportunity while I was there to look around, okay?"

"What else did Angela say about that night?" Faith shook her head. "And who is Jakob-with-a-K?"

"She said that she and Henry fought in the poultry barn, and she wanted to go home, but apparently, he didn't. He grabbed for her scarf, and she left him."

"Well, that explains why they found her scarf at the crime scene."

"According to her, at least," Lilly pointed out.

"I thought you believed she didn't do it," Faith questioned.

"I don't think she did it..." Lilly's voice trailed off. "At least at first."

"What changed?"

"Angela admitted that she was cheating on Henry, with multiple men over the years."

"No way, that's true!" Faith exclaimed. Thankfully, the Attic lacked customers; otherwise, they would have had decidedly unwanted attention.

"Henry was cheating on her, too. I guess they realized their marriage was a farce, and they opened it up but didn't want to leave each other."

Lilly shrugged. "Angela claimed they never got divorced to fulfill some weird will obligation Henry's father put in place."

"Weird," Faith dug a fry through a lake of cheese sauce. "But if Angela killed Henry, she wouldn't see any of that extra inheritance, would she?"

"I don't think so."

Faith began counting off theories on her fingers. "So, money and inheritance are off the table for motive. That would mean Angela was finally tired of their arrangement and wanted out, regardless of Henry's permission. But if Angela didn't do it, that leaves Cecilia wanting revenge for her sister's death. That would connect Owen's death to Henry's and make that make sense. Otherwise, he's just a random act of violence. The cops didn't do a lot back when the death happened, even though the word on the street was that Henry or Owen provided the drugs; there wasn't enough evidence to make it stick."

"So after years of seeing them live their best lives, Cecilia suddenly snaps and attacks them on a bench and at the festival dance?" Lilly asked.

"As good a place as any," Faith licked some cheese from her finger. "Lots of noise and people, easy to get lost in the crowd at the dance. Easy to hide in plain sight on the street. Just walk by and poke him. But why the EpiPen and syringe?"

"It was the easiest weapon she had on her. She said she always carries one for her son's allergy," Lilly replied. "She reaches into her purse and finds the pen, knows what epinephrine would likely do to a man of his size and less than sober condition, and figures why not stab him and see what happens? If he didn't die, at least she'd make his life horrible for a few moments until it wore off. For Owen, she has an extra syringe or something in her purse, sees him on the street, and there's her opening."

"I like the way you're thinking," Faith nodded. "Hey, you haven't explained who Jakob-with-a-K is."

"According to Angela, he's her cousin whom she called upon in her time of need."

"You don't sound too sure."

"She could say he's anyone," Lilly said. "I've never met him before, Will and Gregory stated that they've seen strange cars come and go from the farm. Jakob-with-a-K could be an out-of-town cousin or one of the men she's cheating on Henry with."

"What does he look like?"

"Tall, thin build. Black hair and dark eyes. Likes to dress in all black," Lilly answered.

"Hmm. Could be anyone," Faith agreed. "I don't remember much of Angela's family. Her parents were difficult, and she was an only child. Don't know much of her extended family."

"I wish there were a way to get in touch with Jakob-with-a-K," Lilly lamented as she shoved multiple cheesy fries into her mouth.

"Ask Angela if you can talk to him?"

"Ha! That's unlikely," Lilly snorted. "But... if he's in town, he's bound to stop by here, wouldn't you think?"

"Angela could bring him around," Faith shrugged.

"If they come in, do you think you could tell Jakob-with-a-K that I want to speak with him?"

"If I know who you're talking about."

"You just said that if he'd come in here, he'd be with Angela," Lilly recalled, pointing a cheesy finger at Faith. "And if you see Angela in here with a strange guy, that will be him!"

"That's a lot of 'ifs', Lilly," Faith said.

"Then it won't be that big of a deal for you to relay the message, because odds are it won't happen. Please, Faith, I just need to ask him some questions."

Faith sat quietly, contemplating Lilly's request. "Questions about what?"

"About Angela's most recent extramarital relationship," Lilly answered flatly.

Another sigh from Faith. "Why just Angela? If what she said about Henry was true, he'd have women who'd want him to themselves."

Lilly tapped her fingers on the tabletop for a moment, mulling that point over. "But... really? Do you really think he'd snag a crazy, jealous woman?"

"Weirder things have happened."

Lilly nodded, conceding Faith had a point. Just because she thought Henry married up with Angela didn't mean there weren't women out there who thought Henry was a solid catch. The idea made the fries sour in her stomach.

"So, what happens if neither Angela nor Jakob shows up at the Attic? What are you going to do about your current investigation?" Faith asked.

Lilly grinned. "Then I'll finally have obeyed Cousin Sheriff Mike for once."

Chapter Twenty-three

Lilly woke up Tuesday morning with a renewed sense of purpose and vigor. For some reason, waking up early wasn't much of a chore. She was dressed in her grubbiest pair of jeans and stained T-shirt, and out the door with her chicken feed and egg pails before Ryan's old Chevy truck rumbled up the driveway.

The perplexed expression on his face as he exited the truck cab made waking up almost before dawn well worth it.

Her conversation with Faith the previous day had helped clear her mind of all the theories and questions surrounding them. Having had a chance to talk about her mental murder board was enough to sweep the stale cobwebs from her mind. Faith's promise to contact her if and when Angela or Jakob-with-a-K came into the Attic helped improve her mood as well.

It was the last thing she'd do in terms of investigating this case. She just wanted to know who Angela's previous boyfriend was. Lover? Beau? What do you call the extra wheel in an unofficially open marriage? Lilly shook her head, not wanting to get bogged down in the weird details of the Stilners' love lives. If she got a chance to speak with Jakob and pick his brain about what he knew of Angela and Henry's recent partners, she could begin to tie up some of the loose ends to her theories.

Lilly fought once more with the chickens that morning. Well, more accurately, she fought again with the Colonel. The honeymoon stage of fatherhood wore off during the night, and now he stood guard over all the hens and chicks with his usual frenetic energy. She wore more of her usual battle armor and pads, just to be safe, when getting into the chicken enclosure after she heard how aggressive the Colonel's crows were that morning. She'd almost missed sparring with the large rooster.

Almost.

After depositing her morning eggs and battle armor in the kitchen, Lilly went to the barn. Emboldened by what she saw as a win in her murder theories and investigation with the Jakob angle, she walked into the barn's lower level. It had been weeks since she had ventured into the barn while Ryan did his chores. Usually, his ire greeted her whenever she stepped foot into the barn that early in the morning. Her hired hand was a creature of habit, and he preferred to do things a certain way, so her presence often messed things up in one manner or another.

"Good morning, Ryan!" She called out as she walked down the center aisle of the barn. To her left and right stood ten of the twelve cows of their milking herd. The other two, Peony and Rose, were in a separate pen in the barn. What was usually the maternity pen sometimes turned into a quarantine zone for cows with certain communicable diseases, and summer pneumonia was one of them.

"What are you doing up already?" His less-than-cordial response was nothing new to her; if he had responded in any other way, she'd have been concerned.

"I'm just having a perfect couple of days, that's all," Lilly shrugged as she stopped by the cow he was crouched next to as he attached a tie-stall milker.

"Mm-hmm," was his reply.

"Can't I have a good day, and want to join you for chores?"

Ryan eyed her from under his John Deere cap's brim. He stood, leaned against the cow, and finished attaching the milker. He adjusted his red plaid shirt, picking at an invisible piece of dirt. "Just having a random good day?"

"Yes..."

"It has nothing to do with what you got Faith caught up in, huh?" he asked.

"Faith—"

"Told me about how you asked her to keep an eye out for Angela or that dude she claims is her cousin,"

"Blast her!" Lilly frowned. "She wasn't supposed to tell anyone about that!"

"You're expecting my sister—*my* sister—to keep her mouth shut about you sticking your nose in another murder investigation?"

"It's not about the murder!" Lilly tried to deflect. "I want to know more about Angela's most recent relationship outside of marriage."

Ryan leveled his gaze at her before moving to the milker cart in the middle of the aisle. He hefted another milker to his shoulder and walked behind the next cow in line. "So you're finally feeding into all the rumors."

"It's not a rumor if it's true," Lilly countered. "Heard it from Angela herself that she and Henry were both mutually cheating on each other."

Ryan paused to attach the milker suction cup to the cow's udder. If Lilly remembered correctly, it was Dandelion's eldest daughter, Daffodil. "Then they deserved each other," he said.

"I'm not breaking your and Mike's rule about getting involved in the case if I'm asking about something that's not directly related to the case."

"Whatever helps you sleep at night," he responded.

Lilly opened her mouth to retort when the sound of a diesel engine rumbled from outside the barn doors. A quick honk of the horn caused the cows to reply in kind. Ryan and Lilly looked at each other in mutual confusion. She looked at her watch and noted it was only a few minutes after eight o'clock.

"Were you expecting someone?" Lilly asked.

"No," Ryan's tone turned guarded as he hung the completed milker on the pipeline. "Were you expecting anyone?"

"No."

They caught each other's gaze once more. Now Lilly felt a strange shiver go down her spine as Dandelion bellowed loudly from the stall nearest the door. Ryan started toward the doors, casually reaching for a wrench as he passed by the milker cart. He slipped it into one of his back jeans pockets.

"What are you doing with that?" Lilly hissed as she hurried to join him.

"Shh," he muttered.

"What are you gonna do with that?" She hissed again, reaching for the exposed wrench head.

"Stop it!" He slapped her hand away from his hip. She slapped at his hand and made for the wrench once more. Ryan grunted as he grabbed both of her hands by the wrists.

"Hello, is anyone home?" A loud voice boomed from the open barn doors, only to be answered by more agitated cows.

"Nathan?" Lilly freed her hands from Ryan's grasp and turned toward the vet.

"What are you doing here so early?" Ryan asked.

Lilly whacked the back of her hand on his arm. "Or you could try a 'good morning', seriously."

Nathan did have the decency to appear sheepish as he walked to meet them in the barn aisle. He came dressed in a pair of well-worn jeans and a gray button-down shirt with the logo of his family's veterinary practice on the left breast pocket. "Sorry to come so early, I was on my way to the Grisby's when Jeff called me to reschedule the visit. I figured since I was already in the neighborhood, so to speak, I'd stop by and see if you wanted to do a quick herd check?"

"Herd check?" Lilly looked from Nathan to Ryan. "Already?"

"That's not scheduled until next week," Ryan said. "It wouldn't do much good to check them now; we could get false positives or negatives if we do it now."

"Check who for what?" Lilly asked.

"Pregnancies," Nathan answered, sending a quick side eye to Ryan. "There are three heifers we inseminated a few weeks back, and herd checks often mean we check for a viable pregnancy."

"But it's too early to check," Ryan pushed. "We need to wait at least forty-five days."

"With ultrasound, it can be done in as little as thirty, and we're still well above the threshold for that." Nathan countered with a quick wink to Lilly.

Ryan looked away and shook his head. "Since you're here, whatever. But if there are any mistakes, I want a credit per cow on the invoice."

"I'll run that by the billing department," Nathan said.

Ryan turned and went back to the milker cart. During their quick conversation, three of the four milkers had completed milking the cows and hung uselessly next to the lazily standing bovines. He hurried to transfer the milkers to the next batch of cows, his movements eliciting loud *mrrroowws* of displeasure from the cows as they were forced to wait.

"Want to come with me while I check the three cows?" Nathan asked Lilly after Ryan left.

Lilly glanced at Ryan, then back at Nathan. "I won't be in the way?"

The vet's eyes grew dark as he looked in Ryan's direction. "He doesn't let you do much around your farm, does he?"

"He's very particular about how things are done around here," Lilly knew how weak that defense was as soon as it left her mouth.

"C'mon, you need to see more of the goings on on your farm," Nathan motioned for her to follow him back to his truck.

Once they reached his truck, he opened the passenger-side door and handed her his metal clipboard, again holding the list of the cows in her herd. Lilly stared at the list. The twelve main cows were listed in bold print, with their subsequent calves listed under each mother.

"Why are so many of the calves and heifers not named?" Lilly asked.

"I just go off the list Ryan gives me. You'd have to ask him, I guess," Nathan shrugged. "I'm sure he'd delegate naming the new calves to you."

Lilly made a face. "You'd think that, wouldn't you?"

"I'm sure you would come up with good names." He smiled and tapped a finger on the clipboard in her hands.

"I've named one calf already," Lilly declared with an air of pride. "Ryan didn't rename it, which I was afraid he was going to do."

"I'm going to have a talk with him about that," Nathan shook his head. "We have three yearling heifers to check to see if their inseminations took hold. Wait here while I get my gloves."

Lilly waited for him to grab the long blue gloves from the back of his truck and stuff a pair into his back jeans pockets. He offered her a pair, which she took gingerly from him. "I thought you were using ultrasound?"

"Manual palpation is the best way to check for pregnancy," he replied. "And I don't have my machine with me since I wasn't planning on doing this herd check until next week."

"Smooth."

Nathan led the way back into the barn and down the main aisle. They passed by Ryan as he was hanging the last of the milkers next to the two milking cows. The three two-year-old heifers in question were in the last three stalls closest to the back of the barn. The smell of animal waste and hay grew stronger as they approached the manure pump. Lilly held a hand over her mouth and coughed, trying to clear the offending smell from her nose. She wondered when she'd ever be able to handle being close to the pump.

"Two of Rose's granddaughters are supposed to be pregnant, along with 346's daughter," Nathan explained, pointing out the heifer names.

"Why are they still listed as heifers and not cows?" Lilly asked.

"Female cows are known as heifers until they've given birth. Then they get to be called cows," he explained.

Lilly heard Ryan's snort from further up the aisle. She ignored the nonverbal remark and kept her attention on Nathan. "Is there a similar naming system for males?"

"When they're born, both male and female cows are all known as calves," Nathan began. For males, breeding stock are called bulls. Non-breeding males are often called steers."

"Interesting," Lilly nodded, taking in the information. From the corner of her eye, she spotted Ryan watching them. She raised her voice and continued, "I never got an answer whenever I asked about the difference."

"Because it's not that interesting!" Ryan shot back.

Nathan looked from Ryan to Lilly as he worked the long-sleeved blue gloves over his arms. "You two need couples counseling or something if you're going to work together."

Ryan turned on his heel. He loaded the last of the completed milkers onto the cart and pushed it down the main aisle toward the milk house. Lilly hid her smirk with her hand as she watched him walk away.

"I think you hurt his feelings," she said.

"Good," Nathan snapped the final glove into place. He maneuvered behind a heifer with a yellow ear tag marking her as 156, Rose's grand-daughter, named Rosemary. Gently, he moved his hands over the cow's right flank, staying close to the rump and hips. "He has no right treating you like you don't need to know this stuff. It's good that you are interest-ed in what happens on the farm."

"Thank you!" Lilly exclaimed. "Maybe next time, say it when he's ac-tually around."

Nathan glanced at her as he pushed down on 156's side. "I'm sure he can hear me."

The two fell silent as Nathan continued his examination of heif-er 156. Slowly, he moved his hands to the cow's rear end. "Now here comes the fun part," Nathan grinned. "If you need to look away, I won't think any less of you."

"Look away?" Lilly glanced up from the list of cow names as Nathan inserted his right arm into the cow's backside, clean up to his shoulder. Heifer 156 grunted and squirmed under the intrusion. "Oh, my God!"

"Sorry, I should have warned you better," Nathan grunted. His arm flexed inside the animal. "Got a fetus!" he looked over his shoulder at Lil-ly. "Do you have a pen? We need to mark that down on the list."

"Uh, no, I don't."

"I have one in my front shirt pocket," Nathan gestured with his head to his left side. "Come around this side and grab it."

Lilly groaned as she stood next to Nathan. It was surreal being that close to a cow's backside, especially with a man's arm shoved into it. She quickly grabbed at Nathan's shirt front, fingers fumbling not to touch the heifer if she could help it, and found a pen. As quickly as she could, she stood back in the main aisle and marked 156 *PREGNANT.*

"Good job," Nathan said, giving her a grin as he disengaged his arm from the animal. He peeled the dirtied glove sleeve off and tossed it into the manure gutter behind 156. "Now on to 157."

"These poor things need names," Lilly bemoaned. She wanted to get her mind focused on something other than where Nathan's arm disappeared to.

"You should just name them while you have the list. These are your cows." Nathan stood behind heifer 157 and performed the same procedure on her as he did on her cousin. This time, when his gloved arm disappeared into the bovine, it wasn't such a surprise to Lilly. "Again, he should be happy you're taking an interest in the farm; it means you care what happens to the animals he claims to love so much."

"I don't know if I should invade his space too much," Lilly admitted absently.

Honestly, her mind was more focused on naming the unnamed heifers than pondering the idiosyncrasies of Ryan. She used the pen to scratch out 156 and 157, and wrote *"Rowena"* and *"Ragland,"* respectively. She contemplated what to name the other two-year-old heifer, given that her mother was the, as of now, unnamed 346. Being the first of her family line, at least on the Schmidt farm, Lilly felt honored to be starting a new naming line. She scratched out 346 and wrote *Felicity*, naming her eldest daughter *Fergie* and the newest calf *Francis*.

"One fifty-seven is pregnant, too," Nathan called out as he dislodged his arm.

"Ragland," Lilly corrected while writing PREGNANT next to her name. "I'm giving them names."

"Good," he smiled at her, peeling the used glove off. "Do you still have the gloves I gave you? I need another one for 158."

"Fergie," Lilly stated as she handed him one of her blue gloves. "I'm glad you're not asking me to stick my hand up one of the cows."

"I was going to, but I felt that might be more of a second date sort of thing."

"This is a date?"

"I can't think of anything more romantic than an early morning herd check."

Lilly made a face but ended by flashing him a smile as they moved on to the last heifer.

"My last girlfriend wasn't as interested in what I do as a vet," Nathan said. His gloved arm again disappeared into Fergie. "She'd ask a few questions about procedures. She had animals, too. But didn't seem to be too invested in their well-being."

Lilly narrowed her brows, suddenly intrigued by Nathan talking about his previous relationship. She wasn't sure she wanted to hear about this woman, since she wasn't sure where they stood in the relationship department. One half dance date and one herd check hardly qualified them as anything close to serious.

"Is she someone from town?" Lilly asked, doodling in the margins of the cow list.

He slowly extracted his arm from behind Fergie. The young heifer made a disgruntled noise at the indignity of the herd check procedure. He didn't answer her until he had discarded the soiled glove in the gutter. "No, we dated when I lived in Rochester."

"So that's where you lived all this time after high school?"

"I worked for a local vet out there after graduation. I wanted to get as far away from Lone Tree as I could back then. Rochester was as far as I got. However, that was fine; I could still come back home and visit my family whenever I wanted, which wasn't much at the time." He rolled his shoulders and stretched his neck from side to side. "Around a few months ago, Dad said there was an opening at the family practice, and I accepted. Figured it was time to face the old haunts once again."

"Was your lady's disinterest in shoving your arms up cow's butts what caused the breakup?"

Nathan laughed. He stood next to her, again almost too close. Lilly took an instinctive step back, which he then matched. "I guess you could say that," he shrugged. "I wanted things to get a little more serious, and she wasn't ready for that level of seriousness. Hearing about the nitty gritty of the vet business was apparently beyond what she wanted to know about me. I guess I should have seen the signs."

Lilly tilted her head to catch his gaze. "Will you change your mind about me if I don't want to shove my hand up a cow's butt?"

"Jury's still out on you, Lilly," he smiled warmly. "I'm sure I can convince you to try it at least once."

"I did help pull a calf out," she offered proudly.

"See! You're used to that end of the animal already! Just need to reverse it."

Their laughter was cut short by Lilly's phone pinging from her back pocket. "Hold that thought," she held up a finger as she dug into her jeans for her cell. Her screen held a notification of a text message from Faith Fischer.

242

> **Faith Fischer**
>
> **Guess who wants to meet you for breakfast?**

Chapter Twenty-four

The bells above the door chimed as Lilly entered Grandma's Attic almost sixty minutes later. Thankfully, Nathan bought her little white lie of needing to meet with her cousin, Sheriff Mike, for an impromptu breakfast. She found that having a large kernel of truth was the key to a successful lie. Ryan had gone off to work on the calf chores so he wouldn't notice her absence until later.

After a quick shower and throwing on the closest clean jeans and T-shirt, Lilly hustled off the farm and headed to town to meet her mystery breakfast date. The whole ride to town, Lilly forced herself to keep from assuming it was Jakob-with-a-K. Who else would Faith text that early about wanting to have breakfast with her? It definitely wasn't Faith herself. It had to be Jakob.

Lilly walked through the tables of the Attic, each taken by a group of patrons having a hearty breakfast before officially starting their workdays. Many were truck drivers catching a quick meal before heading out of town on long-haul deliveries. The rest were café regulars, elderly citizens who upheld years-long routines of sitting at the same tables or booths and having the same meal for breakfast on the same day of the week.

Surprisingly, her usual booth, where she would steal a moment of Faith's time, was taken by a tall man with black slicked-back hair, all in black. He sat with his back to the door, but Lilly recognized him instantly.

Jakob-with-a-K.

Lilly caught Faith's hard stare as she returned to the booth. She could tell that Faith was bursting at the seams with anticipation; there was no way the proprietor would let Lilly leave the Attic without filling her in about every single detail of their conversation.

She sat on the opposite side of the booth and gave a nod to Jakob. Faith was over in an instant, handing Lilly a menu. She knew it was a moot gesture, just a way for Faith to insert herself into their bubble of juicy gossip fodder. Faith refilled Jakob's mug with hot coffee and turned over the complimentary mug in front of Lilly. Lilly took the menu and cleared her throat, hoping Faith would catch that as a hint to get lost.

Once Faith finished filling their coffees, she left. Jakob took that moment to look up from the tower of creamers he had constructed before him.

"Sorry to keep you waiting," Lilly said. "I had to clean up after barn chores."

Jakob made a face, his lean features wrinkled in disgust. "Ugh, I don't know how Angela can handle it out here with all those disgusting animals."

Lilly licked her lips, fighting back a sharp retort. "It definitely takes a certain character to be a farmer of any kind," she said instead.

"I suppose," he shrugged. "You want to order anything?"

Lilly's mind flashed unwanted images of Nathan's gloved arm up one of her cows' rear ends, and her stomach quivered. She shook her head. "No, thank you, coffee will be fine. Where's Angela this morning?"

"Let's cut to the chase, shall we?" Jakob replied sharply. "She told me all about your little talk in the library, how you were snooping around the property."

"Just Henry's machine shed," Lilly corrected.

"Toe-may-toe, toe-mah-toe," Jakob drummed his fingers on the tabletop.

"Why meet with me?" Lilly asked, her gaze holding his. "Are you going to tell me to stay away from Angela?"

"I'm not, actually," he said. He held her gaze for a moment longer, then dropped his eyes to the creamer tower. "She's told me a lot about you, how you've stood up to Cecilia and others about the rumors going around town. How she would have quit the farmers' market if it hadn't been for you sticking up for her and just being a civil person."

"Oh... that's nice to hear," Lilly felt her cheeks warm. She sipped her coffee, but it was too black for her taste. She grabbed two of the creamers from Jakob's tower and three sugar packets from the little dish next to the mustard and ketchup bottles.

A precisely manicured eyebrow arched as his tower tumbled to the table. "Because of that, I knew your little Nancy Drew stunt was more of a good intention executed poorly."

"Why does everyone keep comparing me to Nancy Drew?"

"'Cause you ask questions," Jakob shrugged. "And I figured you'd have more questions after seeing me at Angela's the other day."

"Are you really her cousin?"

"Yes, I'm her cousin from the good side of the family," he smiled ruefully. "I could tell by your face that day you thought I was one of Angela's extra men."

"You're okay with her having an open relationship with Henry?"

"No, but that was not my business." He took a sip of his coffee and began to construct another creamer tower. "They seemed to be okay with that arrangement. I was more of a sounding board for Angela than a point of morality. She would complain about Henry or if one of her extra men was being dramatic. Typical stuff like that."

Lilly nodded absently. She tried to imagine that type of relationship with her cousin, Tammy. After her father's fallout with her grandparents, they moved away from Lone Tree and severed every tie with the family who stayed. As she grew up, she had friends who filled the space where her cousin would have been, serving as a sounding board for boy troubles and family drama. "It must be nice for Angela to have a cousin like you. Someone who cares about her."

Jakob nodded. "It's a foreign concept to her, that's for sure."

"Did you meet any of her? What did you call them, 'extra men'?"

"I never met them. She mostly found them online for brief encounters, one-night stands, and similar arrangements. Given that Henry wouldn't give her a blasted divorce and let her go live the life she wanted, she was stuck with less-than-stellar guys. Not many keepers want a long-term deal with a married woman."

Lilly watched his eyes darken, and a frown creased his angular face. "But?" she prompted.

"There was one guy, her most recent extra." Jakob began fidgeting with a creamer package. "I guess she knew him from years ago, and they reconnected on Facebook or one of those platforms. They hit it off, and I guess things started to get too serious for her. She ended it with him, citing the whole lack of divorce thing."

"I take it this guy didn't take it too well?" Lilly ventured.

"Not really, no," he shook his head.

"Did he threaten her?" Lilly asked, a chill going down her spine. How many true crime shows had she seen where the supposedly nice guy the woman met online turned out to be an absolute monster?

"She wouldn't come out and say he did exactly, just that he would make her see that they could be together, no matter what. He didn't care if her husband wouldn't give her a divorce."

She bit her lower lip before taking another sip of coffee. "I guess that could be seen as a romantic gesture?"

"Or delusional," Faith cut in. "Guy's not listening to her boundaries."

"Faith!" Lilly hissed, almost spitting her coffee across the table. Jakob shrank back into the booth, suddenly looking like he would bolt out of the café. "What are you doing?"

"Just happened to hear what you guys were talking about while I was walking by, was gonna ask if you two wanted the last two cinnamon rolls," Faith smiled, her eyes sparkling mischievously.

"Yes, we'll have the cinnamon rolls, now go." Lilly waved her friend off. Faith all but skipped back to the pastry counter.

"I will never get used to small towns," Jakob grumbled.

"She means well," Lilly said. "She hears everything in town and knows when to keep things off the radar."

"Well, it's not like what we discussed was too secret. Everyone thought Angela was cheating on her husband, which was, technically, true."

Lilly watched him silently for a few moments, trying to get a reading on Jakob-with-a-K. "Why did you want to meet with me today? If not to tell me to stay away from Angela or to stop asking questions, and it certainly wasn't to have a dish session about Angela's extramarital escapades. So what's your deal?"

"You're the closest thing Angela seems to have to a friend in this town, from how she talked about you." Jakob glanced at the table, then back at her. "I did some digging of my own, and found out that you're cousins with the sheriff."

"What about him?"

"I wanted to ask you a favor," Jakob said. Lilly took a long drag from her coffee mug. It was almost empty. She risked a glance at the back counter and saw Faith plating up the two cinnamon rolls for their table. Lilly gave Faith a slight nod and raised her coffee mug, signaling more coffee was in order. The restaurateur gave an imperceptible nod and grabbed the coffee pot as she balanced the two cinnamon rolls on one arm.

Jakob didn't meet Lilly's gaze until Faith deposited the rolls before them and topped off their mugs again. The cinnamon spiced sweetness of the rolls filled Lilly's head and made her stomach rumble despite seeing a man stick his arm up a cow's butt.

"Jakob," Lilly prompted. "This favor?"

"I thought maybe since you're the sheriff's cousin, you could talk to him for me."

"About what?"

"About that recent boy toy of Angela's," Jakob's voice came out in a sharp breath.

"Why don't you talk to him first?" Lilly asked.

"I have," he shook his head, picking at the large cinnamon roll with a fork. "He said that he'd take a look into Angela's other men, just like Henry's other women, covering all their bases and all those cop platitudes."

"So why should I talk to him?"

"Just grease the wheels a little more? If he hears something from someone he knows or trusts, maybe it'll give it a little more credence?"

Lilly almost choked on the piece of gooey roll she shoved in her mouth. She cleared her throat and swallowed painfully. "Well... that might not go over as well as you'd like."

"Why?"

"He's banned me from getting involved in the case," Lilly admitted. "If I went to him with any theory or potential lead that I wouldn't know if I hadn't talked to you, he'll know I was asking questions when I wasn't supposed to."

"Technically, I asked you to meet, not the other way around," Jakob pointed out, gesturing with a piece of roll on his fork.

"Mike won't see it that way."

Jakob looked at her and sighed. "Can you at least try?"

Lilly let out a sigh, knowing full well what would happen to her if she agreed. "I'm not making any promises that it'll grease any wheels, but I'll talk to the sheriff."

"Thank you."

The two ate their cinnamon rolls in silence, each lost in their thoughts. Lilly watched as the Attic slowly emptied, patrons having had their fill and heading out into the real world of work and responsibilities. Faith hovered as close as she dared to their booth, but stayed behind the counter, so as not to spook Jakob again.

Maybe if she asked a few more questions about this recent guy of Angela's, what made Jakob think he needed looking into, she'd have a way to sell the lead to Mike. "Where is he from?" Lilly asked.

"Huh?"

"You said that Angela knew this last guy from years ago, is he from Lone Tree?"

"No, he's from some town out east."

Lilly's brows furrowed. "Like New York or D.C.?" Which made sense if they were online.

"No, not that far east," he shook his head. "Almost to Wisconsin, some town in eastern Minnesota."

"That doesn't narrow it down. If he were a local guy, maybe Mike would be more likely to look into it," Lilly sighed.

Jakob shrugged. "All I can tell you is the town started with an 'R'."

"An 'R'?" Lilly swallowed her cinnamon roll hard. "Red Wing?"

"No, that's not it."

"Riceville? River Falls?" Lilly listed eastern Minnesota and western Wisconsin cities that started with the letter R. Jakob, with a K, continued to shake his head with each name. She swallowed, afraid to mention the city-sized elephant in the room. "Rochester?"

Jakob snapped his fingers and pointed at her rapidly. "That's it! Rochester."

"Oh," Lilly said simply, as the cinnamon bun turned to stone in her stomach.

Chapter Twenty-five

Lilly sat in the empty booth long after Jakob-with-a-K left. He stated he needed to go pick Angela up from the police station after her meeting to determine when Henry's body would be released for burial arrangements. He had said he didn't need to be part of that conversation, which led to the surprise meet-up at Grandma's Attic.

She believed she finally understood why she shouldn't ask questions. It was to keep herself safe, not just physically but also emotionally.

Was Nathan Wilhelm Angela's previous boyfriend?

Faith had come and gone, taking Jakob's used dishes away and refilling her coffee as often as needed. Surprisingly, she had nothing to add when she stopped by the table. Feasibly, she had heard the revelation from behind the bakery counter, and she needed time to process the implications of what Jakob had said.

Angela's most recent extramarital affair came from Rochester. Lilly didn't know if Faith was aware that Nathan had been living in Rochester, just like she was, but knowing the café owner, someone close to the Wilhelms would have stopped by the café and spoken about the prodigal Wilhelm coming home and from where.

"It's just a coincidence that Nathan and this guy lived in Rochester," Lilly told herself as she studied the empty coffee mug. It had multiple levels of stains along the inside of the ceramic mug from serving coffee to many customers over the years. Not just one customer used that mug. Just like not just one person who happens to be from Rochester is also the same jealous boyfriend looking for what? To keep the relationship going? To get rid of the block and go to his happily ever after?

Was Nathan that guy? He said he had recently gotten out of a relationship and wanted to be more serious, but could not. But of course, that's not a one-person-specific instance. Millions of people are in relationships worldwide; some enjoy their relationships and want to take them to the next level, while others' partners aren't ready to take that next step.

"You look like someone kicked your puppy," Faith sank into the booth bench across from her.

"Did you hear what Jakob said?"

"Something about Rochester," Faith gave a one-shoulder shrug. "I surprisingly can't hear all that much from behind the counter when you keep shooing me away."

"I didn't want to spook Jakob-with-a-K with you always dropping by. I didn't think he much wanted another set of ears listening in," Lilly responded.

"So what did he want?"

"He wanted me to talk to Mike about Angela's most recent boyfriend," Lilly sighed, pushing the empty coffee mug and saucer away from her. "Being the sheriff's cousin means I have an in on getting leads looked at."

"I assume you told him that your very same sheriff cousin has banned you from looking into this case?" Faith smirked.

Lilly nodded. "He still seemed to think that I could grease the wheels for him, so I told him I would get that boyfriend from Rochester looked into."

"Rochester, New York or Rochester, Minnesota?"

"Minnesota."

Faith's brows twitched. "Oh."

Lilly narrowed her eyes at the restaurateur. "What do you know?"

"Just that Nathan recently came home from Rochester."

"So have many other people in the world," Lilly pointed out. "It could be a strange coincidence."

"Angela said she was dating a vet," Faith blurted out.

Lilly gaped at Faith, mouth hanging slack. "She said that? When?"

Faith cleared her throat. "Well, not in so many words, but one hears things when they run a very popular restaurant in a small town."

"Who said? Angela or someone else?"

"Angela said. She was on the phone, probably with Jakob-with-a-K, about three weeks ago, talking about her latest boy and how he was this hotshot vet from Rochester."

"Jakob also said that they used to know each other from long ago, and they reconnected on a social media site..."

"Nathan, Angela, and Henry were all in the same class in high school," Faith confessed, biting her lip. "It's possible that Angela and Nathan got reacquainted again after all these years online."

Lilly ran her hands through her auburn curls and sighed.

"What's the big deal if he is this other boyfriend? Didn't he ask you out to the Apple Dapple Dance a few days ago?" Faith asked.

"Yes, he did," Lilly nodded. "But it's not like we're super serious... It's just something that Jakob said about Angela's last boyfriend. He seemed to be the possessive sort."

"Does Nathan seem like the possessive sort?" Faith started to put away the creamer tower Jakob-with-a-K had left on the table.

Lilly pondered that for a moment. At first glance, he didn't seem to be the overly possessive type. But then Lilly remembered this morning when they were doing the herd check. He kept moving closer to her and had to stand near her while talking. Did that make him a possessive, dangerous man? Or just someone who lacked boundaries? Maybe it was loud in the barn, and he wanted to stand close to hear her and ensure he was heard.

"I don't think so..." Lilly's voice faded as she struggled to believe it herself.

Faith finished putting the creamer packages into their holding dish on the end of the table, then checked her smartwatch on her wrist. "Oh, shoot, I have to get going. I need to finish an order before I'm done at noon."

"What are you doing after noon?" Lilly asked. She flinched at the desperation in her voice.

"I'm obviously coming over to your house for lunch so we can continue discussing this," Faith smiled as she reached out for Lilly's hand. "Don't freak yourself out. At least not until I get to your place, okay?"

Lilly left Grandma's Attic with more questions than answers. This was always the case when she played amateur detective. The possibility that Nathan was Angela's unknown former suitor sat heavily on her shoulders as she got into her car and drove back to her farm in a haze of rapid-fire questions.

And what if he was? What was that to her? If Nathan had been dating Angela before, did that mean he wasn't truly into her, but only back in town to try and win Angela back? Which was a crazy question. Why ask her to the dance if he wanted to go with Angela? Because Angela was still very married at the time. Going to the dance with one of the rumored 'other men' would have caused the upheaval of all upheavals to the Lone Tree rumor mill. If he genuinely cared for her, he wouldn't have risked her tenuous reputation by doing something so bold.

Lilly navigated the back gravel roads to the farm absently, her mind still mulling over questions and possibilities.

Say Nathan was Angela's mystery man from Rochester, who came home to work at his family's vet practice like he said, and the fact that he and Angela had dated for a time was just that—a simple fact. It didn't mean anything; it didn't mean he was a jealous boyfriend who came to win her back. Perchance, Angela thought that was the case since he came home so soon after their relationship, and it was just a wild coincidence.

But what if it wasn't just a crazy coincidence?

What if he were the jealous, possessive type, and he came back to Lone Tree to get Angela back? And she said no, Henry wasn't giving her a divorce, and she wasn't just going to leave her hometown. Or, heaven forbid, live in her hometown with another man while still legally married to another. The rumors would fly, and they'd never know a moment of peace.

Lilly parked her car in front of the farmhouse and glanced at Ryan's rusted green Chevy down by the barn. Such a difference between the two, Nathan and Ryan. Nathan, if one possibility was to be believed, moved back to his hometown to chase after the woman he wanted to have a serious relationship with, even though there were great odds against them, just because she was someone he wanted to be with, obstacles be damned.

Ryan did not go chasing after her when she left Lone Tree. Didn't make any attempts to contact her. True, he was fifteen at the time. Not many fifteen-year-olds are known for making those grand romantic gestures outside of movies and books. But what about now? Did he want her back as much as Faith claimed he did? His only gesture since she returned six months ago was their dance at Apple Dapple Days.

Is one dance enough to risk one's heart? Is moving halfway across the state enough?

Or do you do something to eliminate all obstacles?

Like, kill your girlfriend's husband?

The next few hours until noon blurred together for Lilly. She vaguely remembered answering emails and confirming with the four canceled reservations that their refund money was still being processed. She even looked through the rest of the 2007 journals to see if anything was mentioned about Abigail Schimmel's murder. It seemed that other scandals and happenings in town, as well as the Schmidts' household, took precedence. The alleged accidental death of a young girl slipped into the ether.

Before she realized it, the grandfather clock struck noon, and barely fifteen minutes later, Faith entered through the kitchen porch door. She carried two plastic grocery bags from the local Fritche's Market.

"Hey there, mopey pants," Faith said brightly as she entered the kitchen, grocery bags held high.

"Ha ha ha," Lilly grunted as she settled at a kitchen island stool. "What did you bring?"

"I wasn't sure how hungry you'd be, but I needed something to snack on while we dish over this whole Nathan thing."

Lilly rolled her eyes. "There is no Nathan thing."

"Not with that attitude, there won't be." Faith set the grocery bags on the island and began to unload them. First came two large bags of tortilla chips, one regular and one with a hint of lime. Next came two jars of dip: one was salsa, and the other was a guacamole-based dip. "Do you have any dishes or bowls for the dip?"

Lilly hopped off the stool and went to a cupboard to grab two bowls for the salsa and a larger bowl for the chips. While Faith poured the dips into their respective bowls, Lilly opened the bag of plain tortilla chips and dumped them into the large bowl. "I have some pop, if you're thirsty."

"Ooh, yeah, whatever you got," Faith nodded as she cracked the lime chips open and dipped one into the salsa. Lilly went to the refrigerator and grabbed a cola for each of them. Faith took hers and popped the tab on the can. "Thanks. Now, what's causing all these new worry lines to mar your pretty little face?"

Lilly regaled Faith with her recent thoughts and concerns about the developments to her theory and mental murder board. Her worries over Nathan being Angela's mystery boyfriend and if he turned out to be the possessive, jealous type. The chance that someone so close to home had the potential to be a murderer.

"Let's simplify this," Faith began. "Let's assume that Nathan is Angela's mystery boyfriend. What does that mean?"

"He could have come from Rochester with the pure intentions of just coming home and starting work at his parents' veterinary office, their relationship status not being a factor," Lilly said. "Or he could have come from Rochester to try to win Angela back, like what Jakob alluded to."

Faith dipped a chip into the guacamole and pointed it at Lilly. "Now the big question: does it make sense for Nathan to kill Henry?"

"If he's the jealous type, yes," Lilly nodded.

"Why would he kill Henry?" Faith asked.

"Because Henry won't let Angela go via divorce," Lilly answered. "And Angela would never have just left Henry to be with someone, out of some weird sense of loyalty or something."

"So we have two possessive men and one woman who's unable to leave or be with the one she wants."

"If she even wanted to be with Nathan," Lilly countered. "He was talking to me about his most recent relationship. He never said her name, but he said she didn't want to be in a serious relationship. That they didn't have a lot in common."

"Maybe he was talking about someone else?" Faith ventured. "He'd be going through a lot of extra work for someone who wasn't a good fit."

"People do crazy things for love."

Faith nodded. "Ryan told me that you kissed him."

"He did not!" Lilly gasped.

"Just a little cheek peck," Faith grinned. "So, what does that mean?"

"It doesn't mean anything," Lilly insisted. "I was just excited over a possible lead in figuring out the case. I got caught up in the moment, and he just happened to be there."

"So if you were talking with me, you'd have kissed me on the cheek?" Faith laughed.

"No!" Lilly hung her head. "I don't know if anything is going on with Ryan. We're finally getting to a civil working relationship. I don't think I'd want to screw it up by trying to reignite any sort of romantic relationship."

Faith nodded, shoving a guac-covered chip into her mouth. "You know if you gave him the green light, he'd be all over you."

"What?" Lilly cried. When Faith looked at her with a pointed gaze, she shoved chips and salsa into her mouth to delay responding to Faith's outlandish statement. "So, what you're saying is my two choices for guys right now are my grumpy hired hand slash high school ex-boyfriend, or a man who used to be in an open relationship with a married woman and may or may not have come back to town to be with her?"

"There are worse choices, I suppose?" Faith shrugged and took a sip of cola.

"Will I ever find a decent guy?" Lilly moaned, running her finger along the rim of the salsa bowl.

Faith leveled her clear eyes at her. "Why would you ever ask a silly thing like that?"

"Oh, I don't know, my husband cheated on me, and I had no clue. This new guy I like might be a suspect in a murder case!" Lilly sighed and dug her hand into the bag for another chip. She pulled out her empty hand. "Things are supposed to get better, right? I think I slipped a few levels lower from cheater to potential murderer."

Faith pursed her lips tightly. She, too, dug her hand absently into the bag and, unlike Lilly, brought out a handful of chips. She glanced down at the pile of tortillas in her hand, for a heartbeat, then thrust her open palm under Lilly's face.

"Look at these!" she exclaimed.

Lilly alternately looked from Faith's hand to her face, her expression turning steadily more uncomfortable. "Uh, okay... why?"

Faith plucked two chips from her palm. "These two, right here, are perfectly paired. They nestled into each other's curves nicely. These two found their mates in the bag, among the jumbled, crumbly mess of chips. These two chips found who they were meant to be with."

Lilly stared up at her friend, mouth agape in disbelief. "And...?"

"They found their mate," Faith declared, dipping the perfect chip couple into the salsa. "If they can find the one they're meant to be with, so can you."

"Did you just say 'there's other fish in the sea' but with tortilla chips?" Lilly's brows arched.

Faith grinned and punctuated her point by popping the salsa-covered chips into her mouth, crunching loudly.

Lilly blanched as Faith chewed. It was a nice sentiment her friend tried to make, and it would have worked had the circumstances been a little different. If her love life wasn't oddly intertwined with murder. She couldn't shake the sinking feeling that watching the chip couple meet their demise was less of a motivational speech and more of a bad omen.

"Oh, and did you stop to think that if Nathan killed Henry and Owen, it was because he took the proverbial fall for the drug party?" Faith asked as she licked salsa from her fingers.

"What?" Lilly groaned and put her head down on the cool granite of the island top. "That just complicates things even more!"

Faith chuckled. "No one said being an amateur sleuth was easy."

Chapter Twenty-six

With her mind filled with questions and thoughts of tortilla soul mates, Lilly bid goodbye to Faith after their theory-hashing session. Neither were any closer to figuring out who killed Owen Perkins or Henry Stilner. Cecilia's wish to avenge her sister's death after a botched police investigation seemed like a perfect reason to kill them. The idea of Nathan killing Henry over Angela seemed plausible, yet somehow not as concrete as Cecilia's motive.

Then Faith had to go and mention that Nathan was also involved in the drug party fallout, though not as severely as the Schimmels' losing a daughter. He did have to bear the brunt of the social ramifications of being the host of the party that killed a young girl. Would Nathan come back all these years and kill Henry and Owen for throwing him under the bus all those years ago? Which was the more plausible motive for Nathan: unrequited love or unfinished justice?

Lilly sat at the kitchen island, polishing off the last of the lime chips and salsa, her brain working feverishly, trying to settle on a suspect and motive. She glanced down at her phone on the countertop, its black screen taunting her with the phone call she promised Jakob she would make. As much as she wanted to make the call, to be a person who followed through on principle, she didn't want to call the sheriff because she didn't want to get yelled at again.

Sheriff Mike Branford may just follow through with his threats and arrest her for interfering with an investigation. This phone call may be the last thing that breaks his resolve. She sighed and spun her phone in a circle on the counter.

"Fine," Lilly huffed as she opened her phone and dialed the sheriff's number. "Hey Mike, how's it going?"

"Lilly, I was expecting your call," the sheriff said with a hard exhale.

"You were, were you?" Lilly matched his exhale. "Did someone tell you I was going to call you, or did you just expect me to break my promise not to get involved in the case?"

"A little of both," Mike confessed.

"I promised someone I would talk to you for them," Lilly said. "Jakob, Angela's cousin. He asked me to talk to you about one of Angela's former boyfriends. He might be the jealous stalker killer type."

Her stomach soured at the description she gave. That could very well be Nathan she was talking about.

"I know, he just left with Angela about an hour ago," the sheriff said. "He told me the same thing about Angela's supposed boyfriend."

"Did Angela confirm who this boyfriend was?"

"Lilly," came the sheriff's gentle warning. "But no, she did not. Jakob spoke to me without Angela present. He didn't want to upset her more than she already was."

"Is Henry's body being released soon?"

"In the next couple of days," Mike confirmed.

"Even if they had a weird relationship, it still must be hard for her to deal with this," Lilly shook her head. Maybe that was why Angela never pushed to leave Henry. There was some level of love there for him. A strange, unusual love, but love, nonetheless.

"As his legal spouse, she had to sign for his body and possessions. I hear his family is working out most of the funeral arrangements." Mike said.

"At least that's one less thing for Angela to do," Lilly paused, biting her lip. "Are you going to look into the boyfriend angle?"

"You know I can't discuss specifics of the case with you."

"It's not specifics. Just a simple yes or no."

"No, Lilly."

"No, you're not going to look into the boyfriend angle? Does that mean there's a girlfriend angle on Henry's side?"

An exasperated chuckle came from the other side of the phone. "I cannot discuss this with you, Lillian."

"Fine." Lilly fought the urge to stick her tongue out at the phone.

"Lilly, you told me about this boyfriend," Mike stated. "You did your due diligence and kept your promise. Now. Will you *please* stop getting involved in my investigation?"

If there was anything that Lilly had learned about her unwilling new hobby of amateur sleuth, it was that the best way to get information is to always go to the source.

After getting off the phone with Sheriff Mike, Lilly got into her car and drove to the Stilner farm. She hoped that after Angela and Jakob left the police station, they would go straight to the farm. There wasn't much else for Angela to do now, with her in-laws taking care of most of the memorial arrangements.

What was she doing driving to Angela's? Lilly slowed her car on the gravel road and almost pulled over to a stop. She promised her cousin that she'd stay out of the investigation, and what was she doing? Driving to the farm of a murdered man to talk to his widow about the identity of the mystery boyfriend who may have killed her husband?

Lilly shook her head and put her foot down on the accelerator. She wasn't going to the Stilner farm to ask about the mystery boyfriend. She was going as a friend of Angela's. The one that Jakob had claimed Angela viewed her as. A good friend would go to her friend in a time of need. She kept that mindset as she continued to drive to the Stilners'.

She finally pulled her car up the long driveway and parked in front of the main farmhouse. Lilly saw Jakob's SUV parked closer to the single-wide trailer. However, now there was a second car parked next to the SUV. A small tan sedan, nondescript and had seen better days. Lilly turned her car off and slowly reached for her phone.

Another thing she remembered after her last time on the Stilner farm and the encounter with Will was to let others know where she was.

She called Faith, but it went to voicemail after five rings. "Hey, Faith, if you get this message, I'm over at Angela's—the Stilner farm." She let out a breath. "I know what you're thinking, but I'm not here about the case. I'm here as a friend." She cast a wary glance at the strange sedan. "But if you were to happen to call me in about thirty minutes and I don't answer, tell Sheriff Mike where I am... okay?"

Lilly hung up, exited her car, and after putting her phone in her back pocket, she made her way up to the main house's front door.

Chapter Twenty-seven

All the campus safety training and years of watching Lifetime movies and TV cop procedural shows told Lilly to turn around at the sight of the front door swinging open ajar, to get back into her car, and call 911. She should have listened to that little voice in the back of her head that repeatedly told her to get off the front porch. But a slightly louder voice urged her forward. *What would Nancy Drew do?*

Lilly stood in front of the open door and listened. Perhaps Angela or Jakob forgot to latch the door when they got back to the house. Maybe they thought the other had closed the door, which had been left open by accident. These were all logical and perfectly safe solutions to why the door stood half open. But the growing rock in the pit of her stomach told her otherwise.

"Angela?" Lilly called out as she crossed the threshold.

Angela's home had a similar layout to her farmhouse. To the left was a former sitting room that had been converted into a living room, and a formal dining room to the right. A central staircase took up most of the lower-level hallway, leading up to the most private quarters of the house. There was one stark difference in this house from her own. It looked as if a fraternity had taken up residence in the house. The floors of the living room and dining room were littered with cardboard beer boxes, take-out containers, and various items of clothing. Various neon signs, now hanging dark, advertised brands of alcohol or smokes. Metal signs that looked like they'd be better suited for a dive bar than a domicile adorned most of the walls in the rooms, readily visible. It was the epitome of a bachelor's pad.

"Oh, Angela, you lived like this?" Lilly muttered as she gingerly stepped over the scattered debris in the entrance hallway.

No, there was a second option. The hired hand trailer is out in the backyard. Instead of suffering with her perpetual frat bro of a husband, she must have moved out into a temporary home, which would explain why she and Jakob emerged from the trailer the day Lilly first came to the farm.

Lilly shook her head, trying to fathom the kind of life Angela lived. The one she chose to live in. Didn't she have the freedom just to leave Henry? Stay legally married to him to fulfill his father's outrageous requirements for the will, but be physically separated from him? Lilly knew that if she were to be shackled to this sort of man-child, she'd certainly escape no matter what.

Even kill for a chance at freedom?

A chill swept through Lilly as she stopped at the bottom of the stairs. She glanced up the rubble-littered steps but couldn't make out any noises from the top floor. "Angela? Jakob? Are you guys home?"

Silence greeted her.

"I should go check on the trailer, maybe they're over there..." Lilly said to herself as she turned around toward the main entrance. She stopped short at the sight of a tall man in the doorway.

"Lilly?"

Lilly swallowed hard in an attempt to calm her nerves. "Nathan, hi!"

"What are you doing here?" Nathan asked, taking a step toward her through the fraternity minefield.

"I, uh, just came to see Angela. Mike told me that the police are going to release Henry's body soon, and I wanted to check if Angela needed help with anything," Lilly said.

He regarded her for a moment before closing the gap between them. "That's mighty kind of you, Lilly."

She shrugged. "What can I say, that's just the kind of person I am!" Nathan caught her in an intense gaze, and her confidence faltered. "What are you doing here?"

"Angela called about some of her goats," he replied, his voice even.

Lilly's smile turned genuinely relieved. "Oh, yeah, she does have goats. I keep forgetting about them."

"Angela and I are a little wrapped up in goat stuff right now. How about I tell her to give you a call if she needs help with anything?" Nathan offered.

Lilly took a half step back to put more space between her and the vet. She still didn't like how closely he stood next to her. It creeped her out even more so now. She glanced at his clothes and couldn't stop the frown from forming on her face. "You're not dressed for working with animals," she said suddenly. Instead of jeans and a veterinary-branded shirt, Nathan wore pressed Dockers and a clean button-down shirt. An outfit better suited for a date than working with livestock.

Nathan glanced down at his clothes, a slight frown creasing his features. "I didn't have time to change."

"Oh," Lilly bit her lower lip. Another chill went up her spine. The warning bells instilled in her from years of Lifetime movies started going off in her brain. "Well, yeah, I should let you guys get back to looking after the goats."

She stepped around Nathan and hurried through the mess to the front door. The farmyard suddenly appeared larger and foreign to Lilly; her car was parked a million miles away, instead of just at the bottom of the porch steps. She glanced to her left, over at the trailer, and noticed the front door and screen hung open on their hinges as well. More alarms went off in her mind as she descended the stairs.

Something caught her eye that she hadn't seen before. She had been so focused on getting into the house that Lilly didn't notice the person sitting in the SUV. It was Jakob-with-a-K. However, now he sat in the front passenger seat, head lolled to the right side. He appeared to be sleeping.

Why was Jakob sleeping? Lilly stopped at the bottom of the stairs, startled by the crunching of gravel beneath her shoes. Maybe he got tired of waiting for Nathan and Angela to finish whatever attention the goats needed?

The pit in her stomach flipped as she heard another pair of feet on the steps behind her. She took a sharp breath and felt Nathan's presence loom close against her back, almost pressing into her shirt.

"Well, it looks like Jakob is taking a nap. I was going to stop by and say hi..." Lilly cleared her throat. "I'll let you get back to the goats."

Nathan's hand dropped heavily on her shoulder. She gasped and froze. He took advantage of her surprise and entangled both her wrists in his other fist. "You should have just stayed out of this, Lilly," Nathan growled into her ear.

"Nathan, please," she whimpered. "I don't kn—"

"This way." He roughly maneuvered her around the parked cars and toward the trailer steps.

Lilly allowed him to direct her toward the trailer. As they passed the cars, she glanced over at Jakob's motionless body. In the fleeting inspection of what she could see of Angela's cousin, he appeared to be sleeping. No apparent injuries were visible.

"Is he dead?" Lilly croaked out.

"No," Nathan responded. "Not yet."

"Nathan, please, you don't have to do this." Lilly dug in her feet at the base of the trailer steps, hoping to do what she wasn't sure of. All she knew was that she had to delay going into the trailer at all costs.

"I think I do," he said, shoving her forward. "You just couldn't stop asking questions? Just couldn't leave well enough alone?"

"You're sounding like cousin Mike," Lilly grumbled.

"Seems like you should have listened to him." His grip on her shoulder and wrists tightened briefly, reminding her who was in charge.

"Where's Angela?"

"She's in the trailer, waiting for me," Nathan replied. "I was supposed to get rid of you, get you off the farm so we could finally head out, but no, you had to poke your head where it didn't belong."

"I can still go, Nathan." Lilly twisted her head, trying to catch a glimpse of him over her shoulders. "Just let me go. Please."

He was quiet as he pushed against her to get her to step up onto the trailer stairs. Lilly dug her heels in, the gravel grinding loudly under her feet. She continued to twist her head, trying to get an indication of where his face was. She could get a good look into his eyes, catch a flash of the old Nathan. Talk some sense into him.

"Nathan, this isn't you. Please let me go," she pleaded again, cranking her chin over her left shoulder.

His eyes were dark and cold. This wasn't the Nathan she thought she knew. He was focused on his one task: tying up loose ends.

"Get up the stairs—" He grunted as he pushed against her once more. Her feet finally slipped, and she stumbled up the first step. "You're making this harder than it has to be, Lilly."

Lilly's back pocket erupted with an upbeat ringtone.

"Now what?" Nathan grumbled.

Lilly, her chin still over her shoulder, saw Nathan glance down at her back pocket. *Faith!* Before she realized what she was doing, Lilly's head snapped back, the crown of her head catching Nathan square in the mouth. He cried out as pain exploded across his face. His hands let go of her and flew up to his nose. "Dammit, Lilly!" he shouted.

But she barely heard him. She spun away from him while he held his nose and ran around the parked cars. Her back pocket continued to sing. She was tempted to answer the phone and tell Faith what was happening, but she knew that would waste precious time. She just needed to get to her car and burn rubber out of the farmyard and get to the police station. Lilly now ran behind her car, digging in her front pants pocket for her keys.

"Ooooff!"

The air exploded from her as Nathan tackled Lilly from behind. With his arms wrapped around her waist, the two crashed to the gravel driveway in a cloud of dust. She landed on her stomach, arms outstretched, keys spilling from her hand like a fumbled home plate catch. Lilly thrashed her legs in an attempt to dislodge Nathan from her. His larger frame pushed her down into the dirt, keeping her flailing legs from kicking him loose.

Lilly dug at the ground with her fingers to pull herself out from under Nathan and grab her fallen keys. All she managed to grab were fistfuls of gravel chunks. She suddenly twisted at the waist and flung a fistful of rocks back at Nathan. Her missiles hit him square in his bloodied face.

Lilly crawled out from under him, taking the brief window of his sputtering and coughing at the gravel. Launching off the ground in a near-perfect sprinter's stance, Lilly scrambled up and away from Nathan. The car keys were a lost cause, vanished in the gravel around her. Again, it would have wasted precious time to try to search for them when Nathan was right on her tail. All she could do now was find a place to hide, arm herself, and call 911 if Faith hadn't done it first. As she ran toward the goat barn, she realized her phone had fallen silent. Hopefully, Faith took her message to heart and now called Sheriff Mike as she had asked.

With her head start, Lilly got to the goat barn before Nathan. She burst into the small red barn and was greeted by small pens filled with roughly twenty little black, brown, and white goats. A chorus of bleats greeted her as she navigated around the unfamiliar barn. Thankfully, a central aisle, much like the one in her barn, separated the two large goat pens. At the back of the barn stood tall towers of hay and straw bales. To the right side of the barn was a side door that led out to the goat's pasture. Lilly quickly threw the door open, making sure it rattled.

"Lilly! Stop!"

She heard Nathan yell over the commotion of the goats as he entered the barn. Lilly ducked behind the straw bales and crouched as low as she could manage. Hopefully, Nathan would see the recently opened door and think she had gone out into the pasture. She crept to the deepest part of the bale pile and waited. She hated to be trapped with her back literally against a wall. If he didn't fall for her door trap, she would be trapped in the barn with Nathan.

And who knew what he had planned for her?

Lilly inhaled deeply and tried her best to do some calming yoga breathing. The last thing she needed to do now was hyperventilate. She needed to calm herself as much as possible, use reason, and try to think ahead for her survival.

"Lilly!" Nathan's voice was louder than before. He made his way slowly through the barn. The goats bleated more audibly as he moved between their pens. "Come out, Lilly, you're only going to make this worse for yourself."

What's worse than dying? Lilly thought as she glanced at her surroundings. *A painful death versus a painless one?* She blanched at the thought.

She crept to risk a look around the tower of bales. Nathan was at the side door she threw open, but hadn't left the barn yet. With his back turned to her, she could have slipped out behind him and exited the barn. However, the goats would have alerted her to her movements. They seemed very reactive to any motion around them.

Damn goats. Lilly frowned. She had to risk it. Otherwise, Nathan would turn around and spot her behind the straw. Lilly moved as silently as she could on the straw. Thankfully, the goats were also making noise, and their little hooves were clattering on the wooden planks and children's playhouses in their pens. She made it around the straw bales before a goat bleated.

"There you are!" Nathan cried as he spun around in the doorway.

The slick floor, slippery with straw and other animal muck, kept her feet from moving swiftly under her. Nathan caught up to her before she had gone a handful of steps toward the barn exit. He tackled her once more and drove her face-first into the grime of the barn floor. She cried out as she fell and got a mouthful of dirty straw for her trouble as Nathan sat firmly on the backs of her legs, his hands gripping each of her wrists to her sides. He roughly pulled on her left arm, wrenching it back as he forcefully turned her over onto her back. She cried out at the twisted angle he forced her arm into. Once more, he sat down on her thighs, gripping her hands tightly.

"Get off me!" she cried futilely.

"Not a chance," he grunted, his legs squeezing hers together so she couldn't thrash.

Lilly glared at him and spat out the filth from her mouth, hoping to hit him with the muck. "You killed Owen and Henry," she said finally.

"Proudly." He dared to grin.

"Why?" Lilly struggled underneath him, only to get his fingernails dug into the tender flesh of her inner wrists. "Why, after all this time?"

"There are so many reasons, it was tough to pick one," Nathan told her. "He threw me under the bus back in high school with the whole Abigail debacle. Everyone knew he and Henry gave Abby the drugs that killed her, but nothing happened. No one had the guts to stand up to Henry and his stupid family."

Lilly stopped struggling and held his gaze, even if it made her stomach flip and not in a good way anymore. His nose bled from where she whacked his face with the back of her head, and red had smeared over his mouth and cheeks during their various tussles. "The syringe and the EpiPen..." Lilly gasped. "So you framed Cecilia for it?"

"It worked out so well, it would have been stupid for me not to," he said, sitting back on her legs, causing her to cry out. "She drops her kid's stupid EpiPen while we're looking at her other kid's stupid chicken, and it hits me. Plant the pen there by his body. By the time the police figured out that the EpiPen wasn't what killed him, I'd be long gone with Angela."

"With Angela..." Lilly swallowed. Where was Angela? Was she just sitting clueless in the trailer, waiting for Nathan to return? Or was she complicit in his scheme? "Did you kill Henry together? Her scarf was found around Henry's neck."

Nathan shook his head. "No, Angela wasn't part of the killing." He confessed. "Her scarf was there, and unfortunately, I used it to strangle Henry after I popped him with the EpiPen. But getting reliable DNA off a scarf is so hard after it's been dragged through multiple chicken cages."

"So you killed Henry for... for Angela?" Lilly asked. "Did she ask you to do it?"

"She didn't ask me." Nathan shook his head. "Although I would have if she did. I would have preferred it if she had straight out asked me to get rid of him. She never would have left the man if he hadn't been removed from the picture."

Lilly swallowed and bucked underneath Nathan to try to dislodge him from her legs. He responded by crouching harder down on her thighs. "You're her mystery boyfriend," she said.

"I wanted to be so much more than one of her short-term flings," Nathan replied, a hint of pain in his voice. "That's why I killed Henry and Owen... they made so many people's lives horrible, back in high school through today. They ruined my life, made me take the fall for the party. Caused Abby's death and ruined that whole family. Do you ever wonder if Cecilia would have turned out to be a somewhat decent human being if Abby were still alive?"

Lilly couldn't fault him with that thought. She had it herself more than once.

"And he ruined Angela's life by not giving her the one thing she needed: freedom." Nathan continued. "He was too chicken to stand up to his old man to give Angela a divorce, even to let her separate from him. Now she's free from that drain on the world. She'll see what I did for her and understand. They all will see I'm the hero in this scenario."

As he talked, Nathan sat forward slightly on her legs. Lilly saw this as her one chance for her freedom. She drew up her feet and arched her back, bucking her legs underneath her. Having most of his weight leaned forward on his knees and her hands, Nathan rocked forward. She pushed the arch of her back and legs sharper and threw him feet over head over her head. He cried out in shock as he launched over her and landed unceremoniously beyond her. She almost was flattened by him if she hadn't scrambled in the opposite direction as he somersaulted over her.

Her limbs screamed with defiance as she ran down the central aisle of the barn. Nathan was collecting himself faster than she had planned. She wasn't sure what she planned with that move, other than being a last-ditch effort at freedom. As Lilly passed the goat pens, she threw open the latches to the pen gates. Almost two dozen little goats flooded the barn's thoroughfare, bleating and crying at the sudden independence. The goats swarmed around her legs, the little beasts running between Nathan and her. They formed a decent living blockade.

Not wanting to outstay her welcome, Lilly rushed to the barn entrance before the goats spread out enough for Nathan to pass between them. Once out of the barn, she sped toward the machine shed. Having been there once, she knew that the shed held a plethora of tools that could be used as weapons. As she ran, she grabbed her phone from her back pocket. The black screen was cracked and dirty. Ducking into the first open bay door of the machine shed, Lilly tried to slide the phone open, praying that the screen wasn't too damaged to make a call. The screen flickered to life, showing Lilly she had three missed calls and five missed text messages from Faith. She hadn't even remembered her phone ringing or making that much noise.

Running for one's life tends to take up most of one's attention.

Lilly ran to an open toolbox and grabbed the first thing with a long handle she could reach. She pulled out a long-handled wrench with a head at least as big as her hand. It was hefty, with just enough weight that if she managed to swing it, it would cause some damage. She moved back to just inside the bay door, positioned just so she could see if someone was coming, but a tall, oversized rolling toolbox hid her.

She controlled her breathing and strained to hear any signs that Nathan was approaching the shed. The crunch of shoes over gravel reached her ears. Slow, tentative steps moved closer to the machine shed. Nathan stayed close to the edge of the door, as she had planned, but was too close. If he turned to his left, he'd spot her.

Lilly stepped back and slipped a hand into an open drawer of the large toolbox. She grabbed what she believed to be a quarter-sized washer and then chucked it across the machine shop bay. Nathan's head turned toward the noise, and he stepped into the machine shed.

Lilly hefted up the large wrench, as if she were holding a baseball bat, and let it fly. Time slowed as she swung. Nathan's head turned again, his face connecting right with the massive head of the wrench. Lilly let go once she felt the impact and spun on her heels. She fled to the back office and heard the wrench hit the cement floor, followed by Nathan's impact.

She dove into the office and slammed the door shut. Surprisingly, thankfully, Henry had thought ahead to install a lock and deadbolt on his office door, even if the rest of the office was a slapdash construction. She flipped all the locks she could find on the door. She sat under the desk amongst the stacks of papers and other junk, trying to swipe her phone awake. She only ended up slicing her fingertips on the broken screen.

In the eerie quiet of the office and adjoining machine shed, Lilly swore she heard sirens in the distance.

Lilly sat in one of the two ambulances vying for a position in the Stilner farmyard alongside the other police vehicles. The ambulance she sat in had been unofficially reserved for Angela, Jakob, and herself. The other ambulance, which was on its way down the gravel driveway, held Nathan Wilhelm and two police officers along with the paramedic personnel. Lilly couldn't keep the smile off her face as she remembered the strangely appreciative groans from the EMTs once they got a look at Nathan's bloodied face.

"You did that with a wrench?" her current EMT companion, Murphy, had asked with a whistle. "Remind me not to get on your bad side."

However, he was on her bad side at the moment. Even though it was his job to examine her, his poking and prodding only served to aggravate her left shoulder. Nathan had done a real number on her shoulder when he used it to flip her over. Despite the EMTs stating nothing was broken and the shoulder joint itself was still intact, she felt as if her arm was about to fall off at any second.

As Murphy worked on putting her left arm into a sling, Sheriff Mike Branford walked up to the back of the ambulance. His usually crisp uniform was rumpled with use. Lilly had heard one of the other officers, as they walked by her sitting on the back bumper of the ambulance, that despite being hit with a wrench to the face, Nathan still managed to put up a bit of a fight when the police arrived.

In his mind, to the very end, he saw himself as the hero.

Lilly looked up at Mike and grimaced, whether from the exertion Murphy put into securing her arm's sling or being caught once again in the middle of one of the sheriff's investigations, she'd never tell.

"Hey, Mike," Lilly said quietly.

"Lilly," Mike gave her a curt nod. He glanced over to Murphy and gestured for him to give them some space.

"I should go check and see if the fellas need help with that guy they found in the SUV," Murphy nodded and hopped out of the back of the ambulance.

"How is Jakob?" she asked once the medic was out of earshot.

"He'll pull through, from what I've been told," Mike answered. He took out his small notebook from his vest pocket and looked over one of the pages. "Nathan confessed to injecting Jakob with some sort of sedative, the same he uses on the animals he treats, but it wasn't a lethal dose. Just enough to knock him out so he and Angela could escape."

Lilly nodded, flinching as she shifted positions on the bumper. She didn't want to sit on the stretcher in the back of the ambulance. She tried to keep it open for Jakob or Angela if they needed the service. Her wrenched arm wasn't on the level of requiring a special seat. "How's Angela doing?"

Mike let out a short sigh. "She's fine. When we found her locked in the back bedroom of the trailer, she appeared unharmed. She's not wanting to leave until they're ready to transport Jakob to the hospital."

"Am I in his ambulance?" Lilly jerked her thumb over her good shoulder.

"It will be needed to transport those two, yes." Mike nodded. "The medics are working on keeping Jakob stabilized before they move him. But I suppose we should get you out of here. They were almost done with him when I walked over here."

Lilly glanced over to where her car was parked, and Jakob's SUV next to it. A throng of EMTs congregated around the vehicles and the stretcher to which Jakob had been moved. From her vantage point, she could see him lying on the white sheet, a matching white collar around his neck to stabilize his head.

"I don't suppose anyone found my car keys?" Lilly asked.

"I'll ask the crime scene guys to keep an eye out for them," Mike said with the faintest hint of a smirk. He reached for the walkie strapped to his shoulder and relayed the message to the other investigators. "Do you want to hitch a ride home with me? We're almost done here."

"Am I officially released?"

The sheriff looked down at his notebook, the very one Lilly knew held her account of the events on the farm. She still couldn't forget the shocked, then angry, then relieved mixture of expressions that crossed his face when he discovered her crouched beneath the desk in the office. When she realized it was one of the police, her cousin Mike, to be precise, Lilly broke down crying in his arms as he ushered her from the office.

"I think we have everything we need from you for now," the sheriff stated as he put away the notebook.

Lilly shuddered. She suddenly felt cold and tired. It must be from all the adrenaline wearing off. Mike reached over her into the ambulance and produced a fluffy blue blanket. He draped it over her shoulders and stepped back. "So, do you want that ride, or should I call someone for you? I'll be needed here for maybe another hour or so."

"How is that almost done?" Lilly asked, her brows bunched together.

"For a cop that's almost done," he smirked. "How about I call someone to come get you?"

Lilly closed her eyes and nodded, growing more tired. "That'd be great, Sheriff Cousin Mike."

The chimes above the door to Grandma's Attic clattered, though the sound was lost amongst the noise of the café. In the two weeks since Henry Stilner's death and the week after his murderer, Nathan Wilhelm, had been captured, the busybodies of Lone Tree never stopped buzzing. Everyone had their theory, whether based on the facts of the case or not, for why Nathan chose to kill Owen and Henry. The old cold case of the death of Abigail Schimmel came to light once more, with one of Nathan's many reasons for killing the two men becoming public knowledge. The Schimmel family was grateful to hear their long-held beliefs that both men were responsible for their daughter's death, but also asked for privacy while they processed this information.

The Stilners also requested privacy after news of their son's involvement came out. Lilly did not know whether they received it, but she hoped they lost a few nights of sleep over it.

Some of the rumors surrounding Angela and Henry's unusual relationship lessened, while others went into high gear. Once hearing the truth of Henry's father's stipulation of staying married, the once negative feelings toward Angela shifted to seeing her in a slightly more positive light. However, others held firm that Angela had brainwashed Nathan into killing her husband for her.

Lilly sat in her usual booth in the Attic, eating her bacon cheeseburger and drinking her glass of iced tea. Her left arm was no longer in a sling, though her shoulder remained stiff and ached more often than not. Thankfully, Ryan had recommended his physical therapist's clinic to help her shoulder return to normal. However, that was the only thing he had said to her in the week since the events at the Stilner farm. Lilly felt he was going out of his way to avoid her more than usual. He probably avoided her over her involvement in what went down at the Stilners' farm. He had told her to stay out of the investigation, and then she got involved in a big way.

As much as she and he butted heads over her engagement with the running of the farm, his daily snark was a highlight of her day. Though they may never return to where they were in high school, their new and developing friendship made her new life in Lone Tree easier. She'd never admit it aloud, but over the last few days, she missed him.

Faith walked by her table with a whole pot of coffee and slowed. "Do you need anything, hon?" she asked. Lilly shook her head, mouth full of burger, and the café owner continued on her rounds with the pot of Joe.

His sister certainly filled in the gap when Ryan pulled away. Faith insisted that Lilly come to the Attic nearly every day. At first, Lilly was happy to oblige, spending her days working on new ideas for lotions and candles for the Accidental Farmer Experience. She could open an online store for all her artisanal sundries and establish an online presence before inviting people to visit her farm and participate in the making process. But by the fourth day of sitting at the same booth in the Attic, Lilly grew tired of being smothered by Faith. Between customers, or some-times even during orders, Faith checked in on her to ensure her food was satisfactory and if she needed anything for her shoulder. She almost stormed out of the Attic the day before when Faith started talking to her like one of her children.

She knew that if Sheriff Mike weren't so wrapped up in closing up the case, he'd somehow find a way to butt his nose in her business with con-stant reminders of what he had told her not to do. The persistent threat of "I told you so"s from so many angles was daunting.

Lilly just wanted things to go back to normal, for her friends to start treating her like a friend instead of a breakable object. This time, she had learned her lesson about getting tangled in a police investigation. Play-ing sleuth was now firmly in her past. She only wanted to focus on reviv-ing the Accidental Farmer Experience, if it could be rescued after Cecil-ia Baxter's smear campaign.

"Visitor coming at eight o'clock," Faith buzzed past her table with an armful of dirty dishes.

Lilly barely had time to register what Faith had said before her near-ly unannounced visitor arrived. She swallowed her burger and quickly sipped her tea to help it go down smoother. Perhaps she thought about her name one too many times, and it manifested in her.

"Excuse me, Lilly," Cecilia Baxter said as she stood next to her booth, her dark blue pantsuit looking very out of place in the country chic aes-thetic of Grandma's Attic.

"Cecilia," Lilly gave her a slight nod. "A pleasure to see you."

"Yes, yes. I came here to... to... well..." At her stumbling over her words, Lilly motioned for Cecilia to sit across from her. After a brief moment, she sat on the opposite bench. She took a deep breath and started again.

"I came here to apologize to you, Lilly."

"Apologize?" Lilly's brow arched. A smart remark danced at the tip of her tongue, and she so longed to say it to Cecilia, especially after all the horrible things the woman did throughout less than a week. But she swallowed it back and smiled.

"It's come to my attention that how I had handled myself recently has been much less than appropriate... desired. It has also come to my attention that the, uh, well, ordeal you recently went through was what brought to light the parties responsible for my sister's death." Cecilia's words came out measured and controlled, as if she had rehearsed her speech before coming down to Grandma's Attic. "And my family is deeply grateful for your role in helping my sister see some justice."

"You're very welcome, Cecilia," Lilly said, genuinely smiling. "How about we just put all that business behind us and start over, hmm?"

Cecilia looked startled as Lilly reached her right hand over the table. "Well, yes, I would like that." She said. She sounded distracted, as if Lilly had interrupted her prepared lines. "I also would like to offer you something in return, to make up for the... well, horrid thing I did to your little business venture."

Lilly sat quietly, waiting for Cecilia to continue. "I am more than willing to email those people back and inform them that I was mistaken about your character, and that they should be more than willing to give you another chance at their reservations for your farmer thingy."

Lilly bit her lower lip to keep from laughing. She cleared her throat and gave Cecilia a nod. "That would be very appreciated, Cecilia. Thank you."

"It's the least I can do," she said, sitting straighter in the booth. "Now, I just had enough time to stop by and deal with that. I must be off, very busy."

"Certainly," Lilly nodded.

Cecilia gave a final nod before slipping out of the booth, although not as suavely as she would have liked. Lilly let out a sigh of relief and nestled back into the booth cushions. Part of her couldn't believe that Cecilia Baxter came to apologize for what she did to the Accidental Farmer Experience, let alone offer to email the four reservations and get them to reconsider their cancellations. She wasn't sure how successful Cecilia would be, but the gesture itself was huge.

"You seem to be a popular person," Faith said as she walked by her booth again, dropping off a fresh glass of iced tea and taking the nearly finished one off Lilly's table.

"What do you mean?" Lilly asked as Faith slipped away once more into the hectic jumble of Grandma's Attic.

"I finally found you," Ryan said, appearing behind his sister and standing by the table. His stained jeans and disheveled T-shirt signaled he had come directly from the farm. In a normal restaurant, this attire would have been frowned upon. However, he fit in with the other farmers and laborers who stopped in Lone Tree daily.

"You saw me earlier this morning," Lilly narrowed her eyes at him. "And if I'm not at home, I'm here. You know that."

"Home," Ryan said softly, the tops of his ears burning. He ran a hand quickly under his John Deere cap and shifted his weight from one foot to the other.

Lilly watched him for a few moments. "Are you okay, Ryan?" He sat quickly in the booth, on the same bench as her. She shuffled a bit to make more room for him. "What are you doing? Why aren't you sitting over there? Sit over there. And I'm not going to share my fries with you," she protested.

"Can you be quiet for one minute?" Ryan asked. He clamped his mouth shut as Lilly gasped, her mouth hanging open. Both were shocked at the sharpness of his words. He was quiet for a moment. "I've been trying to figure out how to say this to you all week, so can you just be quiet and let me say it?"

Lilly pressed her lips together tightly around the straw of her iced tea and slurped. She stared at him intently, silently telling him to get on with it.

"I never really liked that Nathan guy in high school, and even now. When I saw you at the dance with him, the thought of him and you together just ate me up that he could take you away so easily." He closed his mouth and looked down at his hands. He took a deep breath and continued. "And well, it turned out he was a crazy killer and he could have taken you away permanently if he had..."

He was silent once more, his hands wrung together under the table. Lilly glanced down and saw his worried hands. Without a word, she put her iced tea down, slipped her left hand between his, and grasped his hand tightly. Her shoulder muscles protested, but she didn't care.

"I didn't take losing you the first time very well," Ryan confessed. His voice was so low that Lilly could barely hear as she sat next to him. "And then last week... You just don't listen, Lilly. I told you to stay out of things and... I can't always be there to save..."

"Ryan," Lilly gave his hand a tight squeeze. "Just be quiet."

"Okay."

Ryan squeezed her hand back and nodded. The two sat in silence for a moment before Lilly shuffled closer to him. He couldn't help but smile when she rested her head on his shoulder. "You're not going to lose me," Lilly whispered.

They sat in the booth in a comfortable silence for what seemed like forever. Even the numerous walk-byes of Faith, eyes wide and mouth agape, didn't affect them. Lilly sighed and found herself nestling deeper into Ryan's side. He held her hand tighter. Lilly felt herself truly relaxed for the first time in over a week. Just before she closed her eyes, she caught a brief movement out of the corner of her eye.

"Did you just steal a fry?"

THE END

Lilly Schmidt will return in Mazed & Confused

Book 3 in the Accidental Farmer Mystery Series

Acknowledgements

I'd like to thank as many people as I can remember who have helped out with getting *Fowl Play* out into the world!

A huge thank you to my team at Fox Pointe Publishing, LLP: Kiersten Hall, publisher and editor, and Scotty Town, internal designer. Of course, I will never forget my graphic designer, Krista Johnsen, who helped create the fabulous cover. Thank you to my agricultural advisors Brittany Olson and Carrie Mess for helping me keep all things bovine as true to life as possible. I'd also like to thank Public Information Officer Hunter Panning of the Chaska, MN, Police Department for helping answer all my law enforcement/legal procedure questions that came up along the way. And of course, a big thank you to all my family and friends who listened to me complain and go a little crazy about rewrites and plot holes over the last couple of years while working on this book. Thank you for all the encouragement and helping me off the ledge more than a few times.

A huge shout-out to my ARC readers: Susan N., Cheryl M., Margaret H., Mary T., Lynn V., Amanda S., Jordyn K., and the Facts & Fables Podcast, who all helped preview, review, and catch any sneaky typos and mistakes that may have made it to the final printing. Thanks for helping to make *Fowl Play* the best it can be!

About the Author

Amy Gregg is an author of several books, including *Relic Chosen: Magic and Madness* (Minnesota Book Award nominated), *Through the Woods*, and *Next Weekend*. When not writing, she enjoys true crime docs, knitting, and spirited discussions of all things Marvel. A native Minnesotan whose childhood was spent both on the farm and in the suburbs, Amy now splits the difference and lives with her family & 10lb cat near the edge of the Twin Cities.

Keep up to date on future books at:

facebook.com/AmyGreggAuthor

@amylgregg

@amylgregg

www.ingramcontent.com/pod-product-compliance
Lightning Source LLC
Chambersburg PA
CBHW040218170726

48295CB00014B/719